CAROL ANNE DAVIS

was born in Dundee, moved to Edinburgh in her twenties and now lives in southern England. She left school at fifteen and worked at everything from artists' model to editorial assistant before heading off to university.

Her first novel for The Do-Not Press was *Shrouded*, based in a mortuary; followed by *Safe As Houses*, which explored sadism; and *Noise Abatement*, which visited sudden death on the neighbours-from-hell.

She has also written two true crime books for fellow independent Allison & Busby: *Women Who Kill: Profiles Of Female Serial Killers* and *Children Who Kill*.

Carol Anne Davis' small but perfectly formed website can be found at www.carolannedavis.co.uk.

FICTION BY
CAROL ANNE DAVIS

Shrouded
Safe as Houses
Noise Abatement

Kiss It Away

by

Carol Anne Davis

First Published in Great Britain in 2003 by
The Do-Not Press Limited
16 The Woodlands
London SE13 6TY
www.thedonotpress.com
email: kia@thedonotpress.com

B-format paperback: ISBN 1 904316 09 3
Casebound edition: ISBN 1 904316 08 5

British Library Cataloguing in Publication Data. A catalogue
record for this book is available from the British Library.

1   3   5   7   9   10   8   6   4   2

For Ian

AUTHOR'S NOTE

One of the characters in this book, Nick, uses steroids – and usually refers to them colloquially. The terms he uses include gym candy, roids, anabols, Arnies, and being 'on the gear' or 'having had his spike'. He also talks about 'stacking' – taking more than one type of steroid for maximum effect. Although I spoke to bodybuilders who were familiar with steroid abuse, Nick is a product of my imagination. The gym where some of the action is set is similarly fictional.

CHAPTER ONE

He'd scored his knife along ten parked cars before he neared the main road but the strength in his hand said he'd willingly scar a hundred others. His blade was ready to go long and hard and deep.

Reaching the kerb, he glared at the lorries grinding past. They contrasted with his mood, which cried out for speed and action. He ran between them and lurched into the welcome dark promise of Winston Churchill Gardens, the enormous park.

A woman hurried past him with a black Cairn terrier stressing its leather leash. She wasn't much smaller than his own six foot but he was willing to bet that she was a damn sight weaker. He knelt and groped at his bootlaces, pretending to tie them, giving her the chance to go further into the shadowy core. All right for her, with her long coat and Kennel Club canine. She didn't have to figure out where she was going to sleep.

He willed her to stop lingering by the entrance, to walk further on. There were closed-circuit cameras to their left but the area some distance ahead and close to the river wasn't directly overlooked. He'd checked it out when he'd arrived here in Salisbury early that morning, also finding bushes where he could hide his bag and himself.

Nick's right temple pulsed again. He plunged his hand into his jeans pocket for the strip of extra-strong painkillers and crunched two, sharpness overtaking staleness. There was a full packet in his bag and another in the knife-concealing money belt below his shirt.

The woman looked away as the dog lifted its leg against the fence. Nick stayed, crouching, looking like he was pulling up his socks. The backpack probably made him look less threatening, more like a tourist. It would never occur to her that it contained a blanket with which he'd doss down in the park.

Fuck that Claire – she'd be sleeping warmly in the flat as usual, probably with some new stud pushing all her middle-aged buttons. Screw her for telling him to get out when he was only doing his job. *Keep a quiet club*, she'd said, so he'd taken an over-loud clubber and made him quiet. And all of a sudden she wanted him out of her bed and out of Brighton until the uniforms fucked off.

Fifteen minutes until the painkillers kicked in. After that he'd jog round the park a few times then go back to Yurek's and see if the old bastard was home yet. Either that or lift a bag and get enough money to take a taxi to one of the city's hotels. Access to bed and breakfast and a shower would make him look presentable for tomorrow morning, make it easier to get a day pass to a new fitness club or gym.

Damn it, his access to cash wasn't walking along the path. Instead she bent down and let her furball off the leash, then stood there and lit a cigarette as its blackness raced off into the darkness. Nick gave his bootlaces a final tug then straightened up.

She was too near the main road to mug, but there might be more like her in the vicinity. He'd seen two other girlishly small, bright cars in the camera-observed car park.

Park and ride. The twenty-eight-year-old made his way to the bushes and put down his bag then rubbed his shoulders and flexed his elbows. He'd overdone the arm work earlier in the week and now his pectorals felt bruised. They'd have to stay that way till he could afford to get more gym candy. He'd popped the last of it yesterday and needed more so that he could increase his reps.

Nick stood, staring through the bushes, on red alert for a source of cash. After a few minutes he heard a snuffling noise and the black Cairn terrier appeared and barked twice at him. 'Fuck off, you.' He lifted his right foot and aimed it at the animal's exposed throat. The dog backed off and his toecap merely skimmed its chest, a grazing injury. Nevertheless it let out a satisfying yelp. Nick drew his foot back again, ready for the beast to launch at him a second time. 'Come on, you bastard,' he muttered. He'd heard that if you kicked a dog hard enough in the stomach it burst like a balloon.

The furball sneezed twice then raced off towards its owner and the entrance to the park. Nick brushed the leaf-mould away, sat down and quickly located a place where he could peer through the branches. He traced the handle of his knife over and over. Someone else would come along soon.

CHAPTER TWO

'Take me, I'm yours,' Ben said, rolling on to his back and trying to lift an equally naked Dawn on top of him. Somewhat to his surprise, he felt her arms stiffen in resistance then she flopped down at his side.

'Don't feel like it.'

'Don't feel like going on top?' He slid his fingers between her legs but she wasn't as flatteringly wet as she'd been on all their previous sessions. They'd been caressing each other for twenty minutes and it would be no hardship to caress her for twenty more.

'We don't always have to have sex, you know,' Dawn muttered, moving fully onto her back and staring up at the ceiling. Ben noticed how her flushed cheeks made her grey eyes look even larger than they had before.

'No, of course not.' He felt a sense of loss as his erection sank and shrunk. Had he palmed her ineptly or was she tiring of him already? For the first time he felt truly aware of the fact that he was a callow twenty-four-year-old and she an experienced thirty-nine.

Going to bed tonight had been her idea – she'd suggested it as soon as they'd entered her small flat.

'Want me to put the kettle on?' he'd asked casually, not wanting to take over her kitchen without permission.

'I can think of better things we could be doing,' she'd murmured, pressing herself against him tightly and running her hands down his back. He'd been slightly surprised – when he'd taken her hand in the cinema a half hour before, she'd let it lie there limply for a moment then had pulled it away again. And on the way back she hadn't laughed as much as usual at his jokes. In fact, he'd planned just to walk her to her door and arrange a date for later in the week: after all, they weren't at the stage where they spent every single night together. But she'd said, 'I'll get you that book I promised,' and when she'd added, 'Make yourself at home,' he'd asked if he should put the kettle on.

Now he lay there wishing they'd just had a cup of tea and discussed the film. If he got out of bed now it would seem like he'd only been after one thing and that he didn't want to cuddle – but if he stayed in bed and tried to hold her she might misinterpret it and think he was a sex-mad beast.

Aim for a neutral topic, something about the art she did in her spare time. He searched around for a casual tone, one devoid of hurt or frustration.

'So, were you working before you came out to meet me?'

She shook her head. 'Uh uh. Didn't have the time. There was a mix up at the bank about Vitor's standing order so I went in and saw the manager.' Vitor was a Guatemalan child she sponsored. Ben had seen his photograph and a drawing that he'd sent. Now she put her hands behind her head and sighed loudly. 'If only more people sponsored, everything out there would be all right.'

The logical part of his brain said otherwise. 'Not quite.' He propped himself up on one elbow to look at her and felt incredibly grateful that she was his girlfriend. 'I mean, they've got a population problem, a harsh climate and serious underdevelopment.'

He saw that her gaze was unnecessarily confronta-
tional.

'But with child sponsorship they could develop.'

'Some – but it would take much more than that to
make the entire country well.'

He watched as she pressed her lips closer together and
hardened her gaze. 'You're saying that I'm wasting my
time?'

'No, of course not.' She must see in his eyes how much
he admired her. 'I think that what you're doing is great. It's
not a permanent cure, that's all.'

To his amazement she muttered the illogical, 'Go home
to your permanent cure, then,' and turned violently on her
side.

'Dawn?' Ben stared down at her in astonishment and
disbelief. How could his intelligent and easy-to-be-with
new lover be behaving so strangely? 'I think that your
sponsorship is great,' he said again.

'You're just saying that 'cause you want to get fucked.'

'Now you're being ridiculous.' Ben swung his feet out
of her bed and reached for his shirt. She'd started this
session – he hadn't been feeling particularly sexual. He'd
have been happy to go home alone after the cinema and hit
the sack.

He started to put on his clothes, going more slowly as
he got closer to full dressing, hoping that she'd slide her
arms apologetically around his waist.

'Right, I'm ready to go,' he said at last. There was no
answer from the figure in the bed and she was still turned
away from him. 'Shall I phone you later this week?' he
asked tersely.

'Please yourself.'

Fighting the urge to mutter that he wouldn't bother
then, he left the flat, closing the door with a controlled
bang. He took the stairs two at a time, wanting to be
outside in the relative sanity. Christ, these last few weeks
had been perfect and he'd come close to saying that he

loved her. Why the hell had she suddenly spoilt every-thing?

He walked quickly down the street until he came to the Southampton Road that bordered one side of the park. If he turned right and walked for a while he would reach his own house – well, the room in the shared house he was renting. If he walked to his left he'd eventually reach the 24-hour Tesco. It was quite a walk and might wear some of his anger out. There again, he might meet someone from work or from the art club where he'd originally met Dawn, and he didn't want to talk to anyone yet.

No, he'd go to the park for a while, walk alongside the river and get his equilibrium back. There were mole hills in the grass and owls overhead and ducks sleeping in the grasses. He couldn't feel completely bereft when breathing in the October freshness or looking at the improbable fea-tures of an adult duck.

It was 11pm now so the flow of cars was slowing down, though the lorries with their cargoes of supermarket fare were still cautiously active. Ben watched them as he waited to cross the road, and wondered what it must be like to travel all the time. He'd been brought up a few miles from here in the New Forest, had gone to university in Manchester, then had come back to Salisbury to work and live. He'd never been abroad but Dawn had said that he could come with her to an event she was exhibiting at in Brussels. He wondered if that was cancelled now, if she really didn't want to see him again.

Damn it, he had to forget about the row or else he'd never get to sleep tonight and he'd wake up tomorrow with the start of a migraine. He hadn't told Dawn about them yet, didn't want to sound weak or not in control of his life. He could go for three or four months without an attack – and could even hide the milder ones from his colleagues – so there was no reason for her to know for a while.

Would she get to know all about him in time? Or was their relationship truly over? He crossed the road towards the park and wandered in. It was nice at this time of night, tranquil. It looked more like a wildlife sanctuary and less like what it was, an enormous suburban park.

Ben walked past the toilets, past the skateboarding rink. The skateboarders had a platform they could jump up on and skate off. He'd watched them a couple of times and marvelled at their agility. His own body was in pretty good shape, as he walked most places and cycled any really long journeys, but he didn't have the superior suppleness or co-ordination these guys had.

He strolled on through the darkness until he reached the riverbank and stood staring down into the water's depths. It had lost the organic scent it had in summer. In winter, the various stretches of water sometimes iced over for a little while and then he and his current girlfriend would bring the swans and ducks lots of bread.

Twigs crackled behind him. He turned, half hoping Dawn had followed him here. A tall man stood closer than was strictly necessary. If Ben stepped backwards he would fall into the river. Instead he took a tentative step to his left.

'Got a light, mate?'

'No, sorry. I don't smoke.' He noticed the man's skin looked slightly yellow and wondered if it was just an illusion caused by the moonlight.

'Got any money for fags, then?'

Ben hesitated, then decided it was better to say yes. The guy was over six feet and he himself was only five-foot seven. And the stranger might be a combat-trained soldier from the local army base. There were a couple of soldiers who were famous for coming into Salisbury and drunkenly challenging any passerby to a fight.

Ben started to reach for his wallet then realised that wasn't the brightest thing to do. The man might grab it and its contents of eighty pounds plus his credit card. His mind started to work faster. He'd paid for the cinema with a twenty-pound note and had put his change into his jeans back pocket, so… He reached in there instead and brought out three pound coins.

'There you go, mate.' He tried to sound like the older man in the hope that he'd identify with him and wouldn't start punching. It wasn't that he was particularly cowardly, but – like any sane person – he didn't relish being badly hurt.

'Take your jacket off.'

Ben felt his heart start to speed up. The man's eyes were frighteningly devoid of feeling. He stalled for time, said, 'You what?'

'Take your jacket off now.'

Ben looked around for help, but the park was silent. He was too far away to be heard by the occupants of the nearest houses – and by now most parkside dog walkers would be preparing for bed.

'Look, what's this about?' His voice sounded thin and scared and seemed to echo in his ears. If he tried to run, this guy could just reach out one long arm and grab him. And if he fell he'd go into the river and the yellow-tinged man could just hold his face down in the water's depths. Ben reached into every logical part of his being and each logical part said that, for now, he should do what he was told.

'Just take your jacket off.'

'All right.' He tried to sound indifferent to the idea, like a child trying to maintain some dignity when losing an argument with a parent. His arms shook slightly as he pulled them from the sleeves. It was his leather jacket, his newest jacket, bought three weeks into his relationship with Dawn.

He couldn't bring himself to hand it to the mugger, so just dropped it on the ground. As he did so, the man reached out swiftly and grabbed him by the front of his collar and swung him sideways. Ben instinctively reached up to pull the attacker's hands away, but before he could do so the man turned him around again and threw him so that he battered into one of the long riverside seats.

Cannoning into the bench took all of the air from his lungs. Ben slumped, gazing dazed over the back of the wooden chair, one of his feet on the ground and the other slammed awkwardly into the sitting section. He could feel sharp pains shooting up the bent knee and knew that it was either fractured or bruised. He heard noises behind him and figured that the guy must be picking up the discarded jacket. Any second now he'd leave and Ben could run off the opposite way.

'Take off your jeans.' The words were accompanied by a knife pressing against his throat. Ben stilled, kept staring straight ahead. He wanted to look down but knew that the movement would send the blade slicing into his jugular. He could smell the man's breath now and it was tainted with something chemical, some catalyst for rage. The man's long forearm was pressing into his chest, crushing so hard that the fingers felt embedded in Ben's flesh.

There was no point in stalling when he had a knife at his throat. He was just going to have to give the thief his favourite Levis. He'd read of this once, a young man being accosted in a big English city and robbed of his designer clothes. This man didn't have a jacket of his own, and presumably only had the jeans he was wearing. It must be worth mugging someone like himself to get a new set of gear.

His fingers floundered against the buckle, then he managed to undo his belt. The button and zip proved equally difficult. He and Dawn had been eating out a lot during their six-week relationship and he'd gained a couple of pounds.

'Can I stand up now?'

'No.' The blade pressed a little harder. Ben winced and started to edge down the denim, feeling ridiculously stupid. He'd have to take his shirt off and tie it around his waist to hide his underpants, then flag down a taxi on the main road to take him home.

He got his jeans down to his knees, but as one knee was still slammed into the bench he couldn't get his trousers down any further. 'You'll have to let me move my knee,' he said.

'Lie down longways, then,' said the man. He sounded very calm, must know that his knife blade was sharp and that no one was going to come to Ben's rescue. Ben backed up carefully, hellishly aware of the cold cutting metal at his throat. One pull and the big vein would slice open, spurting his life force skywards. Within a few seconds he'd be dying and they wouldn't find his corpse till the following day.

He flexed his injured leg for a second as he got to his feet and the man manhandled him along to the edge of the bench and pushed him over it. Now he was lying along its full length, his jeans bunched at his feet. Ben waited for the mugger to pull them all the way off and run away with them. Instead he felt the man's fingers grazing just below his waist as they grabbed at his Y-fronts and pulled them down.

Christ, was he going to leave him without a stitch to wear? He could ask to keep his underwear, but it sounded so pathetic. Best not to say anything. At least the bastard had removed the knife from his throat. He couldn't get up, though, with the man and his steel blade just behind him. It would be so easy for his attacker to stab him in the lungs.

He stiffened as a new weight fell across his legs. Jesus, what was he doing? Ben started to twist his head back but the man's full weight was suddenly upon him, forcing him fully down. He felt something – *someone* – parting his buttocks, pulling roughly at both naked cheeks. The man was exposing his anus. *Oh God no,* he said inside his head then realised that he'd said the words out loud.

'You know you want it really,' said the man in an oddly cultured voice with an underlying rough trace. His tone had changed so that it sounded like a boy from the wildest side of town after a few elocution lessons. Ben tried to remember the voice so that when he went to the police…

Something nudged against his anus then pushed and pushed. 'Please don't.' The object was withdrawn and Ben untensed ever so slightly. His heartbeat speeded again as he heard the man spitting three times, presumably on his own hand. He felt some of the wetness being spread between his buttocks and tried to squirm to one side but the tall man's weight overpoweringly held him in situ.

'Christ, mate, don't do this,' he said.

'You my mate, are you?'

The man nudged what must be his erection between Ben's cheeks again. Ben felt like he had done when he was at primary school, being bullied in the playground. He'd tried to find the words that would bring about fair treatment but had seen only an inhumane glee in the bully's eyes.

'You can take all my cash, my leather jacket.'

'And now you're about to give up your tight little hole.'

'No,' He realised belatedly that the man must think he was gay. 'I'm not like that. I have a girlfriend.'

The man was trying to push into him. 'And does she shove her fingers up your arse?'

Dawn and he had done most things together, but she hadn't done that. He hadn't even considered the possibility. He'd never had – or wanted to have – anything invade him like this.

'No, and I don't want her to.' He never talked about his sex life with the men at work so it was surreal having this conversation with a stranger. A stranger who was lying heavily on top of him and breathing out chemicals and who had a knife.

'But you want this, flaunting your backside in the park.'

'No, I don't.' He couldn't say no often enough. Every cell in his body and brain was screaming it. 'I'd had a row with my girlfriend, Dawn. I just wanted to think…'

Maybe if he could just keep the guy talking someone would come along eventually. This man was strange but he'd surely run off at the sight of witnesses.

'No, your arse wants it and your arse is getting it.' There was a gloating edge to the mugger's voice. Ben felt the appendage push against his opening again – and suddenly his body opened up a little and he felt the man start to enter him. He cried out in revulsion and denial and pain and it seemed to act as a signal for the man to push harder. Ben felt something give deep inside him and then his assailant was in the full, appalling way. He heard the mugger's grunt of satisfaction mingling with his own agonised cry.

'Oh please, take it out, take it out.' Like a child being vaccinated with an immunisation needle.

'You love it really.'

'If you stop now, I won't tell the police.' He didn't know if that was the right thing to say. His mind was going blurred with the burning and his shame was increasing. How the hell had he let himself be reduced to this?

'Not tell the cops that you took it up the backside? Oh, they'd like to know, pretty boy. I'll tell them you begged for it. I'll tell them you were wriggling your ass like it was a fly on a fishing rod, that you offered me three quid to fuck you hard.'

At the end of the man's speech he thrust forward, pulled back, plunged deeper in. Ben screamed again. He wondered briefly if the mugger was putting the knife rather than an erection inside his sphincter. Then he felt the blade pressing with renewed threat into his shirted back.

'Tell me you love it.' Ben closed his eyes and gritted his teeth. He wouldn't say it. He whimpered as he felt the blade being pulled across his cotton-clad shoulder blades. 'Want me to slit further down, punk? Want me to punch holes in your lungs so you breathe in your own blood? Want me to cut off your balls?'

'No.' He had so little breath left that the word sounded air-starved and vanquished.

'Then say what I tell you to say.'

He could feel the metal tip digging into his flesh. His heartbeat pounded in his ears and his chest at the same time, racing so fast that he expected it to break free of its moorings.

'I love it,' he said brokenly.

'Say it like you mean it. Tell me you want it hard up your arse.'

He said the words. He said everything that the bastard wanted him to – the alternative was bleeding to death in a deserted setting. For what seemed like hours, he echoed back words that he never thought he'd say.

At last the mugger withdrew from his body though the pain went on. Ben felt the man's weight lift off him. He lay there, trembling, his core so open that he wondered if he was internally split. He tried to flex his thighs but they'd virtually merged with the bench, were prostrate. His rapid heartbeat went into further overdrive as he felt still-angry hands in his hair, lifting up his head.

'Lick it,' said the man. Ben clenched his teeth as the mugger tried to force himself between his lips. 'Do it, you little punk.' Ben kept his lips tight-closed but the man pushed harder. Suddenly he gagged twice then vomited over his attacker and the bench.

'You dirty little fucker.' The man stepped back then slapped angrily at the side of Ben's head but his thick hair softened the trauma. As he watched, dazed, his attacker dressed then walked over to the jacket still lying beside the reeds. He took out the wallet, counted the cash and pocketed it, slung the garment over his shoulder then walked stiltedly away.

He, Ben, might never walk again. For an unknown time he lay there, his eyes blurred with tears and his lips smeared with blood, and the overwhelming heat in his sphincter an ongoing memorial to what had just happened. Was he haemorrhaging? Other than the terrible pain in his anus he felt numb below the waist. He briefly wondered what time it was but couldn't find the strength to lift his head and look at his wristwatch. As long as he managed to leave here before light...

Gradually the increasing heaviness in his bladder asserted itself and he moved carefully on to his side, whimpering slightly as the movement sent new needles through him. He hadn't felt this vulnerable since being hit by a car as a ten-year-old kid. He'd crossed near a corner and the car had come round and tossed him up into the air: for a time he'd felt he was flying. Then he'd crashed back on to the road, smashing his glasses and losing the ability to breathe.

He could remember a blurred bending man with a trembling voice saying, 'It's all right, son, my wife's phoning an ambulance.' He'd wanted to smile his forgiveness but he had no breath. Until a few moments ago he'd forgotten how strange it felt to be completely robbed of air.

Time stayed suspended whilst you urged your lungs to catch the breeze, whilst you tried – and failed – to work out exactly where you'd been injured. He could remember thinking that his mum wouldn't be pleased.

He mustn't think of his mum now. She was just a few miles away in one of the villages that survived mainly on American tourists' money. Her world was a nice, safe one in which she worked and shopped and socialised at the same grocer's shop. She didn't know that a young man walking in the park could be accosted by another, that the older man would...

Don't think, don't think, don't think. After he'd been lying on his side for a moment he swung his legs slowly outwards, keeping them as close together as possible. He felt very torn and open, as if some part of his anatomy might fall out. Keeping his movements small and crabbed, he brought his feet down and his body upright till he was sitting normally on the bench.

Normally. He forced back a cynical snort, afraid that if he started to make noises he would never stop, that he'd turn into a child who was crying so hard that he merged his half-phrases. He was a grown-up now so had to deal with this. He got carefully to his feet and shuffled behind the bench and urinated copiously. The warmth of the liquid made him realise that he was very cold. He massaged his upper arms, noting that his shirt was ripped and sticking slightly to his shoulders. He knew that his attacker had grazed the knife along that path.

Wincing, Ben edged his underpants up to his knees, then had to lean against the back of the bench as a wave of dizziness rolled lushly through him. After a moment the faintness passed and he was able to edge the garment over his injuries. He did the same with his jeans and managed to zip them up but his numbed fingers couldn't push the metal button through the buttonhole or fasten his belt. Exhausted, he pulled his shirt-tail over his waist.

Go home. He started to shuffle through the park, getting as near to the main road as he dared without being picked up by the passing lorries' headlights. He prayed that there wouldn't be any witnesses to his dishevelled shame. As he walked he kept the distance constant between himself and the relative light of the pavement so that he could rush towards safety if his attacker appeared again.

When he reached the end of the park he squinted out into the street. There was no one on the pavement. *Do it, do it, do it.* He felt more vulnerable when he stepped beneath the street lights so broke into a pained half-jog. Every fibre of his being wanted to be double-locked in the house he shared with three others. He wanted to bathe away all the sweat and blood from his body, knew that he'd never wear these particular clothes again.

He could pour himself an almost neat vodka when he got in. He could have the entire half-bottle. Each comforting image that he fed himself helped him jog on, on, on. He could feel the increasing clamminess of his skin and wondered if he was running a fever, if infection could set in this quickly. Did anyone have a bottle of antiseptic in the house? He stumbled around the corner, heard an odd little sound and looked up to see that he was about to flail into a very large girl.

Well, a woman. She had dark grey circles beneath her eyes and they were red at the sides, as if she was allergic to something or had been crying. As he cannoned towards her, she moved her mouth into a frightened 'oh', and put her forearm across her chest. Damn. Ben halted then flailed with most of his weight on his toes for a ridiculous cartoon-like moment until he regained his balance. 'Sorry,' he mumbled, stepping awkwardly to one side. Dipping his head again he continued on his stumbling journey, his heart beating even faster than before.

At least the pedestrian wasn't someone he knew. He'd never see her again. He kept telling himself more hollow words of comfort. Inadequate as they were, they fuelled him till he reached his home.

It was a Tuesday night – or rather, the early hours of a Wednesday morning – so there was a very good chance that the others had been sleeping for some time.

Stay asleep, asleep, asleep. His wishes reverberated like a mantra in his head as he tiptoed up the path towards the front door. The house was in welcome darkness. He reached into the side pocket of his jeans and brought out his keys. As he slid the yale into the door he half expected it not to work or to break in the lock, denying him entry. The world felt a hostile and shock-producing place.

His key turned as it always turned. Within seconds he'd stepped into the hall and double-locked the main door from the inside, then hurried to the stairwell and tiptoed up it. Once in the large bathroom, with the door snibbed, he started to feel safe. He stepped under the shower and turned the temperature to medium hot: the first bursts of water both cleansed and hurt him. Hoping to blast away every fleck of dirt, he put the pressure onto full.

There was a carton of shower soap hanging from a hook and he filled his palms with it and started to soap gently at his violated parts. He soaped every hair on his head, every crevice of his flesh – and then he started over. He soaped and rinsed and soaped until the carton refused to yield any more gel.

Only then did Ben leave the wonderful hot spray and dry himself, patting carefully at the unseen hurting. When he took the towel away it was pink with diluted blood. He caught a glimpse of himself in the little mirrored wall cabinet and moved closer, wondering if the man had marked him. He could vaguely remember the bastard cuffing him about the head.

The face that stared back at him was as white as it had ever been, despite the steam from the shower. He looked at himself and tried to feel less traumatised.

Picking up his shirt, he saw the rent that the blade had made. It reminded him to take a look at his shoulders. He turned his back to the mirror then twisted his head around, noting the long, red – but thankfully superficial – scar. Was there some TCP in here? Ralph, the hypochondriacal tenant, was always buying fluoride mouthwashes and antibacterial bubble baths and taking up so much room on the bathroom shelf that none of them had space for their razor blades.

He checked, finding a bottle of liquid antiseptic in the cupboard under the sink. Ben poured some of it onto a tissue then wiped it across the scar. The open tissues burned slightly, but weren't exactly war-wound territory. He hesitated before taking a clean tissue, soaking it with the liquid then pressing it along his buttock crease. Jesus. The sensation was so fierce that he grunted and let his legs take him down and forward till he was kneeling on the floor.

After a few minutes he got new tissues and repeated the process. Each time the tissues came away wet with blood.

But at least he was clean now, cleansed of any germs that bastard might have had on his... that that bastard might have had.

Scooping up his clothes and the bloodied towel, Ben left the bathroom and tiptoed to his room, closing the door gratefully behind him. He threw his clothes and the towel under his bed, knowing that he could put them into the garden dustbin tomorrow whilst his housemates – who all worked for the same estate agency – were still at work. He tended to get home before them in the evenings, had a much-valued hour to himself.

He was going to be all right. Shakily, Ben put on his light cotton dressing gown and tied it tightly then reached to the shelf above his desk for his vodka and juice bottles and a tumbler. He sat on the bed then swiftly stood up again. God, that hurt. The twenty-four-year-old got carefully onto his stomach and lay there, gulping the throat-warming liquid. Having drained his glass quickly, he poured himself a second vodka and a third. His anus burned and pulsed: it was such a stupid, unseemly place to be injured. The stabbing pains went alarmingly deep inside.

The fourth vodka seemed to go straight to his eyelids, making them feel encouragingly heavy. Ben put his glass onto the floor and let his head drop down on the top of the duvet. Going, going... He heard a noise and was suddenly and totally alert. Was his window locked? His attacker could have followed him home, might have other plans for his body. He got stiff-leggedly off the bed and checked that the window latch was on. He locked his door and pulled his little tea table in front of it. If anyone forced the lock and entered he'd wake up hearing the crash.

Sleep, sleep. He looked at his alarm clock. It was 5am. It was set to go off at seven-thirty. Surely even a couple of hours kip would help?

But sleep usually deserts the minds that need it most. After a few minutes of lying under the duvet on his stomach, Ben felt too much like an offering. Holding his breath, he moved slowly and carefully onto his side. Oh, Christ, what was happening to his innards? He could feel liquid trickling down the backs of his thighs.

He had to staunch this or he'd be sticking to the bed-clothes all night. With effort he got up again and put on his bedside light, winced into a new pair of underpants and pressed them firmly against the injured area. As he got back into bed he saw blood smeared on the duvet and the undersheet.

Maybe it's not as bad as it looks. He fought back new waves of panic. The health reports in Ralph's lifestyle magazines told you how to recover from flu or recognise the signs of meningitis – but no one told you how to get over this.

Sleep, sleep. He curled on his side and closed his eyes and immediately saw the man's yellow face leering at him. *Sleep, sleep.* He could remember the bastard's every angry gesture and mocking word. Had he somehow seemed effeminate as he stood there by the river, thinking about his girlfriend? And was he the first person this man had raped?

CHAPTER THREE

The little punk's jacket was much too small. Moments after leaving the bench, Nick prepared to throw the garment into the bushes. Then he realised that he was throwing away hard cash. Hell, soon as he got himself to a new gym he could sell this beauty for at least a twenty, no questions asked.

Or swap it for some gym candy. He totally needed some now. He just felt so fucking wrong in his skin without it. And his legs felt jerky, as if he was walking from the knee rather than the thigh.

Still, the guy had been carrying eighty quid. He could use some of it to get himself a hotel room as it was too late to check in at the homeless hostel. He lurched on through the crackling twigs and ankle-wetting grass of the park. He wanted the moon to stop shining so frigging brightly, wanted that unseen bird to stop making that fucking repetitive nightcall, wanted... wanted his Arnies really bad.

There was no way he could get supplies at this time of night – which meant that his dead strength was popping a few more of the painkillers he took to help his headaches. Maybe he could wash them down with a cherry brandy or three.

Nick kicked morosely at the grass as he made his way back to the clump of bushes that concealed his backpack. He'd had a quarter-bottle of the blood-red brandy in it earlier today but he'd drunk it to give him the energy to keep walking round Salisbury, checking the place out. Oh, he'd been here before for weekends and so on, and had once dossed down at Yurek's, but that wasn't the same as living here.

He could steal some cherry brandy now from the 24-hour supermarket, a straight walk from here. He could also get himself a pack of ham and some bananas. It had been hours since he'd had that bag of chips.

Nick careened towards the promise of lights and the promise of drink, of sweet scarlet vigour. He'd been drinking the stuff since he was ten. His mum had worked in a club and the delivery guys would leave her a bottle in the back yard, hidden in one of the dustbins. He could guess what she'd given them in return.

She'd had Pernod and cassis and something that he couldn't pronounce – but it was the cherry brandy that had attracted him. It was as bright as a jewel and smelt as sweet as a chocolate bar. It made mum and her boyfriends laugh and he'd hoped it might make him laugh too – and it had, for an hour most evenings. He'd felt so warm and unworried that it had been worth the bloated gut later on.

Some of the boyfriends had thought it was funny too. One of them had poured it on Nick's cereal instead of milk. 'There you go, little man. Seeing as it's your usual.' Nice words with a grating, angry edge. The guy had made him eat the brandy-soaked cornflakes until he gagged on them but he'd gotten his revenge later by pissing in the man's shoes.

He'd done a lot of pissing in shoes and spitting in teas before he'd started going to the gym. He'd been so awkwardly thin as a kid that he was a walking hit-me sign. Every stockier boy in the playground had felt duty-bound to have a go. Same with most of mum's lads. Oh, they'd been nice till they got a permanent place next to hers on the pillow. After that, most of them had called him a concentration-camp reject or a thin streak of nothingness. After a while they'd found names for mum too, saying that she was a cunt and that no one else would want her. A couple of the guys hadn't shouted but she hadn't seemed to like them as much.

Nowadays the guys wouldn't be liking her as much. She'd be – what? He was twenty-eight and she'd had him when she was twenty-two, so that made her fifty. And everyone knew that you couldn't drink as much as she did and keep your looks. Hell, she'd probably be unemployable by now and on the invalidity, giving handjobs in back alleys to earn an extra couple of quid.

He'd known a few girls like that. You got the really fat or thin ones who'd been treated like shit all their lives. Buy them a drink and give them a hug and they'd do anything for you. Then you got the other type who thought they were something special and weren't up for it. That was the type he liked – the ones who kept their legs as tight-closed as welded metal, the type he could bruisingly unweld. Now that he popped the Arnies, he had extra-strong arms and it was real easy to prise their slender legs apart.

Fuck, it was even easy to force a *guy's* legs apart. He'd taken that little nancy boy for the ride of his life, split his chocolate freeway. The bastard had been all but crying by the time he'd finished giving it to him up the arse. That'd teach him to ponce about in the park in his good jacket with his wallet full of the readies, looking flash.

The little cunt was probably limping home to Mummy and Daddy by now. Nick bet he'd tell them that he'd left his leather jacket in a wine bar. Stylish blokes like him would never admit to taking six inches up the back. Their talk was of market forces and housing chains and the new beer they'd tried in Spain last winter. They hinted at how much they were making and wanted to be making: he'd listened to it every night in the Brighton clubs.

No, the wanker wouldn't report him. Nick left the park and sauntered along the quiet street towards the all-night superstore. As he walked the skin on his back started to itch, the irritation spreading up and down his spine. God, he needed some stackers. Claire's brothers had shoved him on the train so fast that he hadn't had time to buy anything. They'd wanted him to stay on all the way to Newcastle, miles away from where the heat was, but he'd checked that he wasn't being tailed then gotten off at Salisbury.

He knew Yurek in Salisbury, knew that he kept an open house. As long as you gave him a few cans and kept him company for an hour, Yurek was a happy man. Or whatever passed for happy in an alkie aged between fifty and seventy who didn't speak the lingo very well. He'd turned up today at Yurek's flat, hoping to get cleaned up and get himself a day pass to a Wiltshire gym, find out where to get the anabolics. But Yurek had been out or dead or living at Her Majesty's pleasure, so here he was in the early hours of the morning, mad for a bath or a meal or *something* and still too wired to sleep.

What the hell was wrong with him now? Nick swung his bag from his back and stopped to tear at his overheated shoulders. When he straightened up he found himself staring at the back view of a young, slim girl. She was fifty feet in front of him on the pavement, slim as a model. He could make out fairly high heels and an arse-gripping skirt.

A hooker, perhaps? If so, it was time she gave out a big free sample. But no, she was walking too quickly to be on the game. This surely wasn't the hour for a girl without a car to be doing her shopping so she'd probably had a row with her boyfriend and was walking home. He'd had a couple of such girls himself, who'd run off at the mouth then didn't want to finish what they'd started. He'd had the Harley in those days so had soon caught up with them. A bit of tyre friction to the ankle put an end to their thoughts of having the last word, and neither of them had been sufficiently tired of living to go to the police.

This one wouldn't get the chance to call the cops. There were lots of big shadowy furniture stores and storage depots around here – a man-made sex city. He'd take her behind one of those and get well acquainted for half an hour.

He walked faster, noticing that the jerkiness in his calves had suddenly passed. His long legs and his recently-strengthened thighs made the exercise undemanding. He forced himself not to run, not to draw attention to himself. If she'd had a row with some guy then she'd already be too low for zero, not rating herself too highly. She probably wouldn't put up much of a fight.

He didn't want a fight right now. He wanted her to fold real easy. He'd had all this recent shit from Claire and her halfwit brothers, and had gotten here to find Yurek had fucked off someplace leaving him without a place to crash. And then that leather-jacketed guy in the park with his nice fat wallet had tried to fob him off with a couple of quid.

Closer, closer. That click, click, click she made with her heels was doing his head in. Closer, and he could see the shape of her arse, the fucking tease. *You'll get yours*, he thought and his cock lengthened, hardened. *You'll not be left wanting tonight.*

The girl seemed to read his thoughts, for she turned her head back and glanced at him for a second. *Going places?* He would soon change her mind. He took the knife from his money belt then made a short run to close the distance between them, bringing his forearm up under her throat and pulling her close. 'Keep quiet and you won't get hurt,' he said as he used his other hand to hold the weapon against the side of her neck.

To his surprise, she screamed. She also reached for his arm and tried to pull it away. He tightened his grip and suspected that the blade cut her slightly. She screamed again and he moved sideways and then backwards, taking her with him in a strange four-legged dance. It was a dance that went on far too long in a place where one of these bloody lorries might drive past at any moment. New anger fuelled his limbs and he found the strength to pull her behind a wall.

'I told you to shut up.' How many times had people said that to him when he was a kid? He'd always done it. The girl stopped yelling but still tore at the arm that held the knife. He now had his other arm around her waist, holding her upright. They stayed locked like two fighting insects whilst he tried to figure out how to get her to lie on the ground. Her nails dug through the chambray of his shirt, ten half-moons of sharp pain signalling their presence. 'Quit it,' he muttered, pushing the knife a little deeper into her flesh. She screamed again and the tension scalded his innards like a steam burn and he moved his forearm fast and cut her throat.

As soon as he made the slicing movement he pushed her strongly away. He didn't want blood on his clothes or on his backpack. He leapt back and watched as she stood for a frozen second then collapsed onto the ground behind the wall. Stupid cunt. She should just have given him what he wanted. It wasn't as if she'd never put out before.

He could still… He looked at the fountain of blood and knew it was impossible. Anyway, she'd stopped bugging him now that she wasn't tapping her heels and swaying her arse the way she had before. She looked pathetic lying there, like a wasp after he'd sprayed it with insecticide – a feebly moving, airless thing.

Or, in this case, a gurgling thing. He tensed slightly as she made the sound and peered more closely at her features to make sure that she was dying. The jet of blood had already dropped in pressure and her eyes were open but filmed. He saw a glint of metal a couple of feet away and realised that it was her clutch bag. He kicked it further away from the bloodied body then put part of his shirt over his own hand before he opened the clasp.

A ten-pound note. He manhandled it carefully from the purse and into his jeans pocket. Sad little bitch didn't even have the readies for a good night out.

What the hell. His stomach rumbled and he straightened up, ready to resume his walk to the 24-hour supermarket. Maybe they'd even have an all-night cafe there and he could get tea. He legged it over the wall and back on to the pavement, realising he now had a strong craving for salt. He could have... no, he fucking-well couldn't because the supermarket staff might remember him and he'd appear on their security cameras and end up on the whatever-time-it's-on-nowadays evening news.

Hanging around after giving it to a guy was one thing – staying in town when you'd just iced a girl was something else. Nick stood, thinking, for a moment. He had to get his act together sharpish. He'd keep his head down, walk in the shadows, get his ass to the railway station now. He could take the first train to Southampton or Bournemouth or any other big city and hole up in one of the bed and breakfasts there for a good few days.

It was perfect. Neither Claire, her brothers nor Yurek knew that he'd spent today in Salisbury. There was no one to connect him with this stupid bitch's death.

CHAPTER FOUR

It couldn't be seven-thirty yet. Dawn batted the bleeping clock, convinced she'd only been asleep for an hour. A hard-hearted second later, her other alarm clock sounded in her ears. She pulled the duvet back over her head but the increasing noise of the traffic outside kept reminding her she had to prepare for work.

Feeling like a landed trout, she hauled herself to the side of the bed then patted a widening circle of the carpet searching unproductively for her slippers. Of course, she'd thought that slippers might make her seem ancient to Ben so had started wearing sandals in the house instead.

Rise and shine. Well, rise leastways. Dawn slid her feet into the cool slingbacks then tottered to the bathroom. Her stomach felt as if a kitten-sized animal was trying to dig its way out. She caught a mirrored glimpse of a white-faced woman with tufts of hair sticking out of her head at improbable angles. Her usually large grey eyes were unfocused slits. It was just as well Ben hadn't stayed over, Dawn thought as she removed a small sandpit from the corner of each lid.

Eat and go. Well, eat leastways. She munched a scone with half a jar of jam on it, wondered if she was going down with some sugar-craving new disease.

At ten to nine she reached the post office where she'd worked since her marriage broke up. Already there was a small queue outside, clearly desperate to claw at this week's pension. She smiled at them as she gave her special knock on the door and Peter, her boss, let her in.

'Delivery's just arrived if you want to put it in the safe.'

'I'd rather take it home with me,' she joked before stacking the money in the appropriate sections. Her mood had stabilised now that she was Action Woman, but her body still felt like it belonged to someone else.

And at eleven o' clock she suddenly understood why, when she went to the staff toilet and saw the first bright spots of blood on her off-white gusset. Ah – the start of her period. It was at least a week earlier than it should have been. There again, she'd been having lots of sex and lots of thoughts about being in love and had been eating out at restaurants. They'd probably all brought about a cyclic change. Usually her stomach cramped for a couple of days beforehand but she'd been doing lots of sit-ups and stretches in the hope of tightening and toning everything for Ben.

Ben. What the hell had she said to him last night? Some stupid non sequitur. At the time she'd been awash with irritation, hadn't realised it was hate-filled hormones time. She'd phone him tonight and apologise in triplicate, suggest going somewhere special at the weekend.

The lyrics to *Friday On My Mind* played through her head as she stamped pension books and filled out recorded-delivery slips and weighed airmail packages. She was putting some new international-reply coupons in the main drawer when two of her regulars – who'd recently celebrated fifty years of unhappily wedded hiss – came in.

'I'm just saying to Joe that they should bring hanging back.'

'Hi, Elsie. Oh. Right.' Dawn shut the drawer and accepted the pension books that the woman pushed through to her.

'You know, for that young girl who's been murdered.'

Dawn found the right pages and stamped them twice then tore them away from the counterfoils. 'What young girl's that?'

'Here, in Salisbury. Haven't you heard? I thought he let you play the radio in here.'

'Who, Peter? Oh, that's just when the quiz is on. He sometimes likes to phone in.'

'Well,' the woman lowered both her voice and her head, 'it's been on the TV, on Meridian. They showed the Southampton Road where they found the body. She was only nineteen, you know. They think it happened late last night but she wasn't found till this morning. They've got that many police out there looking for clues.'

'Did they say who she was?' One of her female neighbours was in her late teens.

'Did they say, Joe?'

Joe looked startled then said, 'Nineteen, on the Southampton Road.'

'We're getting his hearing aid checked tomorrow,' Elsie countered then reached with evident relish for the bundle of notes.

Dawn searched for a way to ask the next question without sounding too morbid. 'Did they say how she died?'

Elsie pursed her lips. 'Only that it was very violent and that her killer might be stained with blood.'

What must it be like to bleed to death on a darkened road with no one to help you? What must it be like, feeling your life force fade away whilst your loved ones innocently slept? Dawn knew that Salisbury had its share of bored vandals and purse-snatching drug addicts, but it experienced relatively little serious crime.

'Will you be all right?' Peter asked at the end of her shift and she realised for the first time that the murderer might still be out there, searching for new victims.

'Yes, I've got good locks and if I feel scared I'll just ask Ben to come round.'

In truth, she didn't want Ben to call round tonight, not when she was a whiter shade of pale with an elderly sloth's energy. She wanted to watch *Coronation Street* and eat Death By Chocolate cake and drink lots of tea.

She did, then slept for a half-hour on the settee, ate more cake and felt decidedly better. By 9pm she'd started to rerun the argument with Ben in her head, so decided to phone Angela for a chat. She and Angela had known each other twenty years ago at Art School but had lost touch until recently when they'd attended the same exhibition in town.

It had seemed like a huge coincidence at the time, both of them moving to Salisbury, but with hindsight Dawn realised that it wasn't really so surprising. Artists couldn't afford to live in London and found Brighton too crowded so they settled in Wiltshire instead.

Now she reached for her address book then realised she knew Angela's number by heart. She'd been phoning her friend much more since the recent break-up of her marriage. Angela herself had been divorced for over a decade so was living proof that you could go it alone.

She rang and Angela's teenage daughter Zoe answered on the third ring.

'Hi, Zoe. It's Dawn. Can I speak to your mum, please?'

'Yes, I'll get her.' Zoe was polite as ever though she sounded slightly disappointed or generally low.

'It's just for a quick chat,' Dawn added, not wanting the teenager to think that she was planning on a visit. Not that her visits ever seemed to interrupt a mother-and-daughter chat.

Soon Angela picked up the phone. 'Sorry, I was just bathing Jack.'

At 9pm, Dawn thought that four-year-old Jack should have been in his bed but as usual she kept quiet. Angela wasn't like the mothers you saw on the gravy adverts, but she did OK.

'Should I phone back in half an hour or...?'

'No, I was just drying him when you called. Zoe's said she'll put him to bed.'

Good. Now they could have a Ben-based chat. Dawn reached for her glass of wine. 'Ben and I had our first fight last night.'

She heard Angela's snort.

'Oh, did his mummy tell him to come home early?'

Angela had been making more age jokes than was strictly necessary. Dawn gripped her glass harder. 'No, I'd PMT so I threw him out.'

'In the middle of the night?'

She made the wine swirl round and round until it splashed over the rim onto her baggy pyjamas. 'Well, we went to bed not long after the cinema so it probably wasn't that late.'

'And did you shag the poor bastard before kicking him to the kerb?'

'Uh uh, we started to but then I suddenly went right off the idea. You know how it is when your period's due and you just don't feel like it?'

'I always feel like it,' Angela said.

Dawn grimaced. Her friend's sex drive had ensured that she got pregnant on a one-night stand five years ago, the result being little Jack.

'Anyway, I asked him to leave and lay there hating him all night and felt like Methuselah when I got up this morning. But now I'm starting to feel guilty as hell.'

'Phone him, then.'

'I guess I should. But what if he's still angry?'

'He won't be. Men calm down quickly, especially if you let them sleep on it.'

That was true. She'd spent most of her adult life married to Richard and he'd always been incredibly easy-going. But then he'd been seventeen years older than her, whereas Ben was her junior by fifteen years…

'What'll I say? I don't want to mention periods or anything like that.'

She heard Angela snort. 'Why? He's probably bought tampons for his sister.'

'He doesn't have a sister.' It felt good, knowing things like that.

'Make a joke of it – say that you were hormonally challenged.'

'Hell, no – he'll think I'm going through the menopause.'

She heard Angela laugh and laugh, heard what sounded like Zoe talking in the background.

'I thought I might take him out to a really good restaurant on Friday,' Dawn said.

'Thought you were cutting back?'

'I am, but... well, I think I owe him one. I'll make it the last time I take money out of savings.'

'Yeah, I said that when *my* marriage broke up,' Angela said.

There was no mistaking the irony in her voice; Dawn hesitated. 'Easier said than done?'

'Let's just say it's been a decade since I closed down my savings book.'

Angela must be living solely off benefits then. It couldn't be easy. It was lucky that Jack was going to school in another year and she'd be able to find work.

'I know what you mean. I didn't realise how often Richard bailed me out until he was no longer around to do the bailing.'

'You want him back?'

Dawn hesitated. She'd love to have the old Richard back, the man she'd married. He'd been intelligent, funny and kind.

He'd been a reassuringly solid thirty-seven when they met and she'd been an uncertain art student aged twenty. They both had the same interests and the age difference hadn't mattered a bit. And it had continued not to matter until Richard entered his fifties and started losing his hair and his perspective. He'd swapped his cord trousers for embroidered jeans and combat pants.

'You want him back?' Angela repeated. Dawn wondered if she was taking notes.

'I... well, he's got Rachel now.' She strove for levity. 'And he's probably still wearing that ridiculous baseball cap.'

She immediately felt guilty for voicing an anti-Richard thought. He'd always been so good to her. But she'd mocked his trendy new togs once too often and he'd found himself a girl who didn't laugh...

She heard Angela sigh. 'I saw him in town the other day. He's still wearing it.'

'And the built-up training shoes?'

'I was too busy reading the message on his T-shirt to look at his feet.'

Dawn knew that she was supposed to ask what the T-shirt had said, but she refused to. It didn't feel right when she criticised the man. She'd loved him too long and too hard to talk badly of him for extended periods. She'd always assumed that they'd be together until death carried one of them off. Every one of her acquaintances had been amazed at the sudden break-up. Every one of them had seen her and Richard as the perfect couple, a love match who would never part.

She'd thought that too, had been unable to believe it when she found him kissing Rachel. She'd felt so lonely and scared and washed up until she started dating Ben...

'So you think I should phone Ben?' Dawn knew she was repeating herself but that was what women did. It was one of the reasons that female friends were so vital. Men tried to solve each problem the moment you presented it to them, whereas other women understood that you needed time to talk all the details through.

'Of course. Call him and grovel, girl.'

Dawn forced a laugh. Her relationship with Ben wasn't like that. He admired her because she knew more about art and life than he. She'd once been in awe of Richard so she understood Ben's slight reverence and was in no hurry to fall from grace.

'That's why I thought taking him for a meal would restore the peace.'

'Or keep him in. Give him yourself wrapped only in a ribbon.'

'It would have to be a bloody big ribbon,' Dawn said, contemplating her pyjama-clad curves.

'You look fine. He's nuts about you. You know he is,' Angela said.

She'd met Ben in what was supposed to be a chance meeting in a cafe. In truth, she'd begged Dawn to set it up and Dawn had at last relented. The 'fancy meeting you' had felt awkward and she'd been very glad to leave.

'Right, I'll ring him now. Will I phone you tomorrow and let you know how I got on?'

There was a silence then Angela said, 'Not tomorrow, no. I've got a date. How about Friday?'

'I hope to be out with Ben on Friday.'

'Hell, we girls are just so popular,' Angela muttered in her inimitable dry way.

Dawn thought quickly. Hopefully she and Ben would go to bed after the meal on Friday night and possibly stay in bed for much of Saturday. Best keep things casual. 'OK, Angie, I'll give you a ring sometime over the weekend.' She realised belatedly that she hadn't asked about her friend's hot date. 'So, who's this new guy you're seeing?'

'What?' Angela sounded bemused. 'Oh, just some bloke.'

'I gathered that. So where did you meet him?'

Another pause. Dawn wondered if Angela had been drinking. The local supermarket had been selling off bottles of Romanian wine at three pounds each.

'It was at Jack's nursery. He's a single dad.'

'Uh huh, and where are you taking him?'

'Just a pub,' Angela said.

'I suppose Zoe'll babysit?' Zoe was always babysitting.

'Suppose so,' Angela said.

'Well, don't do anything I wouldn't do.' *Don't turn into the girlfriend from hell like I did.* Dawn brought the phone call to an end then leafed through her address book for Ben's number. She'd been brought up to believe that the man should make the first move – and most of the later moves. Her mother had been very passive and overly proud.

She'd never been as languid as her mother, Dawn reminded herself as she dialled. The receiver was picked up quickly and a male voice said Hi.

'Ben?'

'No, it's Ralph. But I can get Ben for you.'

'That would be brilliant.'

'Who shall I say is calling?'

'Dawn,' Dawn said.

'Dawn the illustrator? Ah, we've heard quite a bit about you.'

'Yeah?' Probably that she turned into Frankenstein halfway through sex.

'Mm. Ben showed us one of your comics and we all thought it was great.'

Dawn felt something expand in her chest. It must be serious then, if he'd told his flatmates. 'I do paintings too. Discount for friends if you ever want to buy one,' she offered happily.

'We're already saving up,' Ralph said with a smile in his voice. 'I'll get Ben for you then,' he continued. 'Just be a mo.'

Dawn gulped her half glass of wine. Finally she heard footsteps approaching.

'Dawn – it's Ralph. There's no answer from his room. I knocked and shouted that you were on the phone.'

'Maybe he's asleep,' Dawn said hollowly. She hadn't realised until now how much she wanted to hear his voice. Suddenly she wanted to apologise profusely and tell him that she cared.

'More likely he's in town. He gets home before the rest of us so he could have had a quick shower and gone out again. Shall I ask him to phone you when he gets in?'

Dawn looked at her watch. She wanted to go to bed soon. Unlike the girls in the adverts, she never felt like roller-skating at this time of the month.

'Better not. Look, can you just tell him that I'll meet him on Friday at nine, take him out for a meal?' She named the restaurant. 'Tell him I'll meet him outside unless I hear from him to the contrary. Tell him I'll pay.'

'Don't want a second, do you?' Ralph asked jokily.

'No, Ben suits me just fine.' She hoped Ralph would tell him that. 'I'm sure we'll meet up sometime,' she added and Ralph said that he hoped so too.

Good. Now she'd made amends for last night's harsh words – and had found out that Ben really liked her. Feeling hopeful about the future, Dawn went upstairs to bed and slept.

CHAPTER FIVE

P   *lease go, go, go…* At last Ralph had gone. Ben stared at his locked bedroom door, his heart pounding. He so wanted to hide away. And he'd succeeded so far, waking up before his alarm and taking his still-bleeding body to the shower. There he'd taken a new carton of shower gel from the cupboard and soaped and soaped. He'd gone downstairs and made toast and tea with exaggeratedly quiet gestures, tiptoeing back to his room with it before the other housemates arose.

Half an hour later he'd lain on his side on the bed and listened to them rising and shining. He wondered what they'd say if he told them what had happened to him a few hours ago.

At last they'd left and he'd gone back downstairs and locked the main door from the inside, then made sure that all of the windows were similarly lockfast. He'd left the answering machine on but removed the page of the telephone message pad that was clearly meant for him. *Ben – you lucky bugger. Dawn wants to takes you for a meal on Friday if you can meet her outside this restaurant.* It was followed by a venue and a time and a little smiling face.

Ben put the note inside his dressing gown pocket. He couldn't think about meals now. He just wanted drink – gallons of it. But first he had to phone in sick to work.

He dialled then gave his name and department. 'I've been ill all night. I won't be in today.'

'What's the nature of your complaint?' The human resources person sounded anything but human.

I got fucked in the arse by some psycho and I'm still haemorrhaging like a pig.

But he'd never tell anyone about that – never, ever. Aloud he said: 'I think it's a stomach bug.'

'Do you think you'll manage in later today?'

Not unless wild horses drag me. 'No, I need to get some sleep.'

'Tomorrow, then?'

Tomorrow was an alien concept. He was just getting through minute by minute. 'I'll let you know.'

He half listened as the women did some spiel about how many days you could go without an official sick note. *Tell it*, he thought dully, *to someone who cares.*

He hung up and poured himself a drink from the bottle of spirits he'd brought downstairs, then went into the lounge and switched the TV on. A grey-haired presenter in his late sixties was flirting with a glum brunette of forty, telling her he still felt young. *Is Age All In The Mind?* read the caption. Did it matter? Ben switched quickly to Meridian. It too had a talk show going on. *Slim Down Or Get Out* was the topic. A flushed, large-breasted woman was sitting next to a pinched and clearly self-conscious man.

No wonder housewives drank. Ben helped himself to another vodka and juice, flicking on to the cartoons. A mouse hit a cat with a mallet then a bulldog with razor-sharp teeth bit the cat's tail off. Feeling increasingly shaky, he switched off the set.

The day passed slowly as he alternately dismissed various TV programmes and dozed fitfully on the settee.

He made himself toast whenever his stomach protested, and searched Ralph's magazines and books in the hope of finding an article on what he'd endured last night. He wanted to know whether he should be on antibiotics, whether he'd need some coagulant cure to stop the bleeding. He wanted to know that he wasn't alone in this.

Articles about impressing women, about improving yourself. Other articles on getting work promotion. There were surveys about men and exercise, men and sex, men and beer. At one stage the word rape leapt out at him but it turned out to be about a man whose bitter ex-girlfriend had wrongly accused him of the crime.

Was there nothing on male rape? He went through every publication Ralph owned until he saw a sidebar with the words 'right up his rectum'. He read it then felt even more sick. An elderly man with gay fantasies had taken to balancing on the slim posts at the foot of his bed, moving down to let the pole penetrate his anus. When he hadn't been seen for a week, police had broken into his flat and found him dead on the protuberance. He'd slipped and the pole had ruptured him.

How long had the pole been? How far in had it gone? He himself had been penetrated for six to eight inches. Was this blood he was losing just from tearing around the rectum or had that bastard actually ruptured something inside?

He should really go to the hospital. Ben showered again in preparation for the visit. When he at last felt slightly cleaner he looked at his white face in the mirror and knew he wasn't going anywhere. He was walking very spread-leggedly, for one thing, and couldn't face the stares of the waiting taxi driver. For another, he didn't want to sit down and risk spreading further blood over his trousers and the taxi seat. He was in that no-man's-land where he wasn't ill enough to phone an ambulance but wasn't well enough to go to hospital by himself.

It had only been a few hours. Give it time. As it grew close to the hour when the others arrived home, he took bread and spreading cheese up to his room and locked himself in.

Thursday and Friday passed in the same slow vodka-and toast-fuelled way. He showered every hour. He channel-hopped the TV and went over and over the encounter in the deserted park.

On Friday night he sat behind his door and listened till the others went out then skulked down the stairs and got onto his side on the couch. His rectum had at last stopped bleeding but was itching fiercely. He'd have to leave the house soon and get more TCP.

He watched the usual Friday night comedies, amazed that they had ever made him happy. The voices hurt his head so he turned off the soundtrack but the colours then coalesced to burn his eyes.

There was a radio built into Ralph's sound system. Maybe he'd find something less mindless on it instead. He found one of Wiltshire's local stations and listened to a phone-in discussion about loneliness. How would they feel if he phoned in and suggested a heart-to-heart about getting fucked up the arse?

The drink he'd finished earlier in his room was beginning to lose its effect. Ben walked carefully over to the two new bottles of vodka that Jim had bought for him. Jim was the hardest drinker of the flatmates so had thought nothing of it when Ben handed him a twenty-quid note and asked him to get stocked up.

He poured himself a glass and added a splash of lemonade. An elderly woman was crying on the radio. His spirits diving even lower, Ben reached for the off switch then stopped as the local news came on.

'...Police want to question a man seen acting suspiciously in the Southampton Road area of Salisbury in the early hours of Wednesday morning, around the time a local woman, Gillian Barnes, was stabbed to death.' The newscaster's voice was replaced by that of a representative from Wiltshire Police. 'A witness has described seeing the man leaving the Gardens. He's described as having dark hair and a pale complexion and is aged between twenty and forty. He was around five-foot nine, dishevelled, wearing jeans and a torn shirt – clothing which is possibly blood-spattered and which he might since have changed.'

Fancy someone being murdered in Salisbury, Ben thought hazily. *I hope they catch him*. He curled back onto his side and poured himself another anaesthetising drink.

CHAPTER SIX

Where the hell was he? Dawn sat in the centre of the subtly lit restaurant feeling like a dildo. Christ, she hadn't felt this vulnerable since being stood up on her second date at age fifteen. All of the other diners were in twosomes, foursomes or sixsomes. Only she was dating the Invisible Man.

'More wine, madam?'

Dawn unpeeled her fingers from her empty glass and pushed her lips up into a polite smile. 'No, thanks. I'll wait for my boyfriend.' She'd told Ralph that she'd meet Ben here at nine and it was now half past.

For the first time she wished that she had a mobile phone or second sight so that she knew exactly what had happened. Was this his revenge because she'd been a bitch on Tuesday after the cinema? Surely he'd have forgiven her after three whole days?

A man alone is simply a man alone – but a woman on her own is often seen as sad or desperate. Soon the waiter was hovering near her again and she was sure that his gaze was of mingled pity and curiosity. At thirty-nine, she was older than most of the madras-munchers. Did he think that she'd always been unattached?

For the first time since leaving Richard, Dawn wished that she still wore her wedding ring. It had given her a sense of security. She'd worn the ring from the time she was his bride until they'd separated a few months ago.

Forget the past. She'd been trying to do just that and had actually been succeeding until this evening. For the past few weeks she'd had a potential man in her future instead of a scary question mark.

Two of the waiters were looking over at her and whispering. She was clearly the main entertainment. Dawn stood up and walked over to them, paid for her glass of house white.

Outside it was exceptionally mild for October. She walked the long way home, taking deep breaths, trying to keep her sadness from showing. Should she phone him in case he hadn't gotten her original message? Wait for him to call her? It was like being a teenager again.

The clubbers were out in force by the time she reached the town centre, the boys from the nearby villages practising their two-syllable vocabularies. The girls, their teeth chattering as they stalked about in their pubis-skimming skirts, said less.

She, Dawn, had a lot to say, but maybe Ben was tired of hearing it. Maybe he wanted one of those perfect-skinned creatures, some rap-loving babe that was closer to his own energised age. He'd seemed so rapt in her that her hormones had gotten complacent. She'd shouted at him and now he was effectively telling her to go to hell.

So be it. She was an adult now, a strong person who had survived a recent marital separation. She could find a new boyfriend or just concentrate on her job at the post office and her illustration work. Or, she could go to teacher training for a year and become an art teacher. Dawn thought of all the wonderful creative years ahead of her, then she went home and howled like a kid.

Gradually she cried herself into a state of calm. She didn't want to be alone tonight but Angela already had a date and Ben was ignoring her. Richard wouldn't ignore her. He'd always laughed at her jokes and admired her art.

She had almost finished her latest serial for *Crisis*, his longest-running humorous magazine. It was as good an excuse as any. Dawn picked up the phone.

It was only when he answered that she realised her heart was beating fast. She'd so wanted him to be home, to be receptive.

'Rich? It's Dawn here. I'm just popping out to the off-licence so I'll be in the area. Shall I bring my latest instalment round?'

'I don't see why not.' She couldn't miss the reserve in his voice, a reserve that had started when their marriage was crumbling. She tried to ignore it, not knowing how to make things right.

'OK, see you in twenty minutes then.' Hurrying to the mirror, she put half a ton of deep-purple eyeshadow over her red-rimmed eyes.

It was odd walking up the path to the bungalow that had until recently been her home. The little front garden was now nettle city. Other than that, everything looked the same as before.

Richard answered the door *sans* baseball cap. That was a good sign. She smiled at him warmly. His white jeans and grandad shirt weren't as kind to his midriff as they could have been, but he looked fresh and neat. At least he'd ditched the baggy knee-length socks and windcheater look.

He grinned at her four-pack of Babycham.

'Repeat after me, my name is Dawn Reid and I am an alcoholic.'

Grinning, she repeated it.

'Were you working when I called?'

'No, I was just preparing a stir-fry. D'you want some?'

He'd never made stir-fries when he was married to her.

Dawn followed him into the kitchen and watched as he threw various exotic vegetables into the wok. 'Prawns?' he asked, then added: 'I have to eat them when Rachel's not around. She's a vegetarian.'

'That must be why she's so undernourished,' Dawn said coolly. 'Prawns would be great,' she added, suddenly realising that she'd only had a glass of wine all night.

They ate at the breakfast bar then moved onto the settee in the lounge where they drank the Babycham. 'You never drank this before,' Richard said.

'So sue me. I just wanted something different.'

I've changed, she thought. *I've lightened up and become more experimental. Can't you see?*

'I thought you'd be out with your toy boy on a Friday night.'

'I saw him during the week.' She thought about adding, *it's not that serious*. Sitting here with Richard, the words wouldn't feel like a lie. She and Rich had so many years of laughter and shared thoughts and experiences. They'd been so foolish to let them go.

She could tell Rich that she and Ben weren't soul mates and then she could kiss him. And then...

Dawn leaned forward. A metallic sound echoed down the hall then a young girl in leather trousers and a red halterneck top appeared in the doorway.

'Hi there,' the girl said.

Richard pulled himself up from the settee. 'Hi Rachel – Dawn just came round to bring me the latest serial.'

'For *Crisis* magazine?' Rachel asked.

Dawn nodded, feeling her face go red then white. Her heavy makeup and the Babycham told their attempted-seduction tale.

She got to her feet. 'Nice to see you again, Rach.' She did her best to make it sound like Roach. Then she turned to her husband and raised her voice by a few decibels. 'Rich – thanks for the prawns.'

It was his turn to go red but the sight didn't bring her much satisfaction. So he was still with that bimbo – and the bitch clearly had her own key. Ben probably had a new girl and Richard had Roach and even Angie had a date tonight. Dawn hurried home and cried herself to sleep, wondering if she was the least loved person in the whole of England tonight.

CHAPTER SEVEN

Nick wept – or, to be accurate, irritated water ran from his right eye. He swatted it away, but it was quickly replaced by further moisture. Fuck it, this sea air just wasn't agreeing with him.

Nothing was agreeing with him. He'd felt increasingly pissed off since arriving in Bournemouth. He'd been here for three days but it felt like a week.

He wasn't used to being conscious in the mornings – that was partly the problem. Normally he'd get up at around 3pm in Brighton, fry up some steak and eggs then go to the gym. He'd stay there for two hours then go home and have a bath and a bit more protein. Then it was on to the club to make sure everything was smooth as a virgin's pussy before going to bed with Claire at 6am.

Who the fuck would she be going to bed with now? A well-set-up bitch like her had plenty of offers. He'd thought that he'd be in there for at least a year. Claire paid well – and she liked to laze around when she got up in the late afternoon or early evening so she'd never hassled him about the hours he spent at the gym. Christ knows, she benefited 'cause when he was in the mood he was so wired that he could go like a piston. Luckily she was one of those broads that could come from getting fucked.

He could do with getting laid now. He'd had a permanent half hard-on since taking these stackers this morning. Maybe the dealer had sold him Viagra rather than anabols.

Nick walked along the wide-paved front of Bournemouth then manhandled his erection so that he could lean comfortably against the metal rail. He stared out at the vast grey sea. Where would a fit man end up if he just started swimming? He'd missed so much school that he didn't have a scooby about geography.

He was finding his way around town all right but he didn't like what he saw. The place was too light for him, too picture-postcard. Brighton was a seaside town too but it at least had a street-fighting, pill-popping side that suited his mood. In contrast, the Bournemouth he'd seen so far was all kids in pushchairs or rich bastards flitting from shop to shop with designer bags.

He'd seen this programme about the lapdancing clubs here but so far he hadn't fucking found them. Not that he planned to pay in order to get a hard-on that wouldn't be satisfied. But these places might need security like himself – or bar staff. He'd have to do something soon as he was running out of cash.

Nick looked at his watch. It was still only midday. It would be hours until the clubs around here opened. What the hell was he to do till then? He'd just spent the last two hours at a gym lifting weights and running on the treadmill. He'd gotten a day pass, so would go back in a few hours and aim for an even greater number of reps. He'd done the same thing at another gym yesterday. The gear was good but he was missing his own bed, his cooker and TV. Well, they were Claire's really, but for the past few months they'd been as good as his.

Was this as good as it was going to get? A bed in a hostel and a walk by the sea? Nick scanned the other side of the road and saw a cinema, crossed over to it. He read the billboards, hesitated for a moment then turned away.

His face didn't fit in places like that. He'd been twice with girls but had felt fucking awkward. He'd sat up straight when everyone else was slouching. He'd spoken in a normal voice when seemingly you were supposed to keep it low. He'd never been to the movies as a kid – never been anyplace. He only knew pubs and clubs because his mum had worked in them. He shivered and fastened the top button of his denim jacket. He hoped that he would never be like her.

No, of course he wouldn't – she was always getting herself fucked whereas he did the fucking. She was always getting herself beaten up and then acting the drama queen. Mum had been one of life's victims whereas he, Nick, was always willing to fight his corner, kick some ass.

He wished he had something to kick now. The salty freshness of this place was making him feel almost dirty. He'd had a shower at the hostel and another at the gym but his armpits were heating up again. His cock was also on fire yet his chest felt cold – and his eye was still watering. Just the one eye, mind, as if he was only partially gutted about something bad.

He hadn't cried since he was ten, since breaking his wrist. He'd been just about to watch his favourite pro-gramme when Vince, mum's boyfriend, got up and told him to get four white rolls from the shop on the corner. White rolls – the alcoholic's haute cuisine. Vince thought that they soaked up last night's bottle of gut rot, that they were easy to digest. Now that he, Nick, was a bodybuilder he knew all about nutrition, knew that white dough was a digestive nightmare. But Vince had known fuck all about anything except how to share his fists.

So he'd run all the way to the shop and all the way back with his usual ten-year-old energy. He dashed into the living room towards the TV – and tripped over Vince who, for some reason, had lain down on the floor. He'd gone flying, put out both hands to save himself and heard a loud snap.

'Stupid bastard!' Vince had snarled.

'Sorry, Vince.' He'd tried to get up but this huge wave of sickness had washed over him and he'd felt so ill that he started crying.

'Fucking stop that.' Vince had lashed out at his head, sending him flying back into a sitting position.

'It hurts...' He'd kept holding his wrist and gulping back the nausea, more and more tears dripping down his face

'Stop whining or I'll really give you something to cry about.'

The blows to his head and shoulders had gone on and on. It was only when his wrist swelled up to the size of an orange that Vince had phoned his mum.

Mum had never liked him to cry either. She always said 'Oh, give it a rest, Nick,' if he wept when one of his step-dads was having a go at him. But Vince was the first of her lads who had made it forbidden to cry, who'd hit him again and again if he wept. After that last beating he'd taken from the man – moments after his right wrist was broken – he'd never cried again.

He hadn't even cried when Vince... when Vince started doing what Vince did. With a plastered right wrist, Nick hadn't been able to do up his trouser zip or his buttons. 'You'll need to help him, Vince,' mum had said. 'I mean, I can't do it. He's a little man.'

But Vince had treated him like a little girl. Vince had... Nick broke into a run towards one of Bournemouth's shopping centres, not wanting to think about what Vince had done.

Vince had taken him to the doctor each time he had to get the setting bone checked. Vince had even come into the surgery with him. Vince had done most of the talking, just as he did at home when mum was around.

One time they'd been in the waiting room when a boy slightly younger than himself left the nurse's unit holding his arm. He was crying that it hurt and the nice woman with him had said, 'Shall I kiss it away?'

There had been a couple of girls later who'd wanted to kiss it away. Problem was, they wanted the sparkly ring, the nice flat, and the squalling baby. They wanted you out of your denim jacket and into the type of outfit that ponced-up actor's wore. They also liked you to stay home with them and watch some braindead soap opera when you'd rather be at the gym.

No, he was better off without a steady girl – or at least, better off without someone clinging to his ankle. Mind you, he didn't like being totally on his own in a strange town like this. He didn't know anyone in Bournemouth and he wasn't going to be around for long enough to really get in with the local dealers. He'd used a few of the code words that a stranger uses to get some gym candy. Other than that, he hadn't spoken to a soul all day.

Back in Brighton he knew everyone Claire knew – all the bouncers at her club, all the regulars, all the bar staff. He'd also known the more streetwise of the trainers at his regular gym.

But he couldn't go back to Brighton. Claire's large-fisted mates would make sure of that. And he sure as hell didn't want to stay here by the seaside. Fuck it, he'd go back to Salisbury and stay with Yurek for a while. It would seem to any passing copper that he was only just arriving in the cathedral city. No one would connect him with that bitch's death a few days before. In Salisbury he'd have a place to live, a mate of sorts and his pick of the gyms in Wiltshire. And he'd soon find some classy little bint to take it up the ass.

CHAPTER EIGHT

Surely the rapist had just been passing through? After all, he hadn't had a local accent. Probably some addict who had already moved on to a bigger town. *He was safe, safe.* Ben told himself as he walked to the door that led to the outside world. It was a bright autumnal Saturday morning and he had to get to the shops for snacks.

He reached for the handle and the movement created a very focused jolt of pain. Ben winced and moved his legs further apart, spreading his weight until the hurt abated. But his cleft felt sticky again, made him yearn for yet another bath.

The shops could wait. Ben walked carefully upstairs and ran the taps and was soon submerged in bubbles. It was four days since the encounter in the park and he'd washed so often that his skin was rough.

At last he left the relative sanctuary of the bath and made his way downstairs. He was turning into a couch spud. What option was there when he didn't have the concentration to read a book, when he couldn't face the cinema or shops? His nose prickled and he reached into his dressing gown pocket for a tissue – and found a piece of paper saying to meet Dawn outside a local restaurant on

Friday at nine. This was... Ben ticked off the days in his head. Hell, this was Saturday. He stared at the scribbled date as if willing it to change.

He'd better phone her now. She was worth more than being stood up. She was special. Until the... *incident* in the park he'd thought about her a lot.

Phone her now, he urged himself again. Since Tuesday night he had split into two people. The grown-up part told him to go to work, to tell the police, to do his grocery shopping. But the wounded little side said to lie on the couch and have a drink instead.

Ben had a drink, then another. He practised saying 'Dawn? It's me,' a couple of times in a calm yet apologetic voice. What the hell was happening to him? He'd never been Mr Universe but now he'd become a home-based, voiceless thing.

He dialled. She answered. 'Dawn, it's...' He realised belatedly that he was speaking to a recording. When the taped voice finished he said that he'd only just found her message, that he'd had a migraine, that he'd been off work. He said how sorry he was, hesitated, then added that next time he'd buy the curry. He didn't feel up to seeing her yet so finished with the words, 'Speak to you later, then.'

Would she phone back soon? He tried to think of things to say. She was part of his old life, part of his outside life. She'd want him to gaze into her eyes and take her places but he longed to stay here and watch the cartoons.

Ben looked at the clock. It was 11am. Was she out shopping? His brain cleared slightly. No, she worked all day today. Some of Salisbury's post offices closed at lunchtime on a Saturday but Dawn worked in the one that stayed open till after five. They'd talked about it before, bemoaning the fact that she couldn't stay in bed late like him after they slept together on a Friday. It had seemed very unfair at the time.

But now he was glad. Ben went to the freezer and found a pizza that belonged to Ralph, Jim or Bart. He'd have to owe them a thin and crispy. He baked it and ate it, washed down with another couple of drinks. He was just finishing off the telltale crusts when Bart came home with a mate.

Ben sat up straighter on the settee and tied his dressing gown cord more tightly around his waist. He wished that he had all his clothes on. He and his flatmates often sat around wearing shorts or towels, but that was before...

Bart seemed to pick up on his discomfort. 'George wants to check out the clay-pigeon sites on the internet.'

'Right.' Bart had only gone online last week and kept bringing people home from work or the pub to see his new techno toy. Ben was less impressed, having had access to the web at work for the last two years. Several of his colleagues checked out various football and horse-racing sites in their lunchbreak but he'd never been particularly interested in anything like that. His own hobby, artwork for the adult-comic market, was well represented but he'd preferred to spend his spare time creating new sketches rather than surfing around to admire existing ones.

No, despite working with computers all day he was never going to be a Net Head. Ben reached for the remote control to turn the volume down as the adverts came on. The movement sent the now-familiar pain up his sphincter and he suddenly realised that he could search online for cases on male rape. Hell, he'd spent the last few days tearing this house apart in case there was a single article in a men's magazine when there were probably hundreds of self help features on the net.

Go, go, go he silently urged, listening for signs that George was fucking off somewhere. He heard voices from the adjacent room for a full hour. Just how many sites could there be about firing at plastic birds?

'Clay man's got a thirst on him,' Bart said, walking to the drinks cabinet and selecting two cans.

'Thought I'd check out some of the comic sites when he's finished.' That was a safe thing to say – Bart thought Ben's comic art was ace.

'Sure – we're off to the match later this afternoon.'

By late afternoon he might be the first man who had died from rectal itching. He might have damn near hung himself because he was so pissed off.

'Whatever,' he said and Bart looked at him strangely.

Ben refilled his glass and wondered if he should book-mark one of the problem-drinkers sites.

At last the avian-killers went away and he stumbled through to the computer and located the best search engine. He paused, wondering which key words to use. If he just put 'rape' he'd find sites aimed at female victims. He thought some more, made a decision, then did some exaggerated listening to make sure that the house was still empty. It was, and he keyed in 'male-on-male rape.'

Immediately, dozens of site descriptions started to appear. Ben leaned forward gratefully – then froze. He had to force himself to keep reading. *Watch Young Studs Being Fucked Up The Ass*, offered one site. *Hot Male Virgins Take A Good Ten Inches* offered another. He pushed down against the chair as if trying to protect himself from some new invader, kept clicking, scanning. Every single site was using male on male rape as porn.

He wanted statistics and medical expertise. He needed to know that other young men had survived this. He needed to know when this hellish fear and disgust would abate.

Ben was still clicking down the numerous descriptions list when he heard a key in the lock. Damn, Jim was away for the weekend so it must be Ralph this time. He quickly exited the machine and walked up the stairs to his airless, curtain-closed room.

Ben lay down on the bed. Ralph could never sit still for long. He'd be out again by teatime. He'd find the help he needed then. He could wait.

He dozed until he heard the door slam shut then he went down to the lounge and stole one of Ralph's bananas from the brown bag on the work surface. He ate it as he scrolled down the screen. *Cum In Tight Teen Boys. Rape A Rent Boy. Hot Male Arses For XXX Climax Now.*

All those jokes about prisoners bending to pick up the soap in the showers... He'd laughed too but until now he hadn't known exactly what he was laughing at. It had seemed such a comical image – but the reality was tearingly different. He'd thought that someone online would understand but instead they just wanted to hurt him further. Surely there had to be at least one other man out there who felt as violated as himself?

Ben surfed on, on, on, keying in different sets of words about men and rape – and constantly finding hardcore porn sites. Why did so many men want to plunge so viciously into other unconsenting men? *Something good will happen soon*, he told himself as site after site offered up unwilling male arses. Surely his life couldn't get any worse?

CHAPTER NINE

Dawn dialled for the fourth time that night. Ben couldn't be on the phone this long. She'd been trying to call him ever since she came home from work and played his message. Her heart – or whatever bit of her anatomy it was that registered happiness – had suddenly felt a whole lot lighter and she was desperate to talk to him direct.

But now her pleasure was fast turning to irritation as the engaged signal bleeped on and on. God, even Angela – whose nickname at College had been Minnie Mouth – didn't talk this much.

Maybe he was playing hard to get? Maybe he'd taken the receiver off the hook because he didn't want to go out with her this evening? Well, two could play at that game. She'd phone Angela now and invite herself round.

It was 8pm before she got to Angela's but four-year-old Jack was still wide awake. He was sitting on the settee between his sister, Zoe, and a somewhat overweight boy of fifteen or so that Dawn hadn't seen before.

'This is Rob, Zoe's squeeze,' Angela said with a brittle laugh.

Zoe blushed and said 'Mum!'

'Pleased to meet you, Rob.' Dawn held out her hand, determined to treat the teenager the same way she treated adults. She could still remember how belittling it was when grown-ups started each sentence with: 'When I was your age...' She and Richard had worked for years on various adult comics and met their readership at twice-yearly parties so she was comfortable around people in their teens.

Zoe, as usual, was fifteen going on fifty. It was strange, Dawn thought, how a slightly wild woman like Angela had produced such a conservative daughter. Zoe was a very nice girl – but youthful experimentation and rebellion had somehow passed her by.

'Cordial?' Angela asked with a lopsided grin.

There was clearly a subtext here – but then there usually was with Angela. Dawn picked up the bottle and read the label of the organic blackcurrant soft drink.

'Love some,' she said.

Angela fetched a fifth glass and poured some of the concentrated juice. 'Rob's family manufacture it, you know.'

Dawn wondered how long it would take for her friend to arrange the teenagers' wedding. She bet Angela was researching countries which allowed child brides.

'If you're looking for berries, Rob, there's these wild bushes growing by the roadside...'

'They'll be full of lead from car exhausts,' said Rob. 'They'd give you lead poisoning.'

'Right.' She'd promised never to patronise teenagers – so she shouldn't feel slighted if they knew more than her. 'Is that where you two met, at the wholefoods store?'

She knew that Angela lived off toasties and coffee but that Zoe saved up her money from her paper round to buy organic fruit and free-range eggs.

'No, at the cycling club,' Rob said.

'I've just joined,' Zoe cut in. It was the longest sentence she'd ever made without prompting.

'You must be cycling for miles most days, Zoe.' Dawn

knew that Zoe cycled on her paper round and cycled to school.

'It's good exercise and it's the transport of the future,' Zoe said.

'You wouldn't like to go cycling now, would you?' Angela muttered, looking pointedly at them both.

'Mum!' Zoe said. 'Rob's here to talk about the school fete.'

Angela raised her eyes towards the ceiling then grimaced at Dawn. 'In our day we got pissed behind the bike sheds. Now they plan how to sell organic cordial for charity.' She looked resignedly at her daughter. 'Want to change the world with Rob in your room?'

'I'll put Jack to bed first,' Zoe said stiffly, turning to her little brother who was now sleeping against her side.

'Did you bring a real drink?' Angela asked Dawn.

Damn, why hadn't she thought of that? Dawn shook her head. 'I was so mad at Ben that...'

'You mean you still haven't made up since Tuesday?' Angela said.

'No, we have. At least, he phoned and left an apologetic message. But each time I phoned back he or one of his flat-mates was on the line.'

'So...?' Angela prompted.

'So, I've given up for tonight and here I am.'

'Seems I'm second choice as usual,' Angela said, pushing her long multi-plaited hair back from her face.

Third choice, as Rich was still seeing fucking Roach. Dawn felt guilty. 'Tell me about your date,' she said. She tried hard to remember further details. Wasn't Angela supposed to be seeing him tonight?

Angela glanced towards the door. 'Oh, it was fine. We had a few drinks and a laugh, nothing heavy.'

'And are you seeing him again?'

'He absolutely insisted on it,' Angela said.

'Way to go, girl!' There was a silence, which Angela ended by making a joke about Jack's project-loving nursery teacher. Angela seemed to hate anyone who had goals. 'I'll pop out and get us that bottle of wine,' Dawn said, knowing that her friend couldn't afford to drink on supplementary benefit.

'Make it a big bottle – I've had a hell of a week,' Angela said.

At least they had that in common, Dawn thought as she scoured the bargain buckets in the off-licence before settling on a bottle of Blue Nun. They'd drunk it by the case in College and the memory might cheer Angela up.

As she waited to pay for the wine, the television in the corner started to relay the nine o'clock news. Dawn watched as a male photofit appeared. It looked somewhat like Ben.

'Police are still hunting the killer of Gillian Barnes...' She listened once more to the details of the Salisbury murder. She'd heard those exact same facts on the radio in the post office every day.

But it was scarier hearing them at night when she was out on her own, and when she'd be walking home later. Dawn still felt especially alert on the streets after dark. She'd been married for so long to Richard, who drove her everywhere in the evenings, that it felt alien being in town late alone.

She hurried back to Angela who already had the corkscrew out. She joined her friend sitting at the table near the fire.

'Reckon I'll have to live on this stuff if Zoe marries into Rob's family?' she asked, putting aside the cordial.

Dawn shrugged. 'Are you sure they're even dating? They didn't seem very...'

'Oh, you know what Zoe's like. She's probably forbidden kissing until the wedding night.'

Dawn nodded non-committally and was glad for the millionth time that she didn't have children. She wouldn't have wanted her daughter being afraid of sex – but she also wouldn't want to push her towards it before she was ready, the way Angela did.

Angela poured the wine.

'Here's to men,' Dawn said, raising her glass. It seemed a safe toast now that Angela had a new boyfriend.

'Here's to money,' Angela replied. 'I've put an advert in the paper to sell Jack's old cot and pram to make a few quid.'

'Right. You'll have a friend with you when strangers call round? You can't be too careful.'

'Hell, I can handle a young dad any day,' Angela said, tilting her glass and drinking with dehydrated haste.

Had they talked about Angela enough? Was it OK to mention Ben? Being with him was brilliant – but talking about him was the next best thing.

'I wonder who Ben was on the phone to,' she asked.

'I'll get my crystal ball out,' Angela replied. She reached for the Blue Nun again.

Dawn ignored the comment but it reminded her why she and Angela couldn't ever be best friends. There was a prickliness about the other woman that got in the way every time they started to get closer. Dawn was grateful to Angela for providing companionship after her marriage to Richard had ended. But she was also aware that if she'd remained married she wouldn't have sought out Angela's company so frequently.

Still, you didn't have to love someone to spend a couple of hours with them. And she'd rather be here than sketching alone in the flat.

Dawn tried again. 'Maybe it was one of his flatmates on the phone.'

Angela shrugged. 'Have you met them yet?'

'Uh uh.'

'Girl, you're taking far too long to get your feet under the table.'

'Well, he lives at the other end of town so I can't stay there during the week or I'd never get to work on time.'

'Saturday night, then?' Angela drained her glass again.

'Yeah, I could manage Saturday. But with me working all day and living in the city centre, it made more sense for him to come to me.' Plus she'd been waiting for him to suggest it, but her take-no-prisoners friend needn't know that.

'Just turn up at his house then.'

She'd done that with Rich and only got a few prawns for her trouble. 'Nah, I'm not as brave as you.'

'A girl of his own age would just turn up.'

Dawn wasn't sure that was true but she let it go. 'I'll phone him again tomorrow.'

'Ask him if he'd like to buy some organic cordial,' Angela said heavily. 'My darling daughter's filled half the kitchen with it.'

'It's good stuff. You could do worse.'

'I'd rather she was dating a gin-maker.'

'Or a Blue Nun baron,' Dawn said, then burped and added a giggled. 'Maybe not.'

'I'm glad she's dating anyone. I was starting to think she was gay,' Angela said.

'Would that be so bad?'

'Guess not – I'm not desperate for grandkids.'

'Me neither,' said Dawn and giggled again.

'You're a lucky cow, Dawn – no responsibilities.'

Dawn thought of her rent, her bills, her six-day week at the post office. 'I'm not so sure about that.' It had been different when she'd been married to Richard and just doing freelance art. Her time had been her own then – and so had most of her money. The adult comic he edited had brought in the mortgage every month.

'I sponsor Vitor,' she said lamely, aware that it was really stretching her budget to sponsor the Guatemalan child nowadays.

'But you've no real kids,' Angela persisted ungrammatically, pouring herself another glass. She grinned, 'Except Ben.'

'Angie – he's twenty-four. Hardly an infant.'

'You were almost fifteen when he was born. That's Zoe's age,' Angela said.

'So?'

'So he's brought out your maternal side.'

'Bullshit.' They could hardly keep their hands off each other and the sex hadn't been Oedipal.

'I think the surrogate mother protesteth too much,' Angela said.

Dawn looked at her watch. It was still too early to go home – but if she and Angela talked much more they'd have a fist fight. 'Anything worth watching?' she asked, indicating the small TV.

Angela shrugged. 'The usual game shows.'

'Maybe there's a movie on.' She wished yet again that her friend had a video recorder so that they could watch pre-recorded tapes.

They watched a film that they'd both seen before, making offhand comments from time to time. Angela finished the wine and made them both another cordial. The movie ended and the late-night news came on.

Dawn was half dozing in the armchair when Angela said, 'That's Ben.'

Thinking that he'd entered the room, she automatically ran her fingers through her hair to make it more buoyant. Then she woke fully and realised what a dork she was.

The photofit of the Salisbury murderer was again being flashed on the screen.

'You mean it looks a bit like Ben,' Dawn said.

'It's the spitting image.'

'You only saw him for fifteen minutes in a cafe.'

'Yeah, but I've seen that photo of the pair of you plenty of times.'

It was true – she and Ben had had their photo taken in a group the night they met, all of the freelance artists grouped together. They'd been flirting at the publishing party for the previous half-hour so both of them looked absurdly pleased. Dawn had pinned the photo to the outside of her fridge to remind her not to eat too much junk food – hell, not too much anything. If you had a younger lover, you had to look your best. Angela would have seen the photo each time she helped Dawn dry the dishes after she'd been round for a meal or a few drinks.

'Well, lots of guys have dark hair and dark eyes like that.'

'Guys who're his height, who also walk home along the Southampton Road?'

'But she was stabbed outside one of the warehouses at the far end of the road – Ben walks in the opposite direction.'

'Unless he was going to the all-night Tesco.'

'Why would he?'

'Maybe he ran out of cigarettes?'

'He doesn't smoke,' Dawn said, and felt pleased with her reply. Then she gave herself a mental shake – why did she have to give her new boyfriend an alibi? 'Angie – Ben's the gentlest man I know. He's really considerate. He'd never stab a girl to death.'

'You'd had a row that night,' Angela pointed out.

Dawn suspected that her friend was playing devil's advocate.

'Yes, but I was the one who was mad. Ben was very controlled about the whole thing.'

'Exactly – the quiet ones are the worst.'

'He's not that quiet.' *Just self-contained.* She forced a jokey note into her voice. 'So when I see him, d'you think I should put the handcuffs on?'

'On him or on you?' Angie asked.

'Whoever,' Dawn replied then grinned. She wondered if Ben was into any of that. So far they'd done it missionary style and on their sides and with her on top. Her breasts looked best when she was sitting astride him. She'd often done it doggy-style with Richard – but now that she had a younger lover she wasn't sure if her hips looked toned enough.

She'd have to join a step class, if they still did such things. Trends changed so quickly. She reminded herself to keep up with the times. These were Ben's exploratory years and she must be a fellow explorer rather than a doppel-ganger for his mum.

'If there was a reward we could turn him in,' Angela said wistfully.

'Just settle for selling off Jack's cot.'

'Well, the advert went in yesterday and the phone hasn't started ringing.'

'People probably don't read the ads till tomorrow,' Dawn said, knowing that Sunday was her own catching-up day. She thought about the crime cases that she'd read where people were raped by strangers who'd called round to buy something. 'Just have a neighbour with you when you're expecting a buyer.' She hesitated, 'Or if it's in the evening, you can even call me.'

'Thanks, but I'd hate to drag you away from your love slave,' Angela said with her usual dry wit.

The wine, cordial and her goodwill finished, Dawn started to say her goodbyes and stepped out into Angela's hall. The other lights in the house were off – Rob had apparently let himself out and Zoe had gone to bed, an atypical teenager.

Dawn jerked her head towards Zoe's bedroom. 'Angie – it's good that she's got someone,' she said.

'I guess. He's not exactly a pin-up, though.'

'Remember the cordial millions.'

'Knowing my luck, they'll give it all away to Greenpeace,' Angela replied.

The two women didn't have the kind of relationship where they embraced, so Dawn touched Angie briefly on the shoulder. Suddenly she felt sorry for her – for all her bohemian makeup and notice-me costume jewellery, she was still a broke, stay-at-home mum.

Dawn left the flat feeling very glad that her own life was less constrained – then her alertness intensified when she remembered that she was on the same midnight streets as a potential murderer. The dark-haired and dark-eyed killer

could be on the next corner, his long, sharp blade waiting
to pierce her flesh.

CHAPTER TEN

Richard listened to Dawn's answering-machine message again. It was 11pm. Where was she? He hated to think of her walking to the off-licence when there was a killer around.

Or was she out with Ben? He'd hoped that they'd split up when she came round on Friday. For an hour, as they'd cooked and eaten, he'd felt the loving feelings creeping back.

Not that they'd ever fully gone away, at least not on his part. He'd fallen in love with her within weeks of their first meeting. He loved her warmth and her humour and her unconventionality. Dawn was like him – she didn't want children or a nine-to-five existence. They were both free spirits. Only now she was free of him...

'You have a caller waiting on the line,' the operator said. Richard forced his thoughts away from Dawn and took the call. Bugger, it was Rachel. 'My cousin's gone home early, so I thought...?'

He felt his stomach tense in a little. He'd never been good at saying no to people. But he wanted to be alone. 'Rach, I'm planning on working half the night.' His studio and editorial office were both in the bungalow so she couldn't dispute this.

'Oh, I thought the new *Crisis* was almost finished?' She named the adult comic he produced twice a month.

'It is – but I'm doing the special *Wild Women* supplement for next spring, remember?' He almost added that she'd seen Dawn's artwork for it – but Rachel didn't like him talking about his ex.

'I could just watch you work.'

Perish the thought. 'No, you'd wear those leather jeans and you'd totally distract me.'

'I could strip out of them.'

She always tried to win him around by using sex. Richard stared glumly into the receiver. Most men were gagging for a horny twenty-two-year-old but at the moment he'd rather snuggle down to sleep with his estranged wife.

'I'll see you tomorrow, OK? I'll cook brunch here at midday.' He put down the phone before she could get tearful. Rachel had seemed very free at first – but now she wanted to be with him all the time.

And he didn't want anyone with him all the time, not even Dawn. She felt the same. They'd always had their own studies, and each of them went out at least one night a week to different work-related functions. The idea of someone being there, making demands, for hour after hour was purgatory.

It was one of the many reasons he'd never wanted to reproduce. It must be hell, having responsibility for someone else on a full time basis. The single mother who did his telephone sales looked constantly stressed. One time she'd had flu so he and Dawn had looked after her little boy. He was a nice child but they'd been worn down by his sheer physical energy and mentally drained through answering his questions all the time.

And the planet was so fucked up that he didn't want to inflict life. Dawn felt just as strongly as he did so had had herself sterilised.

Richard ran a hand wearily through his thick, slightly-greying hair. Three years ago he'd produced a grey hair every day, had feared his energy was fading. 'Toner low,' Dawn had grinned.

It had been all right for her – she still looked, and clearly felt, youthful. He hadn't felt ready to lose all his own verve yet. So he'd gone to a boutique and bought more fashionable clothes – and her laughter had intensified. He'd covered up the grey with a baseball cap and she'd refused to socialise with him.

Which is where he'd made his big mistake. Oh, he'd been right to keep wearing the cap – it helped him feel less conscious about his hair and it made him feel different. No, he'd been foolish in flirting with Rachel during her college placement with him.

It had started as a bit of fun, a way to cheer himself up. He'd dress in the morning and Dawn would say: 'Is the oldest swinger in town home for lunch today?' Then Rachel would come round and flirt with him in his office and in his studio. Dawn had her own studio upstairs and would only pop in occasionally. It clearly didn't occur to her that he'd be fancied by a twenty-two-year-old.

'How's the stick insect getting on?' Dawn had asked one day. He'd felt protective towards young-and-broke-but-not-so-gifted Rach, wondered when his wife had become so joyless.

'She's good – you've got competition.' That hadn't been true – Dawn's art was multi-faceted and natural, whereas Rachel could only manage a slow-won, studied look.

'Going to sack me, then?' She'd looked at him coldly.

He'd risen to the bait. 'I may set an exam to decide which of you I keep.'

It had been a cheap shot, designed to make her re-evaluate their relationship, realise how much she needed him. He was her boss and her landlord yet he felt totally unappreciated. Oh, he didn't want some little woman kneeling at his feet. Hell, he'd hate that. But, like everyone else, he wanted a partner who recognised his worth.

'Maybe I'll get a real job for a change, bring in more cash,' Dawn had muttered.

He'd shrugged and retreated behind his latest comic. 'If you like.' He hadn't thought she meant it. Their shared working and home life suited them both just fine. They had it all – a blend of togetherness and independence. Sure, they worked long hours to meet all their deadlines but at least they were working for themselves.

Then Rachel had burst into tears one day in his studio and told him that she hadn't got some community centre job she wanted. He'd hesitated then put his arms around her, trying to act paternally. She'd raised her lips to his and they'd kissed. He'd marvelled at the softness of her mouth, at the sweetness of her scent, knowing that this wasn't right, that he was married. He'd been about to pull away and apologise when he realised that Dawn was standing in the doorway staring at them.

'Christ, I'm sorry.' He'd pushed Rachel away so fast that she'd gone flying into a table.

'Fuck you,' Dawn had shouted then rushed out.

Later she'd returned to his studio, her face as pale as a corpse, her body shaking.

'I've taken a job at the post office and rented a flat. I'll be out of here in a week.'

He'd said that he didn't want her to go, that he loved her. He'd even tried to put his arms around her. But she'd become so hysterical that he'd backed away.

For the rest of the week she'd refused to speak to him but he'd cornered her on the day she left.

'Dawn, I know things between us are bad but I hope you'll still work for *Crisis*.'

She'd nodded. He knew she'd need the money and that real work, for her, would always involve politicised art.

Her voice had been thick with tears. 'I'll post it on.'

'No, please bring it round.' His voice had cracked. This

couldn't really be happening. He still expected someone to shout April Fool.

'Will *she* be here?' She'd jerked her head in the direction of Rachel's empty chair.

'I hope not. You know she's only here on placement. Once she gets a job and I give her a reference...'

'Oh, you can give her a reference all right,' Dawn had said bitterly, and then the strange little man running the Move-It-Yourself van had come in to say that all of Dawn's possessions were packed.

And now she had her flat and her post-office job and her new young lover so she didn't need him any more. Giving in to the tears that threatened most days, Richard wept.

CHAPTER ELEVEN

Only women bleed – and only women spend half their lives waiting. Dawn waited until almost lunchtime the next day before phoning Ben. When she dialled, she again got the engaged signal. This was taking 'it's good to talk' to extremes. Could there be something wrong with his telephone line? Dawn tried twice more after lunch but the bleeping tone persisted. Deciding to live dangerously for once, she called a taxi and went round.

There were four male names on the door. They sounded like a boy band. Dawn ran her fingers through her hair – she'd spent ages blow-drying the roots to give it a deceptively casual look. She'd also put on her best jeans, which fitted perfectly as long as she didn't make any sudden moves.

Hopefully she wouldn't be wearing them for long. She'd put her new white-lace briefs underneath. His younger girlfriends probably wore thongs but she had her limits. At thirty-nine, you didn't want to be caught in any sudden draughts.

Footsteps raced with youthful zeal down a thinly carpeted stair. Then a lock clicked and the door swung open. She smiled at the ginger-haired youth.

'Hi. Is Ben in?'

'Certainly is,' the unknown flatmate said. He led her into a small cosy room with a computer in it, the screen showing the menu options. 'Oh, he must just have left here. He was on the internet,' the man said. He turned to her. 'I'm Ralph, by the way.'

'Dawn.'

'The artist! We spoke on the phone.'

'That's right.' She hoped he'd like her dry wit. 'You were on the point of giving me a commission…'

'I probably should. Ben tells me there's little money in cartoon work,' Ralph said.

'Well, the creator of Peanuts did just fine. But Ben and I mainly work for the indies. They just don't have the budget of the mainstream press.'

'He said that – said he was very glad it was his hobby and not his full-time job.'

'Yeah – you couldn't live on it,' Dawn said with hard-won resignation. 'I've been doing it for years and still had to take a job in the post office recently.' She didn't add that was after her marriage broke up. She had no idea what Ben had told his friends about her history so it was best to keep things low-key.

'So, which post office do you work in?' Ralph kept the small talk flowing as he led Dawn out of the computer room and up a flight of stairs. Two of the posters on the wall were clearly Ben's handiwork – she recognised his strong use of shading. He had very talented hands…

They reached a closed door and Ralph knocked twice. 'Ben? You've got company.'

There was a long pause during which Dawn feared he wasn't going to answer, then there was the sound of a snib being drawn back and he was there. He looked even more beautiful than she remembered, but exceptionally pale.

'Hi, it's only me. I tried to return your call but kept getting the engaged signal.'

She watched him blink a few times and wondered if he'd been sleeping. 'Ah.'

'That's because you were online,' Ralph said to Ben. He hesitated. 'Right. I'll leave you two to it.' He looked as awkward as Dawn felt. She'd hoped that Ben would look pleased to see her. Instead, he seemed to have forgotten who she was.

'Want me to disappear again?'

Another pause. He was looking in the direction of her face but she could tell that he wasn't focusing. 'No, come in. Would you like a drink?'

He indicated a half-empty vodka bottle and a half-full glass. Strange – she hadn't had him down as a lone drinker.

'No, I'm OK.' She really wanted a cup of tea but feared sounding like his mother. Silence. She searched for something simple to talk about. 'Reckon I had enough to drink last night. I was with Angie and we drank a bottle of Blue Nun in half an hour.'

'Right.' A pause. 'How is Angela?'

She thinks you stabbed a girl to death. 'She's fine.' This was hell. They were like strangers. 'Ben, I'll go. You're tired.'

'It's not… I've had a migraine. I get them occasionally.'

Dawn felt some of the tension leave her legs. A migraine – that explained it. 'My mother got them – you know, the cluster type? They could last for three days.'

She watched him sit down on the foot of the bed then grimace. He was clearly in some pain. After a moments hesitation she sat next to him.

'Mine usually just last for one or two days, but this time…'

He looked as if he'd been a whiter shade of pale for ages.

'So that's why you weren't at the restaurant on Friday night?'

He nodded again then winced. His head must still be

hurting. 'I felt so ill that I forgot all about it. I could have kicked myself.'

'No problem – I could have had my pick of the waiters.' Even if they were just going to drive her to the nearest Samaritans.

He seemed to be staring at her more closely. 'I don't blame them. You look great.'

'You too.' His pallor only made him look more delicate, like a marble statue. Hell, she was starting to think like these older gay men who went on about beautiful boys.

'So, shall I kiss your head better?' It was a clumsy pass but she just wanted an excuse to hold him close, for everything to go back to normal. She sat there expectantly, waiting for him to whisper, 'Which head?'

Instead he just touched her fraternally on the arm. 'Better not – it still feels like it could fall off my body.'

'Have you taken anything?' Bad move – there were few steps between Mother and Nurse.

'Just this.' He indicated the vodka glass on his bedside cabinet.

Dawn knew that alcohol made migraines worse but decided to keep quiet rather than sound disapproving. 'Mum always felt better after she slept.'

'I haven't managed much of that.'

Another silence. Dawn looked around the room, half expecting to find a teenage nymphet peeking from the wardrobe. Something had made him change towards her. Surely a migraine that had started on Friday should be abating by now?

'So were you off work on Friday, or…?'

Another nod. Another wince.

She shouldn't be here. 'Ben, I'll leave you to get some rest. Just phone me when you feel OK.'

She stood up and watched him push himself painfully to his feet.

'Sorry, Dawn – I'm lousy company.'

'You're ill.' She could remember her mother sitting for hours with her hand over one eye, her facial skin stretched tautly. Later she'd vomit for a while then fall into a strange, paralysed sleep. Dad would make sure that they tiptoed around for the next three days as migrainous Mum couldn't stand the slightest sound.

Even when the pain behind one eye abated, the ordeal hadn't been over for she'd been left with a listlessness that lasted for another one or two days. Dawn could still remember Mum sitting about, her stomach bloated and her skin still unnaturally pale.

She could help Ben through this if he would let her – but in her experience men didn't let women help them through their illnesses. Instead, they tried to ignore them or medicated with vodka as he was doing now.

'Phone me when you're better,' she said again.

'I will. I promise.'

'And it's probably best to stay off the internet till your headache goes – the screen's bad for your eyes.'

She watched his face tense in as if he was annoyed or hurt or something. His mood seemed to be veering between distant and dazed. He shrugged and she decided not to push it further. He could do what he liked with his own head.

It was a beautiful head but it seemed to have no current interest in her. Dawn walked resignedly to the door, wishing that she'd worn jeans that allowed her to inhale occasionally. Her new panties were cutting into her arse crease and she felt as low as a stoat.

'See you soon,' Ben said.

Did he mean it? It was only when she reached his gate that she realised she'd forgotten to phone for a taxi home. Rather than go back to Hell House, she walked, her knickers dissecting her crack, the whole way into town.

She wouldn't tell Angie about this. Well, she'd say she'd gone round – but she wouldn't say he'd acted like a passing stranger. She could tell her friend about how nice

Ralph was, about their computer, about the posters on the stairway and in Ben's drink-filled room.

Angela thought that Ben looked like the killer – and the police had said that the killer would start behaving strangely. Ben had certainly passed the 'acting oddly' test. Reminding herself that he was enduring the last hours of a particularly bad migraine, Dawn pushed the damning thoughts away.

CHAPTER TWELVE

Salisbury Station was busy when he stepped off the train. This was good. This meant that there were witnesses to his arrival. Nick went into the cafeteria and looked at the ham and tuna rolls in the glass display. Then he asked for a cheese salad baguette, knowing that they'd have to make one up.

'Been busy?' he asked as the woman behind the counter grated the cheese.

'Not so bad now that the schools have gone back.'

He kept the conversation going. It was just small talk – the type of stuff his mum said from behind the bar. But he needed to say at least one unusual thing so that she remembered him, so that she could vouch he'd only just arrived in Salisbury rather than being there since the night that girl was stabbed.

'I'm going to stay with a friend who lives in town. Do you know…?' He named the area.

The woman looked doubtful. 'Well, you could ask one of the taxi drivers outside but if you're walking…' She fetched a map and showed him the way.

'Magic.' He reached for his wallet to pay for his coffee and baguette.

Not that he intended to eat most of it. Nick sat down so that his back was to the serving woman then pulled all of the doughy white centre from the French roll. Eating that stuff was like pouring putty into your system. It was pointless spending a fortune on gym candy if he was too sluggish to work out.

'If you want sugar it's on the counter over there,' the woman said, coming to clear the next table.

He didn't – he tried to avoid it in its refined form though he was aware that when he drank cherry brandy he was knocking back a plantation of the stuff.

Fuck it, everyone had their weaknesses. The broad sitting nearest him was clearly addicted to cake. She looked like a walking doughnut. In contrast, the guy at the table outside was thin and would get thinner as he puffed constantly on a cancer stick. He, Nick, avoided all of that but wouldn't want to be without his steroids. They made him take it to the max, making each muscle bigger, harder, stronger.

He had enough strength from the Bournemouth pills to help him concentrate now. He'd jog all the way to Yurek's. Nick finished the cheese salad filling and the crustier parts of his baguette, drained his coffee and stood up to go. He slung his backpack so that the weight was evenly distributed across his shoulders. He'd nicked the bag – and this cord jacket and matching black cord bootlegs – from a Bournemouth gym. The cord made him look even thinner and taller than he actually was. No one would connect him with the man who'd been here a few days ago in a waist-skimming denim jacket and faded jeans.

'Thank you. Bye,' the woman called. He left a big tip, smiled widely and waved. She was sorted. Now he just had to hope that fucking Yurek was in. Trust the old bastard not to have a telephone – but then, serious alkies never did.

Christ knows, he knew that already from growing up with his mum. She'd never had much but once the drink had gotten to her she'd had sweet fuck nothing. By the time she got her second ulcer – and kept spewing up – she'd had to give up bar work and go on the social. And the Government didn't give you the readies to buy absinthe from your giro cheque.

The optional furniture had gone first – the walnut sideboard that had belonged to her folks, the drinks cabinet she'd been given as a wedding present, the second-hand standard lamp in the corner. Later she'd sold her bed and then his bed. It had been a particularly bad day when the carpets went.

He jogged on, glad that it was so mild in Salisbury. In Brighton it got really hot – but the sea air could still be bracing. Claire would touch him after he'd been out running and say that his face was as cold as ice.

There was less of it to get cold now that he was growing a beard. He hadn't shaved during his brief stay in Bournemouth. A beard always made him look ten years older. It also made him look harder, wild. That was no bad thing if he was staying with Yurek. That mad cunt would bring home total psychos, providing they had the price of a pint. Nick knew that some of them would roll you for a couple of quid if they thought they'd come out laughing. You had to psych out your fellow dossers, watch your back.

He came to the end of Fisherton Street and ran on past various banks and building societies. He wouldn't be needing them. He'd always just spent what he earned – steak and steroids cleaned you out fast. He crossed the road then raced past the library. if he got bored he'd sit in and read a book on The Krays. He must have read at least four books about them already – and he'd watch the film if it ever came on the TV.

He hurried past a newsagent sign. *Salisbury Killer: Police Release Further Clues*. He wanted to get to Yurek's now but he'd come back here to the library tomorrow and read the papers. He bet the pigs were bluffing as usual –

unless you offed your nearest and dearest and wore a T-shirt saying *I Done It* they usually couldn't collar you for anything. He'd just been unlucky when... when he got sent down that time. But he didn't want to think about that.

At last he reached Yurek's gaff, the ground-floor flat in the land that time forgot. The window was so dirty that he couldn't see through it. He cursed Claire all over again. But this place was close to free – and he needed free until he could get himself some money. Nick walked through the urine stained entrance then knocked on Yurek's name-plate-free door.

Silence – but alkies took an age to open up. It took them a while to wake, took even longer to stand. And if they'd had a bottle of spirits that day, they had to relearn the art of walking. Mummy had taught him the A- Z of life after drink.

At last he heard loath shuffling accompanied by a pro-ductive-sounding cough. The door creaked open and he made himself smile at the unshaven, unwashed and possi-bly unintelligible man.

'Hi, Yurek.' He waited as the alkie's few remaining brain cells started working.

'Hello... my friend.'

Well, the old bastard wasn't falling-down drunk yet – but clearly didn't know who he was. 'It's Nick. You remember? Nick from Brighton. Tommy brought me here before.'

'You want to come in, my friend?'

I want to fucking *move* in, Nick thought. He held his breath as he moved past the old man, avoided searing his nostrils with mingled waste products. He walked towards an open door then walked through it. There was a very thin greyish carpet, held together by various stains. There was also an armchair in the room facing a recess which had clearly once held a TV. There was a carrier bag at the foot of the chair. Nick glanced down and could see it held a single can of beer.

Yurek shuffled in after him and collapsed back into his chair. Nick put his backpack against the wall then sat on it.

'So, how's it going pal?'

Yurek shrugged. 'I am… all right.'

Nick had forgotten how slowly the man spoke when he had a drink on him. Christ, he just wanted to get a big key and wind the old bastard up.

'Brought you something.' He went into the zipped front pocket of his bag and brought out a half-bottle of whisky.

Yurek's face lit up. 'You are… good…' He seemed to search for a final word.

'Nick.' Nick helpfully supplied.

'You… are…'

'Yeah, yeah. Here, let me take the top off for you.' He pushed himself upwards and handed the amber oblivion to the man.

Yurek tilted the bottle and took a long, fast drink. Nick watched the old man's eyes flickering as a little of the spirit ran down his stubbled chin. He wasn't used to the good stuff so it would soon knock him out.

'Yurek – I've got to go out for a bit. Can you give me a key?'

'Key… is…' He kept hold of the whisky in one clawlike hand, reached into his trouser pocket with the other and produced a Yale.

Moments later Nick let himself out of the flat – his new flat, even if it wasn't fucking Changing Rooms. It was time to call on a few agencies, to make sleepy Salisbury his permanent home.

CHAPTER THIRTEEN

There was nothing to fear in the daytime world, Ben told himself as he walked to work. It was a mild October Monday morning, his first day back since... since he'd taken ill last Tuesday night. Schoolchildren rushed past him, followed by their less energetic parents. A queue of cars edged along the road.

He was going to be fine, fine. He'd taken to repeating the word in his head like a silent mantra. Nevertheless, his underarms were swamped by the time he reached his office door.

'Ah, the wanderer returns.' Smiling words from his project manager who'd clearly missed him but didn't want to say so.

'Haven't wandered further than my duvet.' His stomach lurched. He didn't want to talk about bed with other men.

'That new girl too much for you?' He hadn't told his colleagues about Dawn but a couple of them had seen him in town with her.

Ben grinned wanly. 'I've been so knocked out with those migraine tabs that she probably thinks I've died.'

He thought about her as the morning progressed. He must have seemed very distant yesterday. It had been such a shock, her appearing in his room after he'd had so much to drink. He should phone and arrange something. He looked at the telephone but calling felt like a chore.

The hours crept by as he sat through meetings and wrote code and documented everything for the graduate engineers. He went hourly to the gents and cleansed himself with antiseptic tissues. He'd at last stopped bleeding but still felt unclean.

That night he walked home, keeping close to the lights. He could hear the same radio station blaring from many of the cars, a song about being good to your girl or she would leave you. Ben grimaced – he might not care now, but he'd surely regret it in the long term if Dawn told him to sling his hook.

At 8pm he phoned her. 'Hi. It's me. My head works again.'

He could hear the relief in her voice. 'I was worried about you.'

'Not as worried as my project manager.'

'I hope you're not sleeping with him!'

What had made her say that? Did he look gay? He searched for a witty answer but his comic side was out to lunch.

'So, you coming out to play?' Dawn asked.

'Love to,' he lied. He stared out into the darkened streets and knew he couldn't face leaving the house this evening. 'How about tomorrow? I could bring round some takeaway and a bottle of wine.'

He heard her hesitate. 'Tomorrow's fine but I'll meet you at the pub.' She named a central one. 'I'd like to get out of the house.'

'Thought you were just at Angela's on Saturday?'

'Yeah, but it's hardly orgasmic exchanging her house for mine.'

'The pub it is.' He could always have a drink before he went out.

The next day at work passed slowly, then he went home and bathed. Soon it was time to meet Dawn.

He scanned the lounge bar as he walked in but he was first to arrive.

'A vodka with orange and...' He tried to remember what Dawn drank but his mind was an empty vessel. 'And a packet of peanuts, please.' He looked at the bar stool but decided against using it. His body still ached if he moved his legs apart.

'Hi you,' she said when she came in. She kissed him lightly on the mouth. He breathed in her fragrance. He could see how perfectly her scoop-necked black top clung to her breasts but he felt no desire.

'They're having a cocktail hour if you want to...' He waved his hand in the direction of the large pineapple-illustrated sign.

'Yeah – it was market day. I'll have a pina colada,' Dawn said.

She was referring to the fact that coaches and buses brought people from the surrounding villages into Salisbury every Tuesday to do their shopping at the market. They got their pensions and unemployment benefit from one of the Salisbury post offices at the same time. Most only had access to one village grocer's shop, so the sheer variety of stores in Salisbury tended to over-whelm them.

'Did the big family come in?' he asked. She'd told him about them before and it had been genuinely funny. They'd been so overweight that they had to be virtually shoe-horned through the post office door.

'No – but we had the man who can't write so he just signs his giro with a cross. I write *his mark* next to it. Oh, and we had this woman whose clothes are falling to pieces. She paid some money into her savings account – and she's seriously rich.'

'Right.' He wasn't sure if he was supposed to smile at either anecdote. He realised he was watching each person that walked through the door, dreading the arrival of a dark-haired and chemical-breathed rapist. 'I'll get you that pina colada.' He got himself another vodka at the same time.

'Here's to a cure for migraine,' she said when he handed her the glass. She held it high then drank deeply.

'Hopefully it'll be months before I have another one,' he said.

'My mum's were hormonal so she got them at least once a month.'

'Ouch.' He tried to remember if her parents were alive. Best not to ask her. There was a short silence. 'My manager thought I was playing truant to spend time with you.'

'If only – you'd have saved me from Angela and her Blue Nun obsession.'

'Angela's gotten religion?'

He watched her laugh at his joke but he still felt fraudulent, knew he should be home alone.

'One good thing – I finished the artwork for issue 203.'

'That's brilliant. I should stay away more often.'

'I just hope Richard isn't in when I deliver it tomorrow night, then I can just leave it in the porch,' Dawn said.

'You can handle it.' She'd been so scathing about her ex that he found it impossible to feel jealous. She'd surely never go back.

'I know. It's just when he looks at me with those big hurt eyes…'

'Wear shades.'

She laughed again. She was just being nice. He felt weak and forced and boring.

'Knowing my luck, he'll have his teenage nymphet with him.'

'You could always bring your toy boy,' Ben said – then wished he hadn't. He just didn't have the spirit for macho posturing now.

He felt and saw large hands on his shoulders and jumped. 'Sorry mate – there's not much room,' said a male voice.

Ben looked behind him to see that the pub had filled up. He realised his mouth was hanging open and shut it double-quick.

'Did you think that was Richard?' Dawn said.

'Who? No. Same again?' He wanted to stand facing the strangers, to be ready if anyone made a sudden move.

Dawn asked for a white wine and he got himself the same. He pulled his chair especially far in when he returned so that people were less likely to touch him. He made a succession of encouraging noises as she told him about applying for an artist-in-residence post.

His bladder twinged its warning so he looked over a sea of male heads to the door marked Gents. He'd have to squeeze past them. Then he'd have to unzip himself and... his system closed tightly at the thought.

'Listen, there's a good movie on. How about coming back with me? I'll ring you a taxi later.'

Dawn grimaced slightly. 'My house is closer.'

It was – but he badly needed a shower. And the last time he'd walked home from her house via the park...

'I know. But I've got some new work I want to show you.'

'OK. We can flag down a cab,' Dawn said.

They did and she kissed him as they sat in the back seat. He returned the embrace, hoping that his bladder wouldn't give out. He wondered if he'd win an Oscar. He hoped Ralph, Bart and Jim would talk to her when they got back. He wanted Dawn to be part of his future – but he couldn't deal with the present for thinking about the past.

They reached his home and he locked the door once they were inside. Then he checked the locks on the windows.

'I yield – I'm your prisoner,' Dawn said with a wide grin.

'What? Oh right.' He gestured to the lounge. 'Want to go in there and put the TV on? I'll just grab a quick shower.'

Taking the stairs two at a time, he soon reached the bathroom, urinated like a horse then stepped naked under the spray. He closed his eyes as the gel ran down his flesh. He'd find a movie or a video for them to watch and then he'd kiss her a chaste goodnight.

'Is there room for two in there?'

He screamed as the curtain was pulled back.

'Sorry!' Dawn said. 'It's me, not Anthony Perkins.'

'Right. I won't be long.' *In other words, fuck off out of here.* But she was already pulling off her scoop-necked top.

'I've had a long day too.' He watched as she finished undressing herself and stepped under the spray. She slid her hands around his waist. He felt his cock start to lengthen slightly.

'Is he pleased to see me?' Dawn murmured.

Not too pleased, Ben thought.

'You're so silky,' he said. He'd said it to a previous girl-friend and she'd been pleased. He tried to remember what other compliments he'd paid her.

'Richard used to say that,' Dawn said.

'Forget Richard.' *Or go back to him until I feel better.*

'Help me forget him,' Dawn whispered.

Ben took his hands and put them over her breasts. 'So silky,' he reiterated obediently.

'They've missed you,' she said.

'Missed this?' He bent obligingly to suck them. He wondered how long he'd have to caress her. Long enough to reassure her but not so long that she expected full sex.

'Let me soap you.' She took the gel and filled her palms with it and soaped his front then turned him gently round. 'Oh, your back's scarred. What happened?'

A sick fucker traced his knife along it. 'Just an accident at work.'

'But how…?'

He winced as he felt her finger tracing the long red scratch. 'Some of the guys were fooling about with a metal ruler. I just stood up at the wrong time.'

'What with that and your migraine, you have been in the wars.'

He forced a laugh. 'I'm an insurance risk.'

'I'd insure you.' He felt her palm cupping his balls and lifting them up.

'Dawn? You're driving me crazy but my flatmates are due back. Mind if we just watch the film and cuddle?'

He watched the disappointment turn her lips downwards but she rallied quickly. 'Course not. I'll take a raincheck on having my wicked way.'

They dressed and curled up close on the settee. They kissed and smiled and talked during the adverts. He kept one eye on the clock, wanting the film to end, for her to leave.

At last the credits rolled and he pulled himself to his feet and called her a taxi. They hadn't been Romeo & Juliet but they'd gotten by.

Slowly he walked up the stairs to his room, noting that his thighs felt weak. All this lying around had been bad for him. He wondered if he should take up running or join a gym.

CHAPTER FOURTEEN

An hour after he left Yurek's, Nick walked into the social and made his Jobseeker's Allowance claim. Not that he wanted a fucking job just yet – he needed some gym time. But he had to look as if he was desperate to start work this very moment if he wanted to claim any benefit.

'There's almost full employment in Wiltshire. You should be able to find something soon,' the clerk said.

'Right. Cheers.' He grinned his pretend grin. He needed a couple of weeks to get his act together and nick some stuff to kit out Yurek's pit.

'And you're claiming from today?'

'Yes, sir.' It never hurt to play the politeness game. 'I was working in Brighton as I said, but that job came to an end so I went to Bournemouth. But the clubs have their pick of doormen so there's nothing doing there.'

'It's a popular place,' the man agreed. 'Well, you should do fine here. Salisbury has a lot of pubs and a couple of really busy clubs, plus some of the hotels have disco nights.'

Did he look like John Travolta? 'Cheers, I'll soon get sorted.' He was going to get his body sorted out right now.

The man read Nick's carefully-completed form. 'You can have a giro delivered to the house or we can pay the money straight into your bank account for added security.'

People like him didn't have bank accounts. 'Sending it to the house is just fine.' He'd probably have to sit by the letterbox to stop one of Yurek's hangers-on trying to nick it and forge his signature.

He'd have to give Yurek a few pounds to keep him sweet as his living there would affect how much Yurek got from the social. Once he would have winged it, said he lived in the house on his own – but he didn't want to get done for fraud at the moment, couldn't do anything that might bring the pigs rushing round.

'We'll be in touch if we need to ask you anything else.'

Lucky me. He smiled his way out. Fucking bureaucrats. They'd done everything but take a blood sample and a drugs test. Talking of which...

For the next two hours he walked from one gym to the next, asking what a monthly pass cost, checking out the staff and the other punters. He didn't want one of those nancy places full of Rosemary What's-Her-Name looka-likes. He needed a competitive set-up where the punters got pumped and sold gear.

Only when he'd run out of options did he go into a cafe and order a fresh orange juice and an omelette. They had the Salisbury Journal on the paper rack so he read it with his meal. The new clue was that the killer had had his belt undone and his shirt only partially tucked into his jeans.

That was crap for a start. He'd had on a chambray shirt that... Nick suddenly remembered the little punk that he'd fleeced and sorted. This was magic – someone had seen the mummy's boy after Nick had finished with him and assumed he'd offed the girl.

He grinned then belatedly glanced up as a female hand put a bottle of tomato sauce next to him.

'Something funny?' asked the short, round, twenty-something waitress.

'Just remembering a joke.' He told her one that he'd overheard on the train. Then he looked more pointedly at the paragraphs about the murder scene. 'I'm just reading about this terrible crime in Salisbury.' He'd heard the rich guys talk like that in the Brighton clubs.

'That's right. Butchered like a pig, I heard.'

So the waitress was an ordinary joe like him. He added a little tomato sauce to his plate so that she hadn't had a wasted journey.

'Me, I thought this was a safe city to move to.'

'Oh, it is – there were two murders on the same day years ago, according to my mum, but there's been nothing since.'

'You've lived here a while then?'

'Well, in Shrewton. It's a nearby village. Most people live in the villages and come here to work.'

'Yeah? I've just arrived from...' He thought about it and decided to say Bournemouth rather than Brighton. 'I'm staying with a mate. Bit of a dive, really, but it'll do till I get sorted.' That had to be the understatement of the century.

'Great. So will you be working here?'

It was only when she sat down next to him that he realised she was up for it. He looked at her more closely. Twenty or so, gingerish hair that she'd tried to dye blonde. He could tell it was a home job. His mother had had more differently coloured roots than a border's worth of plants.

She was a couple of stone overweight – but unemployed bodybuilders couldn't be choosers. He remembered how recently the Bournemouth-bought anabols had made his cock hard.

'Well, I'm checking out the entertainment scene.' It didn't hurt to exaggerate so he added, 'Back home, I own part of a club.'

'And you want to own one here?'

She'd be mutton to the slaughter, this one. 'Thinking about it, if the price is right.'

She leaned forward. Her breath was stale, as if she hadn't eaten for a while. The brown eyeshadow on her lids had melted into creases. He wondered when she'd last got laid.

'The Chapel – it's a club just up the road. Does a good trade. And there's another club on the outskirts…'

'Yeah, I've heard good things about The Chapel.' The name was new to him until ten seconds ago.

'My sister sometimes comes in from Downton and takes me there.'

Where the fuck was Downton? Did nobody live in the city centre? He nodded like a man of the world.

'She has three kiddies and can't get a babysitter or we'd go more often.'

He was bored and he'd probably feel horny again soon. He might as well take the hint and give her a reason to go on living. 'Tell you what, why don't you come along with me when I check the place out tonight?'

'Yeah? That would be great.'

She'd gone quite pink. He hoped she had her own place. He couldn't exactly take her back to Yurek's. He arranged to meet her outside the cafe at 9pm.

'What's your name?'

'Cheryl.' She looked at him expectantly.

'Paul Prend,' he said. It was a name he used whenever he wanted to keep his head down, the name of an old school friend.

'See you tonight, then, Paul.'

She was never going to win an originality award. He watched as she walked over to another customer. Her legs were quite thick at the top – he liked slim, taut thighs. But maybe if she spread them wide enough they'd thin out a bit. Hell, it was pussy on a platter – and he'd never been one to refuse a free meal.

'See you later, darling.' He did his cute hand-flapping wave. It made him look different to most other guys. He probably was different – he'd had to raise himself from the time he was eight.

He'd been sitting still in this cafe for too long now. If you sat around your buttocks splayed out. Mum's boyfriends had had beer guts and slack, white arses. They'd...

He had a sudden desire to pedal fast, to run on the treadmill until his thigh muscles were hard as metal. He needed the strength to punch and jump and kick.

Nick walked swiftly to his chosen gym, ready to buy a one-day pass. He'd have to make enough tonight to pay for a three-month membership. Luckily he was going clubbing and there should be a shoulder bag or two lying around.

He strolled in wearing his best boyish smile. 'Hi, I've checked the others out, but you're the best.' *In other words, I can do deals here.*

The receptionist didn't exactly wet herself with enthusiasm. 'If you'd like to fill in this form?'

As usual they wanted his life history. *Mother an alkie, father fucked off with mother's sister. Haven't been to a GP since breaking my wrist as a kid,* he thought mockingly. They asked all sorts of questions did the happy families type – but they didn't like hearing the results.

'Thing is, pal, I just want a one-day pass until I can get to the bank.'

'If you want to pay for a year now we can take a cheque.'

Not till I've nicked one. He smiled at her. 'I've just moved here, you see. Haven't sorted out my finances yet.'

'Oh, OK. I can give you a free-trial pass but you'll have to go round with someone. Steve, can you show Mr...?'

'Nick,' he said, giving his first name to appear friendly.

'Can you show Mr Nick the ropes?'

Fuck it, he'd rather have had a girl to show him round. He didn't like those poncy guys with their perfect teeth and their thirty-quid aftershaves. His own teeth weren't so white on account of not seeing a dentist since he was nine.

But Steve was smiling his way over, dressed in the staff tracksuit, wearing state-of-the-art cross-training shoes. He'd have these the first time the bastard unlaced them. He'd check out the changing rooms any moment now.

'I'll just get changed,' he told eager-beaver Steve.

'Right. Have you exercised before?'

'Yeah, but not here.' Christ, did he look like a beginner?

'Ok, well, I'll show you where the changing and shower areas are.'

You would. He'd hoped to check out the petty cash in the snack bar and the staff room for himself. 'Thanks, mate. That'd be ace.'

He kept up the cheerful patter as he surreptitiously cased the joint. Wiltshire folk seemed to be shiny, happy people. But Steve looked like he had natural happy hormones rather than ones made in a lab.

Nick shucked off his cords and hurriedly replaced them with his shorts. He was even quicker at changing his shirt for a T-shirt. His chest was still much thinner than he wanted it to be.

'So, what's your usual regime?'

He told Steve his current exercise programme.

Steve made a poor approximation of a whistle. 'And you're doing that every day?'

He did it at least twice a day but the man didn't have to know that yet. 'Uh huh.'

'So are you in training for something specific?'

For kicking the shit out of anyone that gets in my way. Aloud he said, 'I might do a marathon at some stage.'

Steve seemed to cheer up at the sound of a specific goal. 'The treadmill next to the row of speed bikes – I'll show you it in a minute. It's for longer runs. We have a guy trains for marathons and he runs on it for forty minutes at a time.'

'I want to do more arm reps, too.' *Want to have arms like fucking Popeye.* The sailor man had lied, though – spinach just didn't do the trick.

'If you're aiming for arm mass you should be doing cable curls – but do them at the end.'

Nick nodded. 'I usually start off the arm work with bench dips.'

The trainer seemed to look at him assessingly. 'They're certainly a good warm-up for the triceps. You could go on to do overhead extensions with a free weight.'

He knew some of this. He'd read all the muscle mags that the gym he used in Brighton had to offer. But it was best not to come over as a bigmouth. He'd listen. He'd wait.

Steve showed him the cross-training machines, the rowing machines, the stepper, the various bikes and overhead bars. He demonstrated how to adjust each piece of machinery. Nick dutifully tried out every piece of exercise equipment – but refused to lie down, take hold of a weight and let Steve support it above his chest.

'If you let go, mate, I'm going to be minus a face.'

Steve smiled some more. 'That's why we insist you have a partner for this exercise, so that you can't drop the weight on yourself.'

He'd risk dropping it on himself before he'd have some other fucker drop it on him. Hell, someone you'd dissed could pay your gym partner a few quid for them to let the weight slip.

'Nah, I'll skip that one.'

He also skipped the one where you lay on your belly and used your calves to move weights which developed the hamstrings. With your head, back and backside unprotected, anyone could have a go at you. Anyway, his calves were strong as he walked or ran everywhere.

Steve had just started to adjust a machine to strengthen Nick's biceps when the receptionist shouted, 'Steve – you're needed in the sauna.' Steve excused himself and went into a little huddle with the girl. For a moment, Nick wondered if the conversation could be about him but that seemed unlikely as he hadn't fingered a wallet or bought any gym candy yet.

He looked around the various punters, wondering which was the man with the plan. There'd been a likely contender earlier but he'd scarpered. He'd like some roids now rather than waiting until Rubens mailed him them. For a while, steroids had been in fashion and every girl with a skipping rope had wanted them. They'd made headlines alongside flesh-eating bugs and killer dogs. But now the fad has passed and it was only serious bodybuilders like himself who were on the gear.

'I know how it works.'

Nick jumped slightly and turned in the direction of the voice. An overweight kid of about sixteen stood there smiling shyly.

He was about to say *hoo fucking ray* in his most sarcastic voice then remembered that he was trying to fit in.

'Oh, right. Steve was showing me but he got called away.'

'I heard – someone collapsed in the sauna. Steve's got a first-aid certificate.'

Nick grinned. 'That's handy.'

'They probably have to have someone qualified by law.'

He was a bright kid. Well spoken. His trainers were new and sure as hell weren't from a supermarket. Nick stared at the boy's chubby arms as they adjusted the machine for him. He'd be a nice-looking kid if he just toned up and lost the puppy fat.

'Sorted.'

The word sounded wrong coming from this softly-spoken guy. He wasn't streetwise. Just a fat kid that probably got bullied after school. God knows, he'd been down that road, though in his case they'd taken the piss because he was too thin.

Nick dredged up a half smile. 'Thanks, mate. You train here a lot?'

'This is my first week. I go to this cycling club and one of the other cyclists recommended it.'

'You bunking off school?'

The youth looked shocked. 'No, finished at three-thirty today. I came straight here. I'm going to come here every day after school.'

'They told me just to come every second day,' Nick said. Not that he planned to do what the bossy bastards said.

'They say that to everyone – supposed to be about giving your muscles a chance to rest.' The boy lowered his voice. 'But we had a bricklayer building our extension for weeks and he didn't take time to recover. I reckon the staff just want to avoid the gym being crowded all the time.'

'Good thinking – I'll drink to that.' Nick walked towards the water machine and was pleased when the teenager followed him over. Having a mega-rich fan club suited him just fine.

'They told me to drink at least ten glasses of water a day,' the youth volunteered.

'Is that right?' Nick already knew how to look after himself but he figured it wouldn't hurt to play dumb and then dumber. He let the kid ramble on about the importance of a carbohydrate snack within forty minutes of finishing a session at the gym.

Time to find out if the guy had money to spend. 'So, you working out to impress some girl?'

'No, my girlfriend Zoe likes mc just fine.'

Nick could tell that he was very proud to have a girl-friend.

'Does she come here too, then?'

'No, but she goes cycling with me.'

'Yeah? I used to have a motorbike.' Nick spent the next ten minutes answering the boy's questions about it.

'My parents would never let me have a bike.'

Nick bet they could afford to buy the motorbike factory. He wondered exactly what Mummy and Daddy did to pay for fatso's gym membership.

'Ignore them. In a year or so you'll be able to buy your own.'

'I suppose I could get one when I go to university.'

It was the way of the world – some kids were born to go to university and others were born to be bouncers like him. Only he was going to be the best fucking bouncer on the planet, was going to be so fit that he didn't have to take any bullshit. And maybe if he had enough muscle and stood on enough toes, he could work his way further. Hell, he'd been halfway to owning his own club when he'd been shacking up with Claire.

'You have to pay your university fees these days?' He'd heard it on the news.

'Yes. They changed the situation just after I went to secondary school. Some of the parents can't afford to support their children so the students take out a loan.'

'Reckon you'll have to do that?' They were on adjacent speed bikes now, cycling faster and faster.

The teen looked surprised. 'No, my folks do OK.' He leaned forward and Nick saw that he was putting the bike onto a less strenuous setting. 'Talking of cash, don't leave anything in the changing rooms. Apparently stuff gets nicked.'

You ain't seen nothing yet. 'Yeah, so what do you do with your wallet whilst you're here?'

'Put it behind that desk. See? They have CCTV there.'

Fucking CCTV. It had stopped many a man from earning a dishonest crust. He might have to get a loan from Teen Bank in a mo.

'So, you got a nickname?'

'No – everyone just calls me Rob,' the boy said.

'Yeah? I'm Nick.' He raised his right arm to start the high-five gesture but noticed that Rob took a while to catch on. 'Reckon I'll be here most days about this time. Maybe we can train together?' he said.

The kid flushed with pleasure and nodded like a toy dog. Nick kept working out with him until Smiley Steve arrived to demo the rest of the iron. Then it was time to get himself kitted out for his date.

He'd spotted a store earlier on that didn't have security

guards. Nick walked in, went quickly to the suits and selected a lightweight one. He furtively picked up another in a smaller size – his size – and hid it underneath the first suit. 'Can I try this on?'

'This way, sir.' The young male assistant bounded before him to the changing cubicles. It was almost teatime but Nick had a feeling they hadn't had many sales that day.

He swiftly dropped the smaller suit so that it fell into his bag. He toed it fully inside then made a pantomime of trying on the larger jacket. If the boy popped his head around the cubicle he wouldn't see anything amiss. Then he bent as if to tie his shoelaces but instead reached into his bag and tore off the stolen suit's security tags. He pushed the tags into the adjoining cubicle. It was time to make a break.

He walked back into the store and handed the boy the larger suit. 'I really like it but the sleeves are far too long.'

'We can have them taken in for you.'

'Oh, I know.' He had to act like he spent his entire life in clothes stores. 'But I'm going abroad this weekend.'

'Where to?' asked the youth.

Nick's mind blanked. Why was everyone around here so fucking friendly? 'A cruise,' he said, seeing the poster of a liner on the wall.

The boy frowned. Nick felt his stomach flip.

'Tell you what, I'll have a quick glance round the other shops. If I can't find something suitable I'll come back here and pay extra for you to alter it quick.'

He was breathing fast as he walked to the door. Some clothes had hidden tags nowadays. Some stores shared a security guard between three of them. He concentrated on walking briskly but not suspiciously fast.

Nick only slowed down when he'd put several streets between himself and the outfitters. He scanned the street until he saw a small woman in a long fur coat pulling a shopping bag on wheels behind her. Cue his spending money. He followed her into the supermarket and watched as she approached the fruit and veg.

How charitable – she was leaving her bag at the end of the aisle. He walked up to it, pretended to be examining the bananas. Good – her purse was in a little compartment at the top. Nick reached in, tossed the purse into his bag and headed for the exit. Chances are she wouldn't notice its absence till she reached the checkout. That gave him plenty of time.

He didn't count his winnings until he was almost home. Eighty-five quid. Definitely a night for dirty dancing. And for keeping Britain tidy. He threw the worn purse into the nearest rubbish bin.

Back at Yurek's, he let himself in. As he'd suspected, the old wino was snoring like a hog. Nick unfurled his own sleeping bag and slept for an hour, then attempted to wash. Fuck it – there was no hot water and a quick glance at the kitchen showed that there was no gas coming through the cooker. Yurek must have been cut off for not paying his bills.

Quell surprise, as Claire used to say. She'd been abroad. She'd been most places. She'd had serious money – and it opened doors.

Nick shut the door on the senseless Yurek and used his backpack to keep the bathroom door wedged shut. He soaked a clean pair of underpants in freezing water and used it as a facecloth to scrub his naked flesh. He also washed his hair using a bar of soap that he'd brought with him. From now on he'd shower twice daily at the gym.

He put on his best white shirt and his new suit then wished he'd remembered to nick a bright tie. Christ, and a pair of dress shoes. His old lace-ups would have to do.

He looked around Yurek's before he left. There were two other rooms, both empty save for a few of Yurek's clothes lying at the foot of a built-in wardrobe. The kitchen held four plates, three mugs and a few pieces of cutlery from the Jurassic period. The bathroom contained a chipped bath and an even more chipped wash-hand basin. Deep gouges shadowed the taps.

Someone must have tried to remove the taps to sell them for scrap metal. What a fucking waster. They'd get... oh, at least a quid. Nick wanted to kick out at something but there was nothing to kick. It was like living with his mum all over again – except that Yurek wouldn't be screwing between the sleeping and the spewing. Yurek had the sense to know that he was no use to anyone else.

He, Nick, was of use. His date would be getting ready for him now. He walked and walked until at last he neared the cafe. Even when he was some distance away he could see her standing – well, shifting from foot to foot – outside.

Let her wait. He slowed down a bit. She probably only wanted him for his money. Well, for the money she thought he had. She'd also want something romantic to tell her sister. The single ones with older married sisters always did.

As he loomed out of the darkness he saw her visibly relax.

'Hi. I was worried that you'd gotten lost.'

'Hi, darlin'.' He made a big show of looking at his watch, a present from Claire. 'Walked all the way. Couldn't find a taxi.' He planned to keep the wealth he'd redistributed this afternoon for drink and the gym.

'My sister walks ten miles to her kids' school every day.'

She clearly saw this brood mare who lived in a hick town as a role model. How depressing was that?

'Good for her.' He decided not to mention that he worked out at the gym.

'I suppose I should walk more,' Cheryl said doubtfully.

'You?' He put his arm around her waist and pulled her against him. 'You're perfect as you are.'

'You're just saying that.' She went pink but didn't pull away.

Too fucking right, you fat git. 'No, minute I saw you I thought you were a good-looking girl.'

'You must need glasses.'

Christ, she was going to be so easy. 'Scouts honour.'

'You were never in the scouts!'

'Well, I'm scouting around for a club to buy now.'

'You want to go straight there or...?'

His stomach rumbled. 'Tell you what, let's have a fish supper first.'

She led the way to the nearest chippie and they sat in. She ate her chips as if she had lived through rationing. He mainly ate the fish, leaving half of the batter. He needed the protein rather than the carbs. That was a mistake some of the musclemen made, using most of their calories on carbohydrates. To stay lean and mean you needed chicken and fish.

'It's great eating something that you haven't prepared yourself,' Cheryl said.

'Yeah? You worked in the cafe for a while, then?'

'Since school. My aunt used to work there but she left to have a hysterectomy.'

That was more information than he really needed to know.

They walked on to the Chapel. They drank. He even danced a bit though he felt really stupid. They drank some more. He got her a double every time he went up to the bar.

'So, you often go to places like this?' she asked. Her skin was so flushed that in the club lights it was glowing. Her bra straps were showing at both sides of her vest top but she hadn't noticed them yet.

'Often enough.' He made up the name of a club. 'It's one of the best places in Bournemouth. I'm there most weekends on account of owning forty per cent of it.' That was the way the guys in the Brighton club spoke, never using one word if they could use three.

'That must be brilliant,' Cheryl said.

Brilliant would be thrusting up to the hilt in some hot wet pussy. He looked at his watch.

'Cheryl, would you like one for the road?'

He watched her mouth turn downwards. 'Oh, is it closing time?

No sweetheart, it's opening time for you. 'Not yet, but I've a business meeting in the morning.'

She nodded sadly. 'Should I call myself a cab?'

He shook his head. 'Sweetheart, you're with a gentleman now. No girlfriend of mine goes home alone. I'll get us both a taxi at the rank.'

He did. He murmured sweet things to her in the back of the cab so that she kissed him over and over. She kept patting his hands and his chest as if he was a little dog. He kept up the gentlemanly act – if she ever squealed rape he could have the taxi driver testify that she'd been up for it from the start.

They reached Shrewton and he insisted he'd pay. Hell, it was cheaper than a prostitute. Some of the guys in prison had been in for attacking call girls but it was a source of pride that he'd never paid for it.

'Coffee or tea?'

She let them both into a freezing cottage and turned on the lights. He really wanted some roids but he'd finished his current course and it would be two days till his fix from Rubens turned up in the mail at Yurek's place.

'Coffee would be great.' He wanted the stamina for a really long session. He'd had all the hassle of signing on, of moving into Yurek's squat, of finding a gym and a few quid. He wanted to get it all out of his system, to really let rip.

'I could put a record on,' she said when she came back.

She slid a tape into the deck and the latest romantic rubble filled the room.

'That your favourite?'

She sat down next to him. 'D'you like it?'

'Maybe it'll be our song,' Nick said.

He watched her mouth soften. She'd clearly been on her own for a while. He'd known other girls just like her. Posh people took months to get to know each other – but girls from his neck of the woods did everything at breakneck speed. They fell in love in a day, got pregnant in a month and were usually chucked within five or six.

'I'm really glad you moved to Salisbury.'

'Me too.' It was better than being arrested in bloody Brighton. 'Especially since walking into your cafe…'

Cue time for a kiss. He turned so that he was much closer to her on the settee. Most of her lipstick had come off but her eyeshadow had stayed on, making her face look unbalanced. The colour had faded from her cheeks now and she looked mousy, drab. For a moment he felt so disappointed that he wanted to hit her – but then he looked down at her cleavage and his cock revived.

He brought his lips down on hers, feeling her mouth moving, eager. He felt her hands sliding up and down his back. He put his hands on her breasts. She stiffened then relaxed against him. They were alone now. He could stop trying. 'You've got great tits, babe.'

'Yeah?'

She sounded unsure. He knew girls didn't like slang words. *Too bad, love.*

'Yeah. Let's get them out of that bra.'

'I don't… Not this soon.'

She tried to pull away but he used his full weight to push and pull her down until she lay unwillingly beneath him.

'Don't be shy, Cheryl. You should be proud. You've got a great body.' Acting nice again, confusing her more.

'You too. I couldn't believe how great you looked when you showed up in that suit.'

'What, this old thing?' He hoped he'd remembered to remove the price tag.

'Tall, dark and handsome. My sister'll be so jealous when she meets you.'

She clearly saw them as a meet-the-family item. Nick laughed inwardly. No way. She ate too much and had fuck all of interest to tell him. A bit like his mum, only mum had replaced food with drink.

'Maybe I could take you both out for lunch?'

He edged her vest top right up as he spoke. He reached back to unclip her bra but she pressed down, stopping his hands from doing what they wanted to do.

Fucking tease. Changing tack, he yanked down her silky black trousers and stared at her black cotton briefs and puffy white stomach. It resembled what the muscle-men called *roid gut*, the distended belly some guys got from steroid use. He had such a flat stomach himself to start with that he hadn't gone down that particular route.

'Paul, it's too soon to…'

It took him a moment to realise that she was talking to him. Of course, he'd given her a false name.

'But I really want you, Cheryl. You've been driving me nuts all night.'

He watched pleasure and uncertainty flit across her face. 'I really fancy you too but I'm not on the pill or anything.'

'Nor me,' he said and was pleased when she laughed. He was getting there. He liked a bit of a wrestle but he didn't want a fist fight. He couldn't afford to go around Salisbury with his face badly marked.

'I know what we can do.' He kissed her again then used all his strength, as if lifting to the max, to flip her over. He quickly yanked her panties down to her thighs. She seemed to sense what was coming. Leastways, she tried to rise up but he had his full weight on her, pinning her down. 'Relax, babe. Some girls really like this.' Well, they did in porn movies. He spat on his hand and got her well lubed up.

There was a moment just before he pushed in when all the rage in the world was centred in his cock. He wanted to thrust her right open. He wanted to see the bitch's blood squirt out.

He plunged forward, felt the usual ring of resistance, shoved through it. He could hear her muffled screams as he continued thrusting. She seemed to slacken off, thanks to the blood.

'D'you like that, Cheryl?' He pulled back so that he could watch his cock going back in. He'd always liked to do that. It made it more real somehow.

He couldn't hear a word she sobbed. That suited him just fine. She was just a hot wet arsehole. A stupid bitch out to snare yet another man.

'I'm going to come soon, Cheryl. I'm going to come right up you.' He always found coming difficult unless he was on his own – but it was good to talk.

She's yours. You can do what you like. You're fucking her big white arse and she can't bear it. You can take it out in a moment and shove it up her cunt.

He reached forward and squeezed both her tits, feeling his fingers sinking into their twin softness. She squealed some more and he thrust like a dog and came.

For a few moments he lay there, pressing down on her back, his thoughts still on the pleasure that had surged through his cock. Slowly he became aware of the coolness of his flesh, of the fact that she'd gone quiet. 'Did you like that, angel?' It was time to start sweet-talking her again.

With an effort he pulled himself backwards then rolled off the settee, started stroking her hair. She didn't respond and for a stomach-lurching second he thought she was dead.

'Cheryl? Have you come? You were making enough noise…' Half concerned, half jokey. He was relieved when he saw her fingers reaching back to pull up her clothes.

She moved on to her side and for the first time he was able to look at her. She was very pale apart from one red mark where her face had clearly been pressed into one of the cushions of the settee.

'Want me to make us a cup of tea, champ?' He ruffled her hair. She stared at him mutely. He tried again. 'You were so sexy, you know? Just hearing all those sexed-up noises you made was enough to make me come.'

Keep it light, light. Smile dreamily. He'd seen other men do it in the clubs, the ones who got the most hole.

'I didn't want…'

'I know, love. That's why I went in the back like you prefer. It's a bit too soon for a little Cheryl or a little…' he realised he'd forgotten which name he'd given her. 'Or a little me,' he finished with a suitably boyish grin.

'I…' She scrabbled from the settee. He pushed himself backwards and raised his hands, ready to protect his face. But she was already rushing towards the living room door. Seconds later he heard retching sounds, the toilet flushing, then another retching bout.

Been there, got the T-shirt. He'd often been sick after… but there was no point in thinking about that.

'Had too much to drink, sweetheart?' he asked when she staggered back to the settee. 'You were really knocking it back at the club.'

'It wasn't…' She got back onto her side again, facing him. He knelt up on the carpet so that he could again stroke her hair.

'You've got such silky hair. I bet blokes tell you that all the time.' *Like never.*

She stared at him, further confusion crossing her oh-so-readable face.

'I'm so glad that I went into that cafe. You're not like the other girls at the club. You're different.'

No answer. She was proving to be harder work than he thought. He kept stroking her hair till she half-closed her eyes. 'Sleepy?' he whispered.

'No, I hurt.'

'You were such a wildcat just now, pal. What a session.'

'I didn't mean to…'

'Cheryl, don't apologise for being noisy. I like my girl-friend to have a good time.'

He watched a little of the light return to her eyes. A few

more moments and she'd be back in his corner. She'd never shop him to the police.

'I've never…'

'Nor me, sweetheart, but we aim to please.'

She shifted her position. 'I don't feel right.'

'It's just the drink wearing off. You'll be fine after a sleep.' He took her hand and kissed the palm. 'Want me to go?'

A nod.

'I'll call you tomorrow.' She'd given him her phone number earlier. He bet she'd written it using non-fade ink.

'Paul…'

Ah, so that was his name. 'Yes, love?'

'You really do like me?'

'I'm phoning you tomorrow, aren't I? You've no idea how much work I've got to do then. You know, negotiating to buy a club.'

He watched a pantomime of emotions flit across her face. Security versus loneliness. The single life versus the couple's life. Nights in front of the telly versus nights out in the world with him.

'What time will you phone? I sometimes go out to my sister's.'

'Before four o'clock,' Nick said. Vagueness was his best bet – that way she'd stay in and wait for him to call her. She wouldn't spend the day with her sister and be tempted to tell all about the night's events.

'OK,' she said. She still sounded a little uncertain.

'And we'll arrange to go out one weeknight – maybe for a meal?'

'Uh huh.'

'Chinese or Indian? Take your pick. I'll book it.' He would too – then he'd phone her to say that he was being called away to another town.

'Chinese.'

'The lady knows what she wants. I'll book it for Tuesday. We're going to have such a good time.'

He watched as she got wincingly up off the settee. By tomorrow the drink would have worn off and her ass would be aching. But his pretty phone call would help take her mind off things.

'Till tomorrow.' He kissed her on the lips when they reached the door. She didn't respond but she didn't repulse him either. A few drinks and a fish supper – she was really cheap.

He walked down her path, glad that he'd gotten away with it. He'd gone to prison once when a chick had squealed. Since then he'd picked his women much more carefully. No one else was going to take him for a mug. Tonight he'd been a stallion, the victor. It was only when he reached her gate that he realised he was miles away from Salisbury in some fucking rural retreat.

Should he knock on Cheryl's door and ask her to call for a cab? He looked back just in time to see the living room light go off. A few seconds later another light came on, presumably the bathroom. No, he'd better not disturb her whilst she was showering his spunk out of her arse.

Nick started walking, retracing the route that the taxi had used. After a few minutes he saw a yellow bicycle in a garden. That would do nicely. The gate might creak so he avoided it and vaulted the fence. Lifting the bike back over the rails reminded him that his arms weren't as strong as he wanted them to be – but his roids should be arriving in the post by Tuesday. They'd make him a force to reckon with. People had better get out of his way.

CHAPTER FIFTEEN

'You should come to the gym,' Rob said. They were sitting in Zoe's room. Her mum was out again. He kissed her quickly on the cheek then wished that he'd aimed for her lips like a proper lover.

'You saying I'm in bad shape?'

She had her teasing voice on. He loved her shape so much that he couldn't stop thinking about it, was going through three packs of tissues a week.

'No – but it's really good there. They've got everything. Far better than the school gym.'

'Yeah, but it costs. I've only got my paper-round money,' Zoe said.

'I could pay for us both...' Mum had told him not to spend all his money on Zoe – but mum wasn't psychic.

'No way – I'm not a charity case.'

'I know that. You're my girlfriend'

This time she turned her face to his and her lips were soft.

'Do you love me?' he whispered, not wanting to say it first.

She nodded, eyes all shiny bright.

'I love you too, Zoe.'

They kissed again then lay down on the bed with their arms around each other. It felt so right. Rob wanted to hold her and talk to her all the time but he also wanted to get fit and lose the extra weight that the other kids teased him about. Life would be perfect if she'd just join him at the gym.

CHAPTER SIXTEEN

Perfect. Rachel turned sideways to the mirror and studied her reflection. Her new white shoulderless top accentuated her slight breasts and the white jeans lent a nice roundedness to her childish hips. Richard wore white a lot so it must be one of his favourite colours. He'd lust after her in these.

At least, she hoped he would. Some days he was all over her like an overgrown pup, his hands on her waist and her arse, his mouth nuzzling, nipping. Other times his eyes looked tired and she could tell that his thoughts were very far away.

The phone rang and she raced to answer it, hoping to hear his voice.

'Rach?' It was her cousin, Jill, who doubled as her best friend. Maybe she was phoning to tell her something good.

'So, are you moving in?' She knew by the hesitation that the answer was no.

'Rach, I didn't get the Salisbury job – but I got my second choice, the one in Basingstoke.'

'Basingstoke?' There was nothing left to say. Rachel felt her heart start to beat faster and faster. 'Oh, right.' She tried to keep the flatness from her voice as she responded to the older girl's conversation but it was impossible to keep the panic from flooding through her thoughts. Her cousin had prospects and she didn't. 'Jill, I'll speak to you tomorrow, OK? There's someone at the door.'

That was a lie. There was hardly ever anyone at the door. Even Richard didn't like coming here, and she didn't blame him. These three rooms had to be the smallest and dampest in the whole of Salisbury.

They were also the loneliest. Her flatmate had moved out weeks ago and no one had responded to her advert for a new one. She hadn't found a job since graduating and couldn't afford to keep paying the bills on her own. She'd struggled to obtain a third-class degree so even when she did find a job she mightn't be able to keep it. And she couldn't bear to go home to her mum.

Rachel wiped away a tear. She had to move in with Richard – she just had to. It would be brilliant having the run of that big book-lined house. She could cook the stir-fries and he'd produce *Crisis* and they'd go to art galleries in London. Jill could visit from Basingstoke whenever she liked. Of course, once the children came along they'd take up all her time and she wouldn't be able to jaunt about any more.

The children. She'd brought the subject up very casually, asked why didn't he and Dawn have kids? 'I'm still just a kid myself,' he'd answered, then started talking about something else. But he wasn't indifferent to little ones – he already sponsored a five-year-old from some third-world country. She'd seen several photos of the dark-eyed boy in one of Richard's drawers.

That Dawn had been obsessed with painting, had probably been too selfish to give him a child. She clearly hadn't been doing her marital duty. Richard had seemed sex-starved when they'd started their affair.

Rachel stared into the mirror, wishing she could see – for just one second – into her future. Surely Richard was tiring of the twice-weekly trips to jazz clubs and restaurants? She knew that she was, and she wasn't even half his age. Her own parents had stopped going out when they were in their early thirties. They'd been quite happy to stay at home and look after her.

There was no one to look after her now. Mum had stopped being motherly when dad died, wanted Rachel as a full-time pal rather than as a daughter. On her rare visits home every third conversation had begun with the words, 'If you took your old room back we'd be able to have days out…' But she was too old for patched teddy bears on the bed and faded ballerinas on the wallpaper. She needed an adult life.

After blowing her nose and blotting her reddened eyes, Rachel put on her biggest gold hoop earrings and four mock-gold neckchains. She knew that Richard liked such striking images. Every aspect of his art showed her that. *Crisis* could only afford eight colour spreads per issue but Richard managed to lift the other pages by using monochrome dramatically. He was a larger-than-life type of man.

Rachel wished again that she had half as much talent as he. Her own mum had been really good, a landscape painter. She'd given it up when she had baby Rachel as she no longer had the time. By the time she, Rachel, was at school, her mother had gotten used to going to coffee mornings and organising the local cheese and wine club, though Rachel knew that mum got through a few crumbs of cheese and a river of wine.

Alcohol-fuelled apathy and art just didn't mix. Mum had given up but hoped that she'd passed on her artistic gifts to her daughter. Now Rachel knew deep down that she hadn't. Maybe the gift had just missed one generation and would show up again in her own eventual child? And surely a child that was fathered by an artistic and entrepreneurial man like Richard would be doubly blessed?

Richard might only be producing *Crisis* now, but he'd built up several magazines over the years and sold them on. He had serious funds, a small art empire. Surely he'd want children to leave it to?

He loved her body and the way it made him feel. Now she had to make him love all of her. Rachel went to her makeup box and slicked on the red lipstick and black long-lash mascara she'd been given by Jill.

After another glance – well, a five-minute critique – in the mirror, she removed her bra. Now her nipples strained for attention against the thin white cotton. She walked to Richard's house hoping that within weeks it would be her home.

CHAPTER SEVENTEEN

Life was getting better. Dawn raised her glass to Angela's in the busy bar then started on her third gin. Angela was drinking some designer beer that she'd heard praised at an art exhibition. It was costing Dawn a fortune, but at least her friend was high.

'So, was there anyone interesting at this exhibition?' she asked.

Angela grinned drunkenly. 'No, they were mere embryos.'

'It's certainly the Year Of The Foetus,' Dawn said.

'You should know – you're dating one.'

Christ, Dawn thought, she'd left herself wide open for that one. 'He's the exception, mature for his age.'

'Still love's young dream?'

Dawn hesitated. 'Well, he was a bit jumpy on Tuesday night, but he'd only gone back to work on Monday. You know, after that migraine.'

'He was in the huff, if you ask me.'

Dawn decided to ignore that remark. 'Anyway, we went back to his house and showered together.'

Angela grinned at her. 'Bet you held your stomach in.'

She had. And pushed her tits up, and braced her shoulders back and... much good it had done her. But she wouldn't tell the slightly supercilious Angela that Ben hadn't wanted sex. Still, it was nice getting tanked up with someone you didn't have to try too hard with. When she was with Ben she sometimes wondered if she sounded old-fashioned and if her makeup looked OK.

She changed the subject. 'So, is Zoe looking after Jack?'

'Well, he's in bed but she's staying home in case he wakens. She's got Organic Rob with her again.'

'Aren't you worried that they'll...' Dawn's own mother would never have left her alone with a teenage boyfriend.

'Nah, knowing Zoe she'll show him how to bake wholemeal scones,' Angela said.

'You're lucky to have her, Ang.'

Dawn often thought that Angela didn't appreciate her helpful daughter.

'She's lucky to have me – lucky I didn't fuck off like her dad.'

It wasn't the same thing, but it was useless talking philosophy with Angela. 'Same again?' Dawn asked.

The next day she woke with a dry, pulsing head – nothing that two paracetamol, a gallon of tea and a sultana cake couldn't get rid of. She had to feel great by the evening as Ben was coming to her house for a meal.

Dawn worked all day at the post office then jogged home. She showered and dressed and did everything she could to make thirty-nine look like twenty-four. Dimming the lights helped a lot. Then she set out the wine and put the chicken drumsticks, samosas and prawn wontons in the oven to bake.

He arrived. They ate. She told him about Angela's visit to the art exhibition and he told her about a forthcoming Adult Comics Conference where they could meet the editors.

'I haven't heard if I'm shortlisted for that residency yet,' Dawn admitted.

'A friend applied for one and didn't even have an acknowledgement for ten weeks,' Ben said.

A slight tension permeated the room. They had eaten all the food and drunk most of the wine. It was time for action. Once they had moved together naturally but now Dawn wondered if she should initiate things.

'So, what else can I get you?' she murmured.

'A cup of tea would be fine.'

Pasting on a grin, she went off to find the Indian blend.

She put the cups down in front of the fire and Ben sat down next to it. As he sipped his tea, she told him the latest Tales From Post Office Hell.

'They should make a comedy about that place,' Ben said.

'Or something surreal.'

'Post Office The Movie,' Ben suggested in a pseudo-dramatic voice.

Dawn lent forward and kissed him on the lips. 'Do you know how cute you are?'

'My supervisor never says so.'

'He's just jealous. You could be a male model with these eyes.'

She cheered inwardly as he kissed her back. This was more like the old days. Well, the days of a few weeks ago.

Dawn lay back and Ben rolled on top. She could feel his erection digging into her pubic bone. They kissed for long moments, his lips more demanding than usual. Then she felt his fingers tearing at the buttons of her brushed-denim dress.

'I can tell you missed me.' Smiling up at him, she unbuttoned his shirt then ran her fingers over his warm back. Again, the raised ridge of the scar surprised her. Ben seemed oblivious, though, so presumably it no longer hurt.

They kissed and Ben kneaded and sucked at her curves until her every thought was focused on the heat in her pelvis. Then she lifted her hips so that he could remove her panties and she stripped him of his close-fitting cords.

'I love looking at you,' Ben said.

The feeling was mutual, Dawn thought, as she admired the naked masculinity lying on top of her. She wanted to make a life drawing of him – but she wanted to fuck him more.

She put her right hand down and peeled apart her labial lips. She was soaking. Five, four, three, two... she took hold of his hard cock and prepared to guide him in.

'Wait!' Ben reared back.

'What's wrong?' She had to come. She just had to.

'I can't... I've got a better idea,' Ben said.

Dawn felt the low pull of disappointment in her belly – then her happiness began to peak again as she felt his warm tongue on her clit.

'Christ, that's brilliant.' She closed her eyes and gave herself over to the rippling sensations. Lick, lick, lick, lick, lick. His warm wet flesh teased her warm wet flesh, the sensation building. On and on and on and on and on. He was keeping to an exquisitely gentle rhythm she could rely on. She was going over the edge.

She did, pushing her sex wildly into his face, all decorum gone, caring only about the intensely focused pleasure. The rush of her orgasm spread through her groin and down to her thighs and up to her belly, forcing the hoarse staccato cries from her throat.

At last she opened her eyes to see him staring down at her. His cock was still standing to attention.

'Your turn,' Dawn murmured, taking hold of his shaft, trying again to guide it in.

'No, I've... got a small cut there. Better not.'

'How about this way?' Dawn said. She curled her fingers around his erection and started to move her hand up and down, watching his expression. Now it was Ben's turn to close his eyes and moan.

'Want to come?' she whispered.

He groaned and nodded.

'Want to come all over my tits?'

His groaning intensified.

He was a visual man so she'd make her sex talk visual. 'Want to watch your spunk dripping all down my nipples and...'

He certainly did. There wasn't enough to cover her tits but there were several high squirts of it. She had the feeling he hadn't come since they'd last had sex.

'Jesus,' Ben whispered and lay down next to her. Dawn pulled the cotton throw from the settee over them both and they slept.

When they woke they had cakes and tea and she put the television on. They half-watched a so-called comedy. At the end of it the national news came on, followed by the regional news.

'It's ten days since Gillian Barnes was found stabbed to death in Salisbury,' the male announcer said.

'Just ten days – it seems longer than that.' Dawn murmured.

'Police say the killer will be acting oddly,' the newscaster said.

The scene changed to the HQ of the local police. The detective leading the manhunt stared fixedly at the camera. 'I'm appealing directly to the public. This man won't have come through this incident unscathed. Maybe he's your boyfriend, your son, or your brother. Look at him and ask yourself if he's been behaving differently for the past ten days.'

Dawn grinned at Ben. 'Yep, that's you – you've definitely been behaving badly.'

Ben ruffled her hair then kissed her on the lips.

'Perhaps he's had time off work,' the detective continued.

'You again.'

'Maybe he's shown an unusual interest in this case?'

'Can't tell 'cos you've been hiding away at home,' Dawn said.

'Told you – I had a migraine.'

'Maybe the victim fought back and he's scratched or bitten,' the top cop continued.

'Hell, I'm turning you in – you've got a new scar on your back,' Dawn joked.

Ben grinned and looked at his watch. 'OK if I call a cab?'

He usually walked at least part of the way before flagging down a taxi. The sex must have taken more out of him than she'd thought.

His cab arrived quickly so she had to kiss him goodbye extra fast.

'Phone me tomorrow?' she murmured.

'Tomorrow I'm going to see mum – but I'll try to call you on Sunday,' he replied.

Dawn pasted on her casual grin again – then let it fade the moment he left. Tonight's orgasm had been great but he was still behaving oddly. He'd always wanted intercourse before. Hell, his cock was usually begging for it.

And he'd been rougher with her tits – at the time she'd just put it down to absence making the hard-on grow fonder. But now she wondered if there was some confusion in his beautiful young head.

Get real, she told herself. Ben was a gentle guy – he'd never stab a stranger. He didn't destroy. He loved creating art, the same as she. Thinking of which, it wasn't long until that art holiday for two that she'd won in Brussels. She'd asked Ben to go just before the argument and he'd said yes. Maybe when they were together full time in a strange place he'd relax and forget all his worries. Dawn comforted herself with that thought as she slid towards sleep.

CHAPTER EIGHTEEN

He could have given her AIDS. Ben huddled in the back seat of the taxi as it took him away from Dawn's. He'd been about to enter her when he realised that he could be carrying the virus. Why the hell hadn't he thought of it before?

Because he'd been drunk. Because he'd been sick. Because he'd been too damn scared to think through the various implications. He'd been concentrating on shutting himself away from danger, forgetting that danger might already be lurking inside his flesh.

Even now he couldn't think about it too much. He just couldn't. The thought that something terminal could be snaking through him, destroying his healthy cells...

'Good night, mate?' the taxi driver asked.

That was all he needed – a talker. 'All right. Just a meal at my girlfriend's.'

'A woman who cooks? If I was you, I'd marry her.'

He'd vaguely wondered if one day he'd marry her. Now he wasn't sure if he'd be in any fit state to marry anyone. One thing was certain – he and Dawn couldn't risk full sex.

He realised that the taxi driver was waiting for an answer. 'Me? I'm not the marrying kind.'

'My brother's the same. Got three kids. We keep leaving confetti in his jacket but he's having none of it.'

This was riveting. Ben managed a poor approximation of a laugh. He might not be able to laugh for very long, if AIDS affected his lungs and fuck knows what else. He felt almost paralysed with self-pity. This simply wasn't right.

'You watching the snooker tomorrow?' the driver continued.

He never watched sport, didn't have a clue what the man was talking about. Rather than upset the man, Ben said, 'You bet.' His plans for tomorrow were suddenly a lot more serious. He'd have to find an organisation that could give him an HIV test.

CHAPTER NINETEEN

Nick stood in Yurek's musty hallway and stared at the strips of anabols he'd shaken from the envelope. Christ knows what Rubens had sent him but it wasn't his usual gear.

What the fuck. He went to the kitchen, filled one of Yurek's mugs with water and swallowed two of the roids. He'd take a total of four today and by next week he'd be on six daily. By week three he'd be taking eight a day and his strength would be going up, up, up. He knew he'd get an even bigger pump if he injected but he'd never been one for sticking needles into his flesh. Plus he'd known one guy in Brighton who'd had to have two abscesses cut from deep inside his muscles, thanks to injecting them with roids.

He jumped as his unlikely landlord appeared. 'All right, Yurek?' The old cunt weighed so little that he was like a dead man walking.

'Yes, my friend. I am just thirsty.'

Nick handed the older man his cup of water and Yurek managed to shake some of it into his mouth.

'You have something stronger?'

'Yeah, give's a mo.'

Nick hurried into the bathroom and lifted the lino at the side of the loo. Beneath it was a broken floorboard. He lifted the splintered wood and fetched one of the two cans of Carlsberg that he'd hidden in the gap.

'Had one in my rucksack,' he lied when he got back. Yurek had clearly decided that standing up required too much effort and was now sitting with his back to the kitchen sink.

'You good friend,' he said as he took the can.

A serial killer could be Yurek's friend providing he gave him a bevy. Nick grinned weakly at the old soak and Yurek grinned back with putrid breath.

Nick moved out of the dead zone and watched the old man drink and wondered again if Yurek was fifty, sixty or seventy. How long had he lived like this? Had he ever had a girlfriend? Had he held down a job, cooked proper meals, gone to the gym?

'You Russian, Yurek?'

'No, I'm staying here, my friend.'

The man would be funny if he wasn't so thick. What a fucking state to be in. 'No, I mean, you from the country of Russia?

'No, Poland, my friend.'

'And what made you come here?'

'The council put me here.'

'No, I mean to Britain?'

'Oh, my father bring us here.'

'How come?'

Yurek's eyes began to close.

Christ, the least the alkie could do was talk to him. Nick held his breath as he reached forward and shook Yurek's shoulder, feeling the bones, strangely thin and unsubstantial. Nick was glad that he himself was taking roids.

'Yurek – why did your old man bring you here?'

Yurek opened his watery eyes, stared blankly.

'I do so enjoy our little conversations,' Nick said in his most upmarket voice.

Yurek picked up the empty can and shook a final half drop into his mouth. 'It is good,' he said, looking hopefully at Nick.

'Maybe there'll be more tomorrow,' Nick said tightly and watched the hopelessness return to the Polish face.

Yurek wouldn't leave the house again until his next invalidity pension was due – but he, Nick, had to get out of here for a while before he went mental. He'd go somewhere cheap for breakfast then walk all the way to the gym.

He did, staying well away from the cafe where Cheryl worked. The poor bitch had probably developed piles by now and he wouldn't be her favourite person. He'd phoned her on Sunday and acted real loving but she'd still sounded down.

It was Tuesday now, the night they were supposed to be going out. He'd better phone her at the cafe and explain he couldn't make it. Rapists didn't phone their victims after buggering them so the dimwits she worked with would think he was a nice young man.

There was still nothing nice about the cunt on reception at the gym. She seemed amazed when he handed over cash for a three-month membership. 'We normally take direct debit.'

Well, he'd directly debited that pensioner at the supermarket.

'I'm part of the cash society, love.'

The wankers at the club were always saying they were part of the cashless society.

'You'll want a receipt,' the girl said morosely.

Or a pillow to put over your face, Nick thought.

He smiled dutifully at smiling Steve, the white-toothed trainer. There was no sign of the kid, Rob – he'd be at school.

Living with Yurek was shit but at least he didn't have to sit in a class all day and learn geometry and other crap he'd never need again. Remembering, Nick did his warm-up exercises with added savagery.

He spent the day in Salisbury city centre, just sitting in cafes reading his bodybuilding mag and eating tuna rolls, the muscleman's main diet. By half-past four he was back at the gym again.

This time the kid was there and looked pleased to see him.

'How's it going, Nick?'

He grinned inwardly at the boy's attempt to sound casual. 'It's going good, Rob. I took it to the max when I was in here earlier today.'

That was a lie – he always gave more to his second session. If he overdid the first then his arms hurt like a bitch.

'So, Rob, you getting the results you want?'

The teenager grimaced. 'Not yet – but Steve says it'll just take time.'

'Like he's Einstein,' Nick said. He hesitated, then decided to go for it. 'You know that there are ways to speed things up, build muscle faster?'

'You mean that whey powder?'

'That and... ' He shut up double-fast as smiling Steve approached. Damn, he could have sold the kid half his stack at a healthy profit and used some of the cash to buy his usual gear.

After his workout he went home and took two more tabs. The next day he totalled four. And the next day. He could feel his biceps getting bigger but so was the previously-mild rash on his neck. He kept going to the gym, kept seeing Rob there but what with them both moving from one machine to another and the other trainers hanging around, it was hard to have a really long conversation, convince the boy that taking a stack was the way forward. He needed to get the rich kid on his own.

CHAPTER TWENTY

It would be weeks until he had his results – three months from the date he'd had unprotected intercourse. Ben stared morosely at the gently-spoken nurse and the nurse stared assessingly back at him.

'Most tests are negative, but if you've been indulging in unsafe sex then you may want to consider…' She'd already given him enough leaflets to paper his room.

'It was just the one time.' Ben stood up to go.

'So you'll take precautions with any new partners?'

He nodded. 'That's why I came here. I've no intention of infecting my girlfriend.'

His girlfriend. Once it would have felt good to say these words but now he felt nothing. Or rather he felt like a leper, someone that ought to be shut away. At this very moment the virus might be coursing through his blood, entering his tissues. It would be doing all the destructive things a life-killing virus did.

'Can I phone in for my results?' he asked as he turned to go.

'As I said, we prefer you to collect them in person.'

They probably had a big sponge ready to soak up the blood, sweat and tears.

Slowly he made his way back to work, got through the afternoon, went home and had a half-bottle of vodka. He was lying snoring on his bed, his mouth stuck to the duvet, when Dawn and Ralph appeared at his side.

'Hi, your flatmate was online again so I couldn't get through when I phoned.'

'Uh huh?' He sat up and wiped the saliva from his face. Had he arranged to see Dawn this evening? Maybe the first symptom of AIDS was memory loss.

'I just came round 'cause I got the flight confirmation today,' Dawn continued. 'I wasn't sure if you still...?'

'Uh huh,' Ben said again. His brain felt fogged but he did his best to look enigmatic.

'Oh good. We're going to have a brilliant time,' Dawn said.

They were? Ben took the envelope that she was flapping about. It was from the grants-awarding arts group confirming her holiday for two in Brussels. Hells bells, she'd asked a few weeks ago if he'd like to go with her and he'd said yes.

'We have to fly from London,' Dawn was saying, 'but the group will pay for our train fare there – and they're giving me three hundred pounds spending money. It's going to be ace.'

She sat down beside him on the bed and put her arms around his waist. It was nice being held close by her. Ben kissed the top of her head then nuzzled affectionately at her neck, felt a growing alarm as her breathing quickened and deepened and she slid her right hand over his arse.

'Want me to wake you up properly?' she whispered.

Not if it involved that potentially loaded weapon, his cock.

'I've got a better idea,' Ben murmured, reaching for her jeans zip. Sighing, he prepared to put his tongue into active service again.

CHAPTER
TWENTY-ONE

Rachel stared down at the scarlet phone bill. Had her calls to Jill really been so lengthy? Now that she'd graduated she didn't have other students to go out with so she'd been calling her cousin most nights. Neither she nor Jill had had brothers or sisters to play with when they were little so they'd always been close.

She studied the numbers she'd been dialling. Very few of them were to mum as she had so little to tell the older woman. If only Richard would change all that by presenting her with a diamond engagement ring. She'd been round all the jewellers until she found the one she wanted, was getting ready to drop a couple of hints. She looked at the phone bill again. Lots of the other calls were to him but they were only of a moment's duration. He didn't like talking for hours on the phone.

She glanced at her watch. An hour from now she'd be with him at the bungalow, would at last be warm. It was only November but already her north-facing flat felt like an icebox. Last night she'd worn two jumpers in bed.

Talking of jumpers, she'd better get dressed, find something sexy but casual. It was supposed to be a working day but sometimes he came up behind her as she stretched suggestively over the desk. Rachel had put her mobile and her paintbrushes as far away from her seat as possible so that she had to bend for them, the denim stretching across her size-10 hips.

It wasn't subtle – but then his bitch of an ex-wife wasn't subtle. It had been such a shock, seeing her curled up next to him on the settee. She'd been plying Richard with drink and shoving her big tits in his direction and had cast a spell that had forced him to eat prawns.

It would be terrible if Richard took Dawn back. It would be a catastrophe. She, Rachel, would lose the casual work he'd been giving her, the few extra quid it brought her every week. She'd lose all the nights out and the days in at the bungalow. She'd lose the chance of becoming a mum who could stay home full time.

Richard would make a great dad. She just knew it. He was so easy-going, so patient. And he clearly valued mothers – he was so nice to the single mum who did the phone sales work on commission for his magazine. She'd seen him give the child a piggyback and a pound coin and an ice lolly from the freezer.

She'd listened to him talk about comics to the curious five-year-old.

'You're getting broody,' she'd teased.

He'd frowned. 'Not in this lifetime.' Older guys were like that, had to act like macho men.

'But you're so good with him.'

Both she and the boy's mother had smiled at each other.

'Yes, for five minutes. Full time's too much like hard work,' he'd said, smiling sympathetically over at the mum.

But she, Rachel, would do all the work. She'd buy the rabbit hutch and help the kids to feed the bunnies. She'd go shopping for little dresses and cook vegetarian meals that were free of additives. She'd be one of those creative mums who made happy faces out of mashed potato and vegetables. She'd show the children how to take brass rubbings, how to press flowers, how to live a natural life.

Richard would come round. She just knew he would. Hadn't she almost converted him to vegetarianism? Hadn't she persuaded him to start work an hour earlier each morning so that they could finish early each night? Things weren't perfect just now because she wasn't the best artist in the world and Richard had high standards. Plus there was always the risk that he would go back to the hovering Dawn.

A baby would take care of all that. She'd give up work and be his radiant pregnant fiancée. And as soon as he could arrange the divorce, she'd be his wife. A child would hold their relationship together forever and always give them something to talk about. Richard and Rachel Reid – their names sounded so right together whereas Rachel Lane sounded lonely and cold.

As a single girl, the future was a huge black question mark. As Mrs Reid, the mother of baby Reid, the future looked great. Getting pregnant by Richard would bring her everything she wanted. Mentally re-decorating her lover's bungalow, Rachel threw her birth-control pills in the bin.

CHAPTER
TWENTY-TWO

Brussels here we come. Dawn was grinning inside as she got out of her taxi at Salisbury railway station. She kept on grinning inside until she saw Ben. He was standing with his back to the ticket kiosk, frowning at the other commuters whilst nervously swinging his weekend bag.

What the hell was wrong with him this time? She'd planned to race up to him and hug him but his eyes, mouth and body language were all saying keep away.

Dawn approached with caution, asked if he'd been waiting long. They made small talk for two very long minutes. Her stomach closed in upon itself: she'd been too rushed to have even a cornflake at home. 'Want to buy rolls to take on the train?'

'No, I'm not hungry.'

If she ate alone she'd feel like a gannet but if she didn't she'd be starving by the time they reached London for their flight.

It seemed to set the theme for the entire journey there. He slept on the plane when she was wide awake – then he wanted to talk when she at last felt sleepy. He ordered vodka every time a stewardess came within fifteen feet of him whereas Dawn wanted to keep a clear head.

It was raining when they arrived in Brussels. It rained as their taxi crawled through the many roads to their hotel. She asked the doorman what the forecast for the next three days was and he said, 'Rain, madam,' and added that there were complimentary umbrellas for the guests.

'Nice room,' said Ben and whistled. He bounced on the bed and Dawn hoped he was about to put his bionic tongue into action. She hurried into the en suite bathroom to freshen up – but halfway through sponging her crotch she heard him snore.

It was early evening in Brussels. She should be wandering through the darkening November streets holding hands with her admiring lover. They should be dining at a French restaurant or dancing in some candlelit club. Instead, Dawn sat in the armchair and ate the complimentary bourbon creams and wished she was somewhere else.

At last he awoke and showered and changed. 'Let's explore,' Dawn said. She'd read the travel books and knew that Brussels had lots of exotic restaurants.

Ben looked out into the darkness and shuddered. 'Would you mind if we just got room service? I don't feel like going out tonight.'

Dawn felt her spirits drop further. 'But we're here for such a short time.'

'You go, then.' There was an angry set to his jaw.

They settled for room service, pretended to watch the pay-per-view horror film then slept at opposite ends of the king size. The next morning breakfast arrived in their room as Ben had filled out two breakfast-in-bed cards. Dawn munched sadly at her cold hard toast, feeling like something from Prisoner Cell Block H.

'You know I'm meeting the proprietor from the art gallery today?' The gallery was showing some of her paintings. They and the arts group back in Britain were co-sponsoring this trip.

'I can't wait to see your work there,' Ben said.

At least that was something. Maybe he was in a better mood today, fuelled by last night's steak sandwich and double fried chips with mayonnaise. Dawn had wolfed down the slimmers special – a flavourless prawn salad – then had lain awake with hunger pangs half the night.

Her young lover seemed to relax at the gallery. At least, he looked less pale and made constructive comments about several of her paintings.

'Bet you're the one exhibiting here next year,' Dawn said, then noted his look of alarm.

'Ben – what's wrong?'

'Nothing.' He stalked to the other side of the room. *Fuck it*, Dawn thought, and spent the rest of the hour flirting with the gallery owner. She only went back to Ben when it was time to leave.

Should she ask him if he wanted lunch? He'd acted strangely last night when she suggested going out to dinner. Maybe he had some eating disorder that involved foreign food.

'So, what do you want to do now?'

'I thought lunch,' Ben said, 'I'm starving.'

'European?'

'Whatever suits you.' He smiled but she had the impression that he didn't quite see her, that his thoughts were with something or someone else.

Dawn gave in to a malicious moment. 'Let's have snails.'

The gallery owner phoned them a taxi and they raced to it to avoid the torrential rain. Dawn stared out of the window as they crawled past tall, wet buildings. She glanced at Ben, planning to comment on the large scale, but he was staring at the taxi meter. 'Don't worry – the cab fares are on me,' she said.

'I didn't realise the city centre was this way.' He looked edgy again.

Dawn shrugged. 'I'm sure the man's done the sprout equivalent of The Knowledge.'

'There was a taxi driver in Mexico took couples into the desert, shot the man and raped then killed the woman,' Ben said.

'Hell, I'll take my chances – there isn't a desert in Brussels as far as I know,' Dawn joked. She slapped lightly at his arm, watched him quail. 'Ben, what's wrong? You seem so jumpy.'

'I'm fine.'

'No, you're not.'

'It's just that I've never been abroad before.'

'But you had a passport.'

'My boss insists on it. We can be sent to international conferences at any time.'

'Well, you had advance notice of this so I'm breaking you in slowly.' She watched him wince. Dawn searched for more encouraging words. 'It's not so different here. I mean, half of the menus are in English and I've got my phrase book to deal with the rest.'

'Leave it Dawn, OK?'

No, she fucking wouldn't leave it. 'Look, I need this break even if you don't so lighten up and start enjoying things.'

'You just don't have a clue,' Ben said.

'So tell me what's wrong.' So far he seemed to assume that she was damn near psychic.

'I'm just not at my best right now.'

'Is it a migraine?'

'No, just leave it.'

'Is it me?'

This time he sounded angry. 'It will be if you don't get off my case.'

Feeling her throat start to tighten, Dawn backed off. She stared out of the window at yet more rain-darkened buildings. She'd dreamt of this holiday since receiving the award letter but had never envisaged it being like this. She and Rich had always had such good times abroad, spending their days window-shopping and gallery hopping and their nights wandering around the clubs and cafes.

Ben watched TV in their room when they got back to the hotel. Dawn locked herself in the loo and cried. She gradually let her muffled sobs develop into louder cries in the hope that he'd walk in and comfort her but she snuffled in vain.

The next day was the same, as was the next. On the night before they were due to go home, Dawn tried again. She chose her words very carefully. It was so easy to upset him these days.

'Ben, I really like you and we had great times at the beginning but I feel you've changed.' She watched his face tighten, felt her own stomach tense up. He said nothing. She kept using the honest approach. 'I wondered, have I done something to upset you?'

'No.'

'You have to admit that things are different.'

'I'm going through a difficult time.'

Dawn put her hand on his arm. 'So tell me about it.' She'd had fifteen more years than he on the planet to get through difficult times.

'I can't talk about it now.'

Dawn tried aiming for lightness. 'Well, at least give me a clue.'

'No, let's forget it.'

'I can't forget it if it's making you act like this.'

'Can we change the subject?'

'Fine,' Dawn said tightly, 'but you're the one who's fucking this up, not me.'

She'd had enough – but she wouldn't tell him now. He was too unstable. Plus it would add even more awkwardness to the plane journey home.

She played the lyrics of *I Will Survive* in her head during the flight, trying to block out how beautiful he looked as he slept in the adjoining chair. She spoke to the stewardess and to the man behind her when he panicked during a nosebleed. She bought enough chocolates for one person and tried to adjust to the fact that she was going to be on her own.

'See you later,' she said to Ben at Salisbury Railway Station as she walked towards the first of the waiting taxis. Then she went home and wrote him a goodbye note.

CHAPTER
TWENTY-THREE

These backstreet pills were turning him into a sponge. Nick stared in disgust at his bloated stomach. He was also developing bitch tits, where fat accumulated behind the nipples and made them stick out. His usual gear came from Romania – but Rubens had sent him some Thai shit that was probably aimed at ladyboys.

'You have any drink, my friend?'

Nick opened the bathroom door. It was Yurek, aka the broken record.

'No.' *But give me a month and my breasts'll be producing pints.*

'Ah, I may need my key back to give to other friends…'

There was always a hobo in need of a place to crash – and his landlord knew it. 'Here – get your own bevy.' He took his last fiver from the little inside pocket of his jeans. His giro wasn't stretching very far as it was costing him a few quid a week to eat out in cafes. The alternative was to eat here in Salmonella City, a house so vile that it even repulsed the rats.

He should nick another handbag or three, but the pills made him feel sort of tired, not up to sprinting. Oh, he could still do his reps at the gym, he just wasn't in a racing-away-from-an-active-pensioner mood.

'See you later, mate.' He put his shirt on over his bitch tits, grabbed his jacket and left Yurek's. It felt odd, walking into town without a single coin on him.

The last time he'd been this broke was in prison before he earned his first prison wage. They'd given him a two-pound phone card, said it would be deducted from his earnings. That made him a debtor within minutes of them unlocking his cuffs. Then they'd marched him to the showers, told him to strip naked. Standing beneath the spray, he'd felt cold and thin and scared.

'Got a light, mate?' A stranger's voice broken into his thoughts.

'Sorry, no.' He eyed the man up, wondering if he was good for something. But the guy looked even more broke and pissed off than he. No meal ticket there, no nothing. Life was so hard that some people just gave up.

Fuck it, he mustn't give up. He had to get to the gym, build his body really strong. He had to look tougher. And he had to be able to run fast so that he could snatch and go. Strength would also help him to get and keep another job as a bouncer, bouncing the village idiots all the way to Stonehenge when they got out of line.

He did his morning stint with the weights then went to another cafe – where you paid on the way out – and had a roll and a large black coffee. He had chicken rather than tuna in the wholemeal roll but it was hardly living danger-ously. Sitting in a quiet corner, he read the local paper, which said that the police were following up promising leads in the Salisbury murder. That was double-speak for they didn't have a clue.

Deck the hall with boughs of holly sung the singer on the cafe's music tape. He didn't have a hall and he sure as fuck didn't have the cash for any holly. Not that he'd have wasted any money he did have on some spiky leaves.

The waitress seemed equally low on festive cheer. The two other early morning customers left and she started giving him dirty looks, probably wanted him to pay and go so that she could have a fag break. But he couldn't pay, didn't have a penny to his name. He hid behind the newspaper till she at last went into the back shop then he raced from the building, running until he was several streets away.

Where now? The racing and the roids were making him sweat so he didn't want to be indoors for a while or upwind of anyone. He walked, scanning the landscape for a likely hit. He strolled past women with busy faces and gift-filled carrier bags. He walked past overdressed businessmen.

Later he strolled past shops with fake-snow window displays that screamed *buy me*. He slipped past restaurants with tantalising turkey scents. Every street was so fucking mobbed that snatching a bag would be madness. He'd be up before dozens of witnesses.

After walking for Christ knows how long he saw an old guy with a coin-filled cap lying at the entrance to an alley. That would do nicely. Nick bent as if to add a coin to the dirty headgear, snatched it up and ran and ran and ran. He could hear the old drunk shouting – but no one listens to an old drunk shouting. When he at last stopped to count his winnings he found he had a grand total of four pounds and five pence. Still, if he spent it on cheap tinned tuna and a bag of apples it would keep him going for three days. It was a pity that Yurek's oven didn't work 'cause baking your own potatoes was really cheap.

He'd live cheaply, if not cheerfully, until after Christmas Day, Nick decided. Then the streets would quieten and he'd make a serious smash 'n' grab.

The days passed in a dull repetitiveness until December 25th.

'Not got the decorations up yet, Yurek?' he asked scornfully on Christmas morning.

'Cans?' Yurek said.

'Santa's not brought cans.' He stiffened as Con walked in with belching Betsy close behind him. 'So, you doing anything special today?'

'Back home we always go to the pub on Christmas Day,' the younger man said.

Yeah? What a surprise. Nick kept his thoughts to himself, not wanting to piss off the hard-drinker. Con's capacity for cheap wine seemed to grow daily. So did his knuckles. At least, he was always cracking them.

'You coming?' Con asked. Betsy and Yurek were already stumbling towards the door.

'Nah, I'll stay in and roast the turkey,' Nick said.

Even Betsy knew that was a joke. He could hear her strained laughter as they all traipsed out of the close. He wondered if Con would treat them to a pub lunch. Some alkies didn't like to eat as it spoiled the affect of the booze.

'Happy fucking Christmas,' he said to himself as he opened the ringpull of a small can of tuna and ate it with his cold-numbed fingers. Then he did two hundred press-ups, knowing that tomorrow he was going to use his muscle to get rich.

He was woken by the rumbling of his stomach on Boxing Day. God, he felt weak. He scrabbled into his ruck-sack and found his last two apples. He ate them then sneaked into the kitchen for a glass of water. It was only 7am and the others were still sleeping their hangovers off.

The world was his. He walked into town, at first passing wooden curtains then moving on to the better areas which had window-based Christmas trees. He wondered what it must be like to be given lots of gifts. Mum had got him a small toy car and a join-the-dots book most years. There hadn't been the cash for anything else. The first year he'd used a pen to fill in the book then had nothing to play with for the rest of the school holidays. The next year he'd joined the dots with pencil so that he could rub the marks out and fill them in again and again.

He needed someone to complete the bigger picture now. Just some rich kid out with his fat new wallet or a grandmother on her way to her grandkids, bringing them Christmas cash. He walked past all the closed stores with their posters of fat, smiling Santas. He walked past pictures of angels – yeah, right – and his mood grew increasingly dark.

At last he reached a cemetery and walked in. Hallelujah. He'd gotten lucky in such places before when some howling mum left a new doll for her dead kid. Others left big bouquets of plastic flowers and big bright vases which he'd sold to a junk shop for a couple of quid. OK, so it wasn't Rogue Trader but it would get him a cup of tea and some chips.

He patted his jacket pocket. Yep, he still had the bin liner in there. Yurek, a man without a bin, had lots of the black plastic liners in his flat.

Stop, look and listen. He could hear two birds calling to each other from the trees, a future feathery shagging. Other than that, he seemed to have this section of the cemetery to himself.

It was grave-robbing time. The first few graves had built-in empty urns or ones filled with not-so-fresh flowers. He walked further in, saw a few wreaths, several bunches of flowers they'd had in the clubs called Christmas roses. A squirrel sidled towards him twitching like an alkie but he kicked out in its direction and it scampered away.

Fucking glorified rat. He'd catch it and eat it if he got the chance. Pure protein. What with the price of roids and the smallness of his giro, it might come to that.

Where the hell was this going to end? He'd go off his head if he spent many more weeks at the old Pole's place. But he daren't go back to Claire's yet and he couldn't afford a place of his own. He could get a clubbing job but he wasn't sure if he could keep it, what with his sweating bouts, his neck rash and his new bitch tits.

The gym candy was to blame but if he came off it he'd be back to square one, built like a pencil. And if he went back to jail these cunts wouldn't just kick sand in his face. Not that he was going to go back – not ever. He'd just snatch so quickly that no one would ever identify him.

He scanned the near distance, mentally rejecting the various floral tributes dying on the better-tended graves. Some other poor fuckers hadn't had a visitor in aeons. His mum had always said that she wanted to be cremated. He'd settle for that himself. What was the point in wasting good ground that could be used for vegetable growing or for a sports field or something? Graves were yet another reason for people to feel guilty and sad.

There was nothing sad about *her*, despite the bent posture of her head. He stopped and stared at the side view of a kneeling woman. She was decked in a big furry hat, probably the uncle of the squirrel he'd seen earlier. The collar of her grey suede coat was also trimmed with fur.

Clothes R Us. He'd have these for a start, get quite a bit for them in the pawn shop. There again, if he was caught on his way out with such clearly female goods... Nah, he'd go for her bag, pocket the readies and throw the actual purse away.

Closer, closer. He edged sideways so that he was behind another set of gravestones, no longer on the path that cut along the centre. He'd walk behind the stones until he was parallel with her then rush down and go for blitzkrieg. He'd be running towards the gates with her cash before she even stood up and there was no one around whom she could call for help.

Almost, almost. He couldn't see her when he was behind the bigger stones but he could still sense her. Tread slowly, carefully. Draw parallel, observe, *run*. He dashed down the slope, adrenalin taking over when the pills failed him. Damn her, she was already standing up.

She turned and saw him, stepped back. He could see the alarm showing in her panicked step and open, lipsticked mouth. She was older than he'd first thought – in her sixties. Maybe her old man had given her a few hidings for she put up her arm to shield her face.

The gesture brought her handbag closer to his hands. He grabbed at it, expecting it to slither from her elbow without resistance. Instead, the strap tautened but she maintained her hold by clutching at her coat.

'Let it go,' he yelled. His voice sounded guttural in the vast green calm. Still soundless, she stepped back, back, back, forcing him to follow her behind the gravestone. Snaking out his foot he entwined it around one of her boot-clad ankles, expecting her to start falling and relinquish the bag.

Gotcha. She fell, but she went down so fast that he didn't have time to reassess the situation. Worse, the force of her fall pulled his grip free of the bag. She landed on top of it and he knelt and tried to roll her sideways. But the grieving widow had apparently been eating for comfort and was a dead weight.

'Fucking give me it.' He tried to reach under the suede but she started to scream. He could smell her talc and see brown-and-grey hair escaping from her hat, but most of all he could hear her screaming. Christ, if a parkie was to appear he'd go to jail…

'Shut the fuck up.' He tried to get his hand over her mouth but her teeth scraped his palm and he let go pronto. Some of mum's boyfriends had liked biting chunks out of him and he fucking hated that. Snatching his hand away, he felt it brush his pocket, heard a welcoming rustle. Thank God for Yurek's binbag – that'd shut her up.

It took seconds to open it in the wind, to shove it over her face. He held it tight, knelt on her back to keep the rest of her from moving. It was a bit like riding a horse that was lying down. She seemed to move at the knees as if she was trying to stand up and she jerked at the waist as if she was convulsing. Her arms didn't move, though, presumably trapped beneath her weight.

Even the two birds had stopped singing now. It was as peaceful as could be. For a moment he just wanted to lie down and not get up again. Then his stomach rumbled, reminding him that he'd walked for miles since eating those apples. He needed carbohydrate and protein, preferably meat. This bitch might have serious cash, especially if she planned to take a taxi home after visiting her dear departed. That fur hat alone would pay a man's rent for a week.

Cautiously he pushed back from the suede coat. She didn't move. This was probably the most excitement she'd had in her lifetime. He reached beneath her and dragged her handbag free.

Nice bag, shame about the contents. He shook a lipstick, a powder puff and a handkerchief onto the grass. There was also a small tin of barley sugar. He emptied them into his pocket – that was tea taken care of. He was about to give her a kicking for not carrying any cash when he saw the built-in compartments for notes and coins.

Sixty-five quid. He could eat out for ages on that and have money over to keep Yurek in Carlsbergs. And he could spend twenty of it when the gym reopened, getting himself some decent gear.

He stuffed the notes into the lining of his jacket in case the cemetery police asked him to turn his pockets out. Hell, there were transport police and football police so it was only a matter of time before the wankers patrolled the graves.

He rolled Mrs Fur Hat over. 'Don't tell anyone about this or you're dead.'

She was keeping nice and quiet so she'd clearly got the message. He pulled the liner from her face and put it in his jacket pocket. She kept her eyes closed but one of her eyelids twitched.

'I'm still watching you,' he said menacingly. In truth, he felt a lot better now that he had her cash. He clearly had the place to himself – and even if someone did come along, they couldn't see him from the pathway. The gym was shut so he had nowhere to go, could have a little fun with her.

'I don't suppose you've had any for a while,' he said, and began to push up her coat. Her legs looked quite long in their near-black nylon. His cock flickered slightly. Maybe a good come would make him forget the hell of the past few weeks. 'Guess that's why you were here alone – because you wanted it really.' He shoved her black skirt up around her waist.

She continued to pretend to be asleep. He'd had other girls do the same, especially schoolgirls. Most had been the sisters of his mates. The one he'd gone to prison for had been some clubber's little sister. She was twelve but looked sixteen. Big on flashing it about but not so big when it came to delivering. He'd had to prise her right open, give her a slap.

He could try slapping this one or holding her nose till she opened her mouth. Nah, he'd have a look at the merchandise first, try to get a proper hard-on. There wasn't much point in loosening her lips when he wasn't ready to stick it in.

She had fucking horrible wooden buttons on her dress. He pushed them out, pushed up her bra, stared at... oh Jesus. The old cow only had one tit. There was just slightly mottled flesh where the other should have been, almost a hollow. He pulled her bra back down, feeling sick.

'Count to a thousand before you stand up,' he said as he got to his feet. No answer. He nudged her thigh with the point of his shoe. Still she didn't move. 'Lady? You all right?' He knelt down and stared fully into her face. It was devoid of expression. Then he saw the urine seeping down the inside of her tights.

Damn it, she'd only gone and died. Just his luck. At this rate the Salisbury police would be working overtime forever. Unless... unless he could make it look like a natural death.

Thinking faster now, he rearranged her clothing and rolled her so that she was lying on her face. She could have passed out and suffocated. He'd bet most doctors wouldn't say any different. He'd met the prison doc – and he'd been a drunk. Plus some of the other prisoners had sisters who'd been offed but who the autopsy guys said had died of natural causes. It was only when some patsies confessed to the murders that the bodies were exhumed and showed clear signs of being knocked about.

Nick hesitated – if he was to make things natural then he really should put some notes back in her purse, but his need was greater. Anyway, some gravedigger could have found her corpse and nicked her cash.

Her missing tit had robbed him of his appetite so for a while he just walked, putting more and more distance between himself and the cemetery. Finally he reached a burger joint that was open and his hunger reasserted itself. He could have the double McEverything for a late Boxing Day breakfast, washed down with a large cappuccino. The caffeine would help him to walk home faster and the milk would strengthen his bones.

Nick ordered a sit down meal then discarded most of the anaemic white bun – it was a myth that bodybuilders needed endless carbohydrate. The body could convert protein to carbs if it tried hard enough. After all, once upon a time man had eaten roasted dinosaur, hadn't heard of Mothers Pride and had gotten along just fine.

There was very little that was fine in here. Most of the mothers looked pale and pissed off, the kids loudly happy. He tried to remember his own childhood, couldn't imagine getting so excited over a carton of thin chips. Not that he'd ever eaten out – mum had just brought in pokes of chips from the chippie. She and he would eat a few but her lads always nicked most of them.

No one would nick anything from him now. In fact, they kept well away. He noticed with some satisfaction that no one tried to take the empty seat opposite him. He must look hard, then, a force to be reckoned with.

The next day he took that same force to the gym. The kid – Rob – was there again but this time he wouldn't try to tap him for money. Burgers were cheap so he still had most of Mrs Fur Hat's sixty-five quid. He kept seeing her lying there and tried to turn his thoughts towards her pricy clothes and her easy lifestyle. He didn't want to remember her missing tit.

Think nicer thoughts. He'd told himself that so often as a child. *Think about...* but there was rarely anything good to think about. Too many memories of adult fists connecting with his head and arms, of being told that he was shit.

'How's it going?' he said to Rob.

'Going good.' The boy was hanging onto the cross-training machine as if it were a lifeline.

'Didn't see you just before Christmas. You have one of these winter breaks somewhere?'

'No, my father doesn't like us to go abroad at peak times,' Rob said. 'Zoe's mum at last got a buyer for a cot so we had to stay home with her.'

'I thought your Zoe was fifteen?'

'She is – but she has a little brother age four. It's his cot they were selling. A man was coming round to view it and Zoe's mum didn't want to be on her own.'

'Very wise.' There clearly wasn't a Zoe's dad or he'd have been acting bodyguard. 'So, did Zoe's mum give you anything for your trouble?' he asked, letting a slightly lustful note slip into his voice. Some of these single mums really went for randy teenagers.

Rob clearly had his mind on cakes, as per usual. 'No, she never cooks.'

'If she's anything like my mum was, I'll bet she's always hanging around when you want to be with your girl. You know, getting yourself an extra Christmas present?'

Rob smiled widely and shook his head. 'She's not like that, not like a mum. She's really cool about everything.'

'Yeah? How old is she, then?'

Rob stopped to think. 'Well, she must be in her thirties but she doesn't look it. She has long red hair and still wears jeans.'

She sounded a shag, but it was a shame about the lack of cooking. He liked a woman who was friends with her frying pan.

'Sounds like you've got your feet under the table,' he said and Rob blushed and shrugged. Nick searched for a further way to bring sex or drugs into the conversation but his thoughts were clouded. 'Want to see who can cycle most miles in five minutes?' he asked, indicating the stationary bikes.

'You're on.' Rob got off the cross-trainer, seemed to have a momentary dizzy turn, then straightened. He walked on his rounded legs towards the bikes.

A few more talks and Rob would be happy to tell him where Zoe's sexed-up mum lived, Nick thought. At the image, his cock lengthened a bit. It sounded like she could use a strong male lodger – and he wanted a womanly hole to enter regularly and a nice new place to live.

CHAPTER
TWENTY-FOUR

'So what was she doing in Brussels?' Richard looked blankly at Angela and Angela looked wide-eyedly back.

'She won that competition – you know, that post-millennium image thing with council funding?'

'Funding from Brussels?'

'No, England, you dork.'

'Gotcha.' Richard tried to wake up his brain. There were various art schemes offering bursaries and none of them applied to comic artists. But Dawn also produced pop art so could have won a bursary for that.

'And she went there on her own?' It was hard to imagine his wife doing the *me, myself, I* bit in a foreign country. Dawn liked to eat out and to tour galleries, things that usually involved two.

'No, she roped in her toy boy,' Angela said.

God, he'd never win her back now. The hurt that cut through him was so strong that it felt physical. A little acid rose into his mouth and he wondered if he was going to be sick.

Richard looked weakly down the street. They were very near a burger bar. 'Look, do you want to grab a coffee? I've been shopping for the last couple of hours, could use a seat.'

'Sure.' He watched Angela lift her long hair back from her neck. The winter sun showed up a few grey glints amongst the auburn. *We're all ageing quickly*, he thought, and felt another rush of despair. People could die so suddenly. Only today he'd been reading of a local woman who'd been found dead at her husband's graveside. She'd only been sixty-two, six years older than himself.

'Last one there buys the drinks,' Angela said, taking off like a child.

Richard followed more slowly. If he went running just now she'd probably have to call for an ambulance.

'I needed a head start – I'm an old man,' he joked when he caught up with her at the door of the cafe.

'You're not so old. Dawn tells me you've got a babe of a girlfriend.'

The word *babe* hadn't been hip for ages. He realised Angela wasn't as modern as she liked to make out.

'Rachel?' He was about to say that it wasn't serious then realised that his words would get back to Dawn. 'Yes, she's young but she's very mature for her age.' That made her sound like a cheese. He tried again. 'And good company.'

'Some kind of student?'

'A new graduate.' They reached the head of the queue and he happily turned the conversation to strawberry sundaes and large cups of tea.

'Dawn said that she's a hard worker, too,' Angela said as soon as they sat down.

'Well, she certainly puts in the hours.'

'And she's taken over Dawn's sketches?'

He shook his head. Rachel was good at running her artist's brush over his skin but she wasn't so hot on graphics. 'No. But I'm lucky she helps out informally whilst applying for work.'

He'd be even luckier if someone got her a real job and he could get in an artist that could draw quickly and come up with new angles. Now that Dawn was determined to hold down her post office job she simply couldn't provide him with as many sketches as before. She'd been late with her November input – hardly surprising given that she'd spent part of that month in Brussels. He hadn't seen her when she delivered her last two sets of sketches as Rachel had just taken them from Dawn at the front door.

He realised that Angela was saying something about Rachel now and forced his thoughts away from Dawn.

'Sorry?'

'I said why not take Rachel on full time?'

'It's complicated.' Richard shrugged and changed the subject. In truth, the student had dropped numerous hints that he employ her but he kept sidestepping the issue as she'd hold production and sales right back. As it was, he got her to produce the smaller sketches that relied mainly on the word jokes and he put in additional hours drawing the main features himself.

Everything was a mess. Richard looked over the table at Angela and tried to force a smile. Angela clearly wasn't psychic as she grinned happily back.

'So, did you miss the happy wanderer?' he asked, masochistically needing to hear more about Dawn.

'Well, it was a really short trip and as I don't see her that often…'

'I suppose this new kid on the block takes up most of her time?' He wasn't the swords-at-dawn type but couldn't bring himself to use his rival's name.

'Ben? Yeah, she's either at his house or he's round at hers.'

Again he felt old thinking of Dawn crashing out in some studentish place. He'd stayed at Rachel's once and hated it – no double bed, no bath, no music system and practically no food.

'Will you keep the bungalow on now that you've split up?'

Angela was clearly going to give him the third degree. Richard tried to eat his sundae in a rush but choked on a frozen berry.

'Yes, it's my home. Why would I sell it?' he asked when his voice returned.

'It might be too big for one.'

'I often have Rachel staying over.' That was true, though it wasn't usually by invite. It was a myth that older people needed company. He liked a lot of time to himself whereas Rachel wanted to be with him almost constantly.

Angela's eyes seemed to be widening by the moment. 'So it's serious, then?'

'Time will tell.' *But I'm not telling you*, he thought wearily. It would be in the *Salisbury Journal* by ten the next day.

'Only, if you need another artist I'll be going back to work in the summer when Jack goes to school.'

Of course – Angela had been at art college with Dawn. For the first time the day showed promise. OK, she was a gossip but he didn't have to marry her. 'Have you worked on comics before?'

'Sort of – a friend and I produced three graphic novels six years ago,' Angela said.

'If you could put samples in the post?'

Angela looked at her watch. 'I can do better than that. I live just five minutes' walk from here. Want to come back with me and see them now?'

He went. Her flat was on the ground floor and smelt of rosemary. There was a child's teddy bear lying in the middle of the hall. 'Jack spends half his life chewing that thing,' Angela said matter-of-factly then kicked it out of the way. 'Have a seat,' she added, ushering him into a small square lounge with black and metal furniture. 'I'll go get the books.'

Five minutes later she was back with them in her arms and dust on her cheeks. For the first time she sounded nervous. 'You don't have to give me the verdict now.'

Richard tensed, half expecting some Rachel-like mediocrity. He opened the large colourful tome. The opening graphics were very good. He looked carefully at every page. 'I really like them. And you're equally good with colour and monochrome.'

'The market's probably changed since...'

'No, they've the same kind of dynamic we use in *Crisis*. You're what I need.'

'I can produce work like Dawn's if that's what you're looking for,' Angela said. Suddenly she seemed to be really lacking in confidence.

'No, keep your own style – as long as you can keep up with the writer's brief and the schedule then we can definitely work together,' Richard said.

'And I'd be starting next August?'

'You can start now if you like and work from home.' He thought things through. 'Do you want to help produce one issue on an informal basis? Then if it works out for us both you can tell the DSS.'

Angela looked like she'd seen the light. 'And I'd be paid a wage?'

'It would be up to you what you earned, within reason. I'd pay you per drawing and provide all your art materials.' He told her his standard rates and she seemed really pleased.

'Zoe and Jack are going to be so impressed when they get back from the cycle club.'

'Jack cycles?' He thought she'd said the child wasn't even at school.

'No, he goes in this little buggy that Zoe has attached to her bicycle. She wanted to go cycling and as I had to go out to the shops...'

There was probably a sketch in there about the ways that mothers escaped from their kids. He forced back the more bizarre images and shook her hand.

'Welcome to *Crisis*.'

'Thanks, you won't regret it. Dawn's going to be amazed when she finds out.'

Hell, he hadn't thought about Dawn's reaction. Richard thought about it now as he left the flat. She'd probably be shocked that he'd employed such a meddler. But he'd needed a talented artist – preferably one like Angela who could work from home.

He let himself into the bungalow and someone called 'Surprise!' For a second he hoped his wife had come back to him. But no, it was only Rachel emerging from the kitchen looking pink-facedly pleased with herself.

'I've made us an onion pizza.'

Richard looked at his watch. It was 7pm. He tried to avoid onions after lunchtime. But twenty-two-year-olds with perfect digestive systems didn't think of things like that.

'Well done you.'

'And I've done the cover for your sports issue. It's on your desk.'

'Have you really?' She had to bend over the kitchen unit really far to reach the spatula hanging on the wall. He found himself thinking idly that she must have very short arms. If she'd been a permanent fixture in his life then he'd have moved the utensils closer to her reach.

But there was no way that he and Rachel would be an item for long. She'd hopefully find a job soon and stop working in his studio. At that stage he could legitimately take his key back and just see her at night. He's slowly reduce the number of evenings that they spent together until she found herself a new man or accepted that they'd never make the grade.

Richard watched her as she cut the thin 'n' crispy in half. She was a nice girl and would make someone an ideal girlfriend but that someone would never be him. He needed a woman who dared to challenge life, someone alternative. Rachel, for all her tight clothes and big jewellery, was desperately conventional and not in the least politicised.

'You were in town for ages,' she said as he chewed each slice of onion twenty times.

'Yeah, I met one of Dawn's friends and went for an ice-cream.'

'Dawn wasn't with her?'

'No, probably recovering from jet lag,' he joked. 'Apparently she was in Brussels last month.' His throat tightened and he reached for the wine that his girlfriend had poured.

'The post office must pay more than I thought,' Rachel said.

That wasn't fair – Dawn had taken the post office job because she needed instant cash. He didn't know how much she made but he doubted if it was much more than shop work. Most of the students he'd employed over the years had worked in shops and earned only a fiver an hour.

'She won a competition for her art,' he said. *And it's more than you'll ever do*, he thought sadly.

'All right for some,' Rachel replied. She cut off another triangle of pizza and wolfed it down. 'Maybe we could go to Brussels sometime?'

He'd been twice before on his own and didn't think it would be third time lucky. He managed a shrug. 'It's really dull at this time of year.' *Unless you're my ex-wife with her toy boy*.

'But you'd like the art galleries.'

Once he would have done but now he felt tired at the thought of even packing a suitcase. 'Too much like a busman's holiday,' he replied.

'So what would you like to do? You know, when spring comes around?'

Hibernate, he thought. 'Don't know. It's ages yet.' He realised how often the word 'age', or some variant of it, entered his talk. The age gap between him and Dawn had somehow felt comfortable whereas the larger gap between himself and Rachel was just too big.

'I've only been abroad once, with Jill,' Rachel said. 'You know, to Portugal like I told you.'

She'd told him over and over. It had been a cheap flight, an even cheaper hotel that was miles from the centre. She'd hardly seen the country at all. He'd seen so much more than she. He'd done so much more. He'd participated rather than observed life – and he didn't want to do it all again with her.

And yet he felt he owed her something, if only for the numerous orgasms she'd given him. He only had to look at her perfect smooth arse and firm tits and he went hard with wanting. He'd only had sex once a fortnight with Dawn but with Rachel he sometimes surprised himself and managed it twice a day. He wanted to give her a holiday abroad as a thank you. He just didn't want to travel alongside…

'Penny for your thoughts,' Rachel said.

She was always saying such old-fashioned things. He bet she heard them from her mother.

'They're in euros,' he said and she looked nonplussed.

'Did I tell you I phoned mum? She'd like me to go to her for the New Year.'

'Have a great time,' Richard said. He poured himself more wine that he didn't want, just so that he could avoid looking at her. He knew she'd have gone pink with disappointment or rage.

'You don't want to come?'

'Why would I want to meet your parents? To meet anyone's parents?'

'Dad's dead, as you know. It's just mum.'

'I'm sure she'll enjoy her shortbread just as much without me.'

He never celebrated New Year, Valentine's Day or any other man-made celebration that tried to prescribe how he should live.

'But it's Hogmanay.'

'I don't care.'

He knew without looking that her lower lip was jutting out. 'But, Richard, you should care.'

'Why?'

There was a long pause then she mumbled, ''Cause you should.'

She went to the bathroom then. Every time they had a discussion she locked herself in there. He wondered wearily if she cried or stamped her adorably small feet and called him names.

He was unpacking his carrier bags when she walked up behind him. He stiffened, half waiting for a knife in the back.

'What did you buy?'

'A linen suit, a short-sleeved shirt and canvas shoes. They've got their summer stock in already. Everyone must be broke after Christmas 'cause I got the changing room to myself.'

'Going to wear it to Jill's house-warming party?'

'Could do.' He'd been in a good mood when he agreed to that particular night out.

'You always look really sexy in a suit.'

He watched – and felt – her right hand slide past his waist and over his belly, before brushing his flaccidness. Richard groaned as the sudden sparks of heat ensured the area was no longer lax. Rachel silently but arousingly repeated the gesture. Dawn had always talked through foreplay whereas…

His thoughts ebbed away to be replaced by further sensation. Christ, the girl knew how to touch him. He turned and wrapped his arms around her, moving his palms to cup her small cheeks. He traced a finger down her divide, reaching into the cleft through her silk trousers. He hadn't see them before so she must have bought them with her boutique credit card.

'Shall we do it over the settee?' Rachel asked. She must have watched various bad sex scenes in movies. So far she'd suggested they do it on the kitchen table and in the bath.

'I insist on it.' He steered her to the couch and leaned her over the back, pulling her hips back until they jutted towards him. He caressed her through the silk for long moments, telling her how perfect her arse was, before pulling her trousers down.

'New panties,' Rachel said.

He'd probably have to give her an extra fiver this week or she'd come to work looking even hungrier than usual. She sometimes made a sandwich to take home with her at night so he'd started to buy her a bagful of groceries when he did his shopping.

'Nice.' He caressed the high-legged black briefs that had the day embroidered on them.

'I bought a whole week's worth,' Rachel added.

Richard mentally increased his input to twenty quid.

'You must be feeling down if you're shopping. I'll have to cheer you up.' He slid his right hand into her briefs and found her clitoris already peeking out of its hood. 'Does this take your mind off things?' He circled the outside of her clit and in answer she wriggled like an eel then pushed against his fingers. 'I think these are surplus to requirements.' He pulled the new knickers to her knees then played with her until she came.

And then it was his turn and he unzipped himself and slid into her accommodating hot wetness. And she closed her thighs together to increase the friction and he bucked and thrust. She made encouraging little cries and he looked down at her small, smooth, oval buttocks and was encouraged further. He reached for her breasts and held them tightly as his orgasm began.

Afterwards they showered together then lay down on the settee where she slept like an infant. Richard held her and stared at her long lashes and full lips and cute nose, wishing desperately that it was a face he loved.

'Can I stay?' she murmured when she woke up.

'It'll only take me five minutes to run you home.'

'But if I'm here then I can start work first thing in the morning.'

Richard groaned inwardly at the thought. 'Rach, you know what I'm like first thing. All these early starts are already killing me.'

'Then I'll bring you breakfast in bed and start work on *Crisis* by myself.'

Sadder and sadder. 'You've got it all worked out. How can I refuse?' He'd have to refuse her soon, when his new artist started working for him. Unable to face the tantrums, he decided not to tell her about Angela yet.

CHAPTER
TWENTY-FIVE

What the fuck was wrong with him now? Nick wiped the sweat from his hairline but it was immediately followed by hot new rivulets. His thirst increasing, he decided on a third cup of tea. That had been a tip in his bodybuilding magazine – drink caffeine half an hour before a workout. He should really have had strong black coffee but his guts felt too upset.

When he reached the self-service counter the girl grimaced and took a step back. Glaring, he gave his order. The hot liquid burned his throat and one of his eyes started watering again.

Maybe he'd feel better after a session at the gym, just working off some tension. He pulled himself upright and his vision blurred. Christ, if he was to pass out in public... He had to get back home now. Nick made his unsteady way back to the counter and faced the girl for a second time. 'Can you phone me a taxi, pal? I'm not feeling too bright.'

He gave the cab driver Yurek's address and the cabbie immediately demanded the money upfront. 'Nothing personal, mate, but I've had quite a few runners in that area.'

'No problem.' He gave the man some of the money he'd taken from the cemetery bint.

'You feeling all right?'

He thought he might have flu. 'Yep. Tiptop, pal.' You never wanted to show strangers that you were feeling down.

'Soon get you home.'

If only he had a proper home with a woman and carpets. Nick closed his eyes.

He opened them again when the taxi drew up outside Yurek's condemned-looking building. It might be a dump but for once he was glad of it, a quiet place to get his head down for a couple of hours.

Nick unlocked the main door then walked into what he'd come to think of as his room. The first thing he saw was a hairy arse moving up and down. There were trousers at the knees and bare feet and an even mustier smell than usual. He stared, not quite taking it in.

Then he looked further up and could see a woman's face. It had the purplish tone of the wasted alkie. One of her eyes was half shut and she had some kind of sore on her lip. The man on top of her looked slimmer and younger, from what Nick could see.

''Lo there,' the woman said.

The butt-naked guy looked back and stared at Nick expressionlessly.

'I'll make tea,' Nick said and went into the kitchen before remembering that the electricity had been cut off.

He poured himself a drink of water and took it into the living room. Yurek was snoring in the chair, an empty bottle of supermarket wine by his side.

He'd get the full story later. Nick unravelled his sleeping bag, put his sports bag under his head so that no one could steal it, and tried to get some kip.

But, tired as he felt, he couldn't sleep. The dossers in the next room could come in at any time and overpower him. He hoped they'd shag and go.

He sat up and stared morosely at Yurek until the old bastard woke up.

'Yurek, who're the wasters next door?'

'Friends,' the old man said vaguely, tapping the wine bottle.

'How long they staying?'

A shrug. 'They have nowhere else to go.'

Nick was about to make some brutal suggestions about where they might go when the lovebirds themselves appeared. They were clearly allergic to soap powder and showers. Nick tried not to wrinkle his nose.

'Hi there. So, how do you two know Yurek?'

'From drinking in Browns,' the woman said.

'Right.' With its bare floorboards and dark walls, Browns must be like a second home to Yurek. 'So, where are you off to next?'

'We're staying here,' the man said. He had various blue dots on his hands and his neck, the kind of tongue-biting tattoos you did yourself in prison.

'You a friend of Yurek's too?' Nick asked. He looked at Yurek for confirmation but the old man was staring blankly through filmy eyes.

'Na, me and Betsy just got it together. Isn't that right?'

Betsy mumbled something through her swollen lips.

'You from round here?' Nick asked.

Betsy looked like she didn't know but lover boy answered.

'Nah, I'm from Andover – but they've just knocked me flat down so a mate from the army dropped me off here.'

'You're joining the army?' The thought of this guy being given a gun was a new level of scary.

'Nah, he said they've got spaces in the hostels here.'

'They've got good ones,' Nick said encouragingly. He looked at Andover Man hopefully but there was no response. 'And Betsy?'

'She's been staying in the Sallie Army but they kicked her out for bringing in booze.'

Just his luck – a jailbird had picked up an alkie whore and the two were dossing down at Yurek's. Two living here wasn't company – but four was definitely going to be a crowd.

'Right, see you later, guys.' He was still feeling wasted but the shock of seeing Pinky and Perky shagging had at least dried up his sweat glands. As he was in funds, he decided to take a taxi to the gym. But areas like this weren't exactly a cab driver's wet dream, especially in January when everyone was extra skint, so he scanned the roads in vain.

After half-an-hour's walking he saw a teenager speaking into a mobile phone.

'Hiya pal, can I borrow your phone to call a taxi?'

'Sorry mate, it only takes incoming calls,' the guy said then did the four-minute mile.

Did it bugger. He hated these ponces with their tune-playing mobiles. It wasn't right, kids having them, when the likes of Yurek and Rubens didn't even have an ordinary phone.

At last he reached the gymnasium and lurched in. Usually he put on his training T-shirt right away but today he went straight to the cafe. He sat there, drinking black coffee and nibbling the chocolate bar that apparently kept lorry drivers pounding the road from coast to coast. He kept waiting for the lift to kick in, but it fucking well didn't. Nick watched the strong men lifting and holding and he started to sweat again.

He'd taken his morning steroids and shouldn't take more until lunch but he desperately needed their energy. He took two of the pink tablets from his jacket's inner zipped pocket and swallowed them down.

He sat there for two long hours, waiting for his strength to appear and drinking coffee after coffee. He watched other iron men come and go, and still he couldn't work out. His entire body trembled with some hellish weakness that made the thought of standing up feel like a marathon. How could he possibly lift weights?

Maybe lunch would help. Walking like an OAP, Nick left the gym and went into the first cafe he found. He managed to eat half of a roast chicken dinner and drink a family-sized bottle of water. Usually he avoided anything with the fucking word 'family' on it.

At last he felt strong enough to leave the cafe and even managed a weak wave at the pretty waitress. He lurched towards the street – and almost cannoned into Cheryl.

Christ, he was supposed to be on an oil rig or some such shit. Nick stepped back into the doorway and Cheryl walked on, staring straight ahead of her. It was lucky that he'd chosen a dozy bird to bugger. A wiser one would have had him up on charges by now.

He daren't hang around the town centre whilst she was around and he couldn't go home to Yurek's and face the gruesome twosome. There was nothing for it but to go back to the gym.

By now he felt so dirty that he showered before his workout. Then he sat on one of the wooden benches in the gents changing rooms and waited for his body to cool down.

A big-armed guy walked in and sat across from Nick. They nodded at each other. The guy started to ask Nick about his training schedule, all the time eyeing him up.

Nick sat more firmly on his arse whilst he told the guy that the results were taking longer than he'd expected.

'You tried whey powder?' the bodybuilder said.

'Yeah, and protein shakes and…'

'Go natural, right?' the guy said with a sarcastic laugh.

Nick realised that this bloke was on the juice like him. 'And stuff from Romania that I get from a mate.'

'Same here. What're you on?'

Nick told the guy about his gear but kept it in his zipped pocket. This giant could take it off him any time.

'You really want to start stacking,' the guy said.

'Yeah, I've been thinking about that.' It meant taking more than one type of pill each day but it could be worth it.

'You'd keep taking your Pronobal and stack it with Sustanon,' his new friend explained.

'And d'you know where I can get…?'

The iron man winked. 'I'll go into the first gents cubicle. You go into the second and push a twenty under the door.'

'How often do I take them?'

The dealer told him how many to take. 'The main problem's remembering to take so many but if you want that rippled look…' He lifted his right arm, displaying a bicep that bulged like a water balloon.

He'd soon get rid of Yurek's dossers if he had muscles like that. Nick followed the dealer into the bogs and paid for the steroids. He sat staring at the pills long after he heard the other man leave.

Then he tried to urinate but he couldn't. It was something that was happening more and more often nowadays. He'd been drinking tea and coffee all morning and had even had that full bottle of water but hadn't produced a drop.

Somehow he had to get fitter and sort himself out. Maybe these new steroids would do it. Why take one type of magic pill when you could take two? Stacking would give him extra strength and aggression and staying power. Anyone who crossed him would wish that they'd never been born.

CHAPTER
TWENTY-SIX

There was a limit to how much ice-cream you could eat whilst watching TV but Dawn hadn't found it yet. She channel-hopped as she worked her way through a tub of Chocolate Chip Wonder. The only wonder was that she'd gone for weeks without buying this – but she'd been trying to tone up for Ben.

Was someone else now toning up for Ben? She'd half expected him to get in touch when he received her 'it's over' note but he hadn't ever phoned to explain or apologise. She'd had to accept that it was totally over and was now cheering herself up with the break-up diet and with elasticated-waist clothes bought at the January sales.

Never mind death by chocolate – she seemed to be death to reasonable men. Ben had been a man who talked easily about many things, yet he'd suddenly become a silent witness. By Brussels his catchphrase had been, 'Change the subject, Dawn.'

At the start of their relationship he'd had an almost permanent hard-on. By the end he clearly thought her vagina had grown teeth.

He acted differently in public as well. At first he'd seemed at ease in cinemas and bars but later he'd been jumpier than a circus flea. And though his cock no longer stiffened, his shoulders did.

Dawn spied three chocolate chips that had merged together, and liberated them from the ice-cream. The flavour made her momentarily happy. But it would take more than a sugar high to block out the many lows of life with Ben.

There was a doctor-nurse romance coming on. Yuck. She quickly switched channels. The news had started on the local programme, Meridian, the latest farming problems reminding her that her own life wasn't so bad. Yet another farmer had had enough of mean supermarket prices and even meaner animal diseases and had turned his gun in the direction of his adenoids.

'There's been another death in Salisbury,' the newscaster continued, and explained that Renata Bristow had been found lying behind her husband's grave on Boxing Day. 'Police originally thought that the widow, who had heart disease, had died of natural causes.' The camera zoomed in closer. 'But the coroner has now found evidence of suffocation and Wiltshire Police say that it's become a murder enquiry.'

The newscaster adopted an even more serious face. 'This is the second murder within months to terrify the city. ' He gave details of Gillian Barnes who'd been found stabbed to death on the Southampton Road last year. 'Police are still hunting the killer for whom they issued this photofit.'

They flashed up the picture that looked horribly like Ben. Dawn shuddered and set down her ice-cream. She turned the sound up. 'Wiltshire police held a press conference earlier today.'

The scene shifted, this time to a room with a long table and a bank of mikes.

'We need to find this man urgently before he strikes again,' a detective said.

'Do you have a description?' a female journalist asked.

'Not yet but we think that the underworld will be shocked by the death of this elderly lady who did a great deal for charity. She'd fought her own battle with cancer and had only recently regained her health when her husband died.'

There was a pause but no members of the underworld came rushing up.

'Was the motive sexual?' a male journo enquired.

'No, this may even have been a robbery gone wrong. Friends say that Mrs Bristow always carried a bundle of notes with her, yet her purse only contained coins.'

'And are you linking this with the murder of Gillian Barnes last year?'

'Well, the killings were very different, so we can't definitely tie them to one killer. There again, Salisbury has a very low murder rate so it's unlikely that there are two killers operating here. We're keeping an open mind.'

'And you expect the killer to strike again?' the journalist who'd asked about the sexual assault prompted.

'Yes, this woman was attacked in a public place so this man is clearly desperate. If he wants more money – perhaps to support a drug habit – then he's liable to do the same thing again.'

It was lucky she didn't have any dead relatives to visit at the cemetery, Dawn thought, given that it had become a killing ground. Her mother had died when she was twenty and had been cremated. She'd never known her dad.

She realised she'd missed a question and answer, forced herself to concentrate.

'This man will have been acting oddly since the murder on October 6th or the murder on Boxing Day,' the detective said. 'Perhaps he's been withdrawn or using alcohol more or not sleeping. Has he got more money than usual? We urge anyone who has their suspicions to phone this number now.' A number was flashed up on the screen as the broadcast switched back to the newscaster, who said, 'You can also find these details on Teletext.'

Dawn sat there for several minutes, feeling numb. Ben matched the photofit of the Southampton Road killer, something she'd laughed off until recently. But he would have walked home along the Southampton Road – albeit in the opposite direction to where the body was found – on the night that she'd thrown him out. And afterwards, he'd started to drink large quantities of vodka, and had migraines and time off work.

He'd also started to behave oddly in both sexual and social ways. He'd changed completely. And he'd been even odder during their trip to Brussels just weeks before the cemetery death. Could he have killed Gillian after he'd had a fight with Dawn, then killed Mrs Bristow because Dawn had finished with him?

Feeling like she'd been pinned to the settee, Dawn turned to Teletext and found the relevant page. *Do you know anyone who has been acting in this way?* asked the headline. It was followed by a list of the killer's likely character traits. It was a nightmare in print – Ben matched every single one of them. *You can phone anonymously but please help us catch this man before he kills again*, the statement said.

She'd never forgive herself if a third woman was brutally slaughtered. Dawn picked up the phone and gave the operator Ben's name and address then quickly hung up without leaving her name.

CHAPTER
TWENTY-SEVEN

There weren't enough hours in the day to take the number of steroids he was stacking now. He was well into his latest Pronobal course, which meant taking eight of them daily. Plus he had to take four Sustanon. They were best swallowed with a meal or a snack but he was finding it harder and harder to face food.

Maybe he'd get himself some vitamin tabs, help get his strength up. He was still feeling spaced and wasn't sleeping too good. Betsy and Andover Man were dossing down in the bedroom between noisy blowjobs, which meant that he and Yurek were both crashing out in the lounge.

Yurek slept in the chair and Nick lay in his sleeping bag on the floor and tried not to listen to Yurek's guts complaining. The old man's stomach rumbled almost constantly, plus he flailed about and snored. Last week he'd had the DTs so bad that he'd rocked back and forward in his armchair moaning for eight long hours. The next morning Nick had bought him a bottle of the world's cheapest sherry to shut him up.

Hearing the living room door open, Nick quickly pulled his jeaned legs from his sleeping bag. He wore trousers every night now in case his new flatmates tried to have an early-hours go at him.

''Lo,' Betsy mumbled.

'Hiya.' Nick waved his little wave.

'It's fuckin' freezing through there. We thought we'd be warmer in here,' her unlikely stallion said.

'How come? There still isn't any heating.'

'Warmer on account of it being south.'

The guy had his pretend-posh voice on. Sometimes guys used that voice when they were getting mad, going to give you a hiding. Nick kicked the sleeping bag fully out of the way and flexed his ankles and wrists.

But the man sat down with his back to the other wall, facing Nick but several feet away from him. Nick relaxed a little and wondered how he could find out the bastard's name. It wouldn't be right to ask, could seem a bit too homo. Yet if he didn't know it was harder to act like a mate.

'So, Betsy, you off down the pub today?'

Betsy's mouth turned downwards and either her lower lip split slightly or Nick noticed a little river of blood he hadn't seen before. Christ, how could the other man bear to touch her? After a nerve-shreddingly long pause she shook her head.

'What about you, mate?'

'Only if you're offering,' the guy said.

'I'm brassica, me.' It was true – he'd long ago spent the readies from the one-breasted widow on roids and in cafes. And it was too soon to risk snatching another bag. If he just did it occasionally then chances were he'd get away with it. If he did it all the time then the police would build up a good picture and he'd get nicked.

A silence descended. The sleeping Yurek's stomach growled and everyone laughed too loud.

'What's he like?' said the man.

'Sad, innit?' Nick muttered. He hoped he sounded tough, a fighter, someone to be reckoned with.

'He's been all right with me,' Betsy cut in.

Hell, Nick thought, she's actually mastered the English language.

'You been necking with him or something?' her lover asked with a sarcastic grin.

'No, Con, just with you.'

So the con's name was Con. Nick forced back a smile. He realised it gave him an excuse to find out about his unwanted flatmate. 'Con, you called that 'cause you've been inside?'

'Could be,' Con said. Nick wasn't sure if he was trying to be mysterious or if he was just plain thick.

'So, where you been?'

'Perth, Barlinie, The Scrubs.'

'Yeah? I did a stretch in Wandsworth,' Nick said. Not that they'd wanted him to stretch. They'd made him… He dug his nails into his palms, knowing that if he did so hard enough the pain would temporarily take his mind off the memories.

'You all right, mate?' Con asked.

Nick nodded, aware that one of his eyes had started watering again. 'So, how come you did time in Scottish jails?'

'I was living up there at the time.'

'What'd they get you for?'

'A bit of this, a bit of that,' Con said.

He'd probably been beating up whores, Nick thought, looking at battered Betsy. He wondered what they'd say if he told them he'd killed a girl and a woman in the past few months. Not that he'd meant to off them – it had just happened. They'd been loudmouths who he'd quietened down.

'So, what did *you* do time for?' Con asked.

Fuck him. 'A bit of this, a bit of that,' Nick said and grinned to take the cheek off it.

'Yeah? I used to visit me brother in Wandsworth. He was kept in the hospital block. You ever have truck with a warden called Clegg?'

Nick shook his head. He couldn't remember any of their names and didn't want to. He had to forget about his time inside.

How to change the subject? With his thin arms and legs he'd never been one for playing football. He couldn't even talk about footie scores, especially now that he didn't have a TV.

He could talk about working out at the gym – but then he'd lose the advantage. It was better if Con thought he was really weak.

The silence went on and on and on. Everyone looked at the dusty floorboards. Yurek snored and Nick, in a moment of inspiration, threw a shoe at him. The old Pole grunted and sat up, opening his eyes and looking blankly at them.

'Rise and shine, Yurek,' Nick said.

For a good five minutes their landlord rubbed his pink lids and scratched under his arms and cleaned out one ear with a bitten finger. Then his brain must have woken. 'You have breakfast for me?'

Nick knew the old alkie wasn't talking bacon and eggs. 'Nah, we're all skint.'

'Then perhaps some would fall off the back of a lorry?'

Nick played it for laughs. 'Doubt if any lorry's daft enough to come round here.'

It was true enough – any vehicle left on its own for half an hour would be stripped until there was SFA left.

'Then maybe I have to find friends that can see me all right,' Yurek said.

Shit, that was all he needed, another two or three dossers moving in.

'Right, you leave it with me,' Nick said. His guts cramped and he realised that for the first time in ages he was hungry. He had a packet of eccles cakes in his bag but didn't want to eat them in front of the lodgers from hell. 'Off to see a man about a dog,' he added, and took his bag with him to the bathroom. He ate all three cakes whilst sitting on the loo and thinking about ways to get rid of Betsy and Con.

Yurek wouldn't throw them out 'cause they'd brought him some Carlsbergs recently. Now it was his turn. Nick put on his shirt and shouted that he'd see them all later then he walked into the city centre and went into a cafe for a cup of tea. It was one of these places where you got refills for nothing. He managed six cups before the waitress told him to sling his hook.

He was slinging his hook in the direction of the gym when the word *wine* leapt out at him from a bookshop window. He walked closer. 'Book-signing today.' This was followed by a name he'd never heard of. 'Free cheese and wine.'

Fuck the cheese – it clogged you up like cement. But the wine would do him nicely. He wandered nonchalantly in and found himself facing a long table. It had a dozen or so disposable tumblers on it.

Nick made his casual way over and picked up a tumbler. He started sipping it. 'There's white if you prefer, sir,' a female voice said. He turned round and saw a woman in her late forties wearing a light-blue skirt suit. She had on a ton of makeup and the type of perfume that cost a working man a week's wage.

'Thank you,' he said in his best upmarket voice.

'Are you a fan or is it for your wife, sir?'

'For my wife,' he said, not wanting them to think he was a poof.

'And would you like a dedication or…?' She looked to her left and he followed her gaze, saw another woman sitting behind a second table. This table had a large pile of books.

Fuck, did they expect him to buy one right away? He thought you got the cheddar and chablis before you made a decision.

'Thing is, I have to buy some other books first.'

'I understand.' She looked like she didn't. Nick eye-balled the lady author and saw she had an equally downturned mouth.

He walked into another section of the store, keeping his hand over his tumbler. This cup's worth was no good – this would just give Yurek the taste for it. He had to get the old bastard a bottle of the stuff.

He wandered around the store until he found a vantage point where he could watch Sooty and Sweep. The minder kept rushing forward every time someone walked through the door. At the same time the author would paste on a smile and straighten her shoulders. But the punter would walk on to the Cookery or Science Fiction section and both women would go into a decline.

One of them would have to go to the loo eventually – and the other just had to start daydreaming for a moment. He'd already seen full wine bottles behind the trestle table, three in all.

At last the minder scurried off. Nick approached the author again. 'The wife has all your books. She'll be green when I tell 'er I've seen you.'

'Couldn't she be here?' asked the author, smiling.

Well obviously she fucking couldn't, Nick thought. Aloud he said, 'No, she's not feeling right.'

'Maybe a signed copy would cheer her up.'

Didn't she listen? He'd already said his wife had all her frigging books.

'Naw.' He had to speed this up before the Creature From The Black Lagoon came back. He walked towards the empty bottle. 'I'll just take this, pal, OK? As a souvenir, like. She puts candles in them, you know, to make lamps?' His mum had done that at first but the house had been like Blackpool Illuminations in six months.

He took the empty bottle, reached down to tie his lace and substituted it for a full one. Then he walked out of the shop and raced most of the way to the gym. As soon as he got there he put the wine in his locker and locked it in.

Then he went upstairs and tried to lift the weights he'd lifted last week. He couldn't do it. Nick went to the cafe and bought himself a Mars Bar then tried again. Christ, this wasn't helping him to work, rest or play. He wondered if they'd give him a refund. He needed energy but he still felt crap.

He switched to the bike, knowing it was good for building stamina but his legs felt weighted. After five minutes he moved on to the treadmill but set it at a walking pace. He wanted to get fit but he couldn't afford to start running, for then he'd burn fat that he simply didn't have. The last thing he wanted was to get any thinner. He'd already lost weight since moving into Salmonella Court, aka Yurek's house.

And now there was Con's semen and Betsy's pox to add to the filth. He might do better living in a hostel. But then the police came round the hostels and checked people out.

No, he had to find the strength to crack their heads together if necessary. He also had to find the energy to keep them out. The likes of Con might hang around the close of an evening waiting for Nick with a baseball bat.

He patted his pocket. His knife was still there. He never let it leave his body. When he washed his jeans – in cold water with a piece of soap that he'd nicked from a public toilet – he put his knife in his shirt pocket or even in his underpants. The blade was hidden when the knife was closed so he was in no danger of cutting his wedding tackle off.

Not that he was using it much nowadays. There'd been no one since Cheryl. He just hadn't felt very lively. Maybe a few minutes on the stepper would help, get his circulation up?

He stepped. Later he rowed. He still felt feeble. After an hour and a half he decided to call it quits. He was putting his shirt back on in the changing rooms when the guy on the bench opposite said, 'How they hanging, mate?'

Nick looked at the guy – and could see from his pushed-out gut and the acne across his brow that he was a serious roids user.

He listened but there was no one in the nearby shower room that could overhear them. 'I'm stacking,' he admitted quietly, 'but not feeling so great.'

'Tell you what you need.' The guy started walking towards the bogs. Nick followed him, hopefully. 'You need a dose of Deca. All my regulars swear by it.'

'Yeah? I'm skint just now but I could owe you.'

The big-armed man hesitated, then said, 'First one's on the house.'

Nick went into one cubicle and heard the dealer go into the next. He watched for the strip of tablets to slide under the door. Instead, a syringe appeared.

'Hell, no. I don't inject.'

There was a stunned silence then the dealer said, 'You want results or what?'

'Well, yeah, but…'

'Thought you said you were on Sustanon?'

'Yeah, tablets, mate.'

'I only sell injectable Sustanon. You sure you're not being ripped off big time?' the guy asked.

'No, someone here gets it for me – at least he used to. Haven't seen him recently. It works, whatever it is,' Nick said. 'Pronobal and Sustanon, both in strips. Not a needle in sight.'

He heard the dealer sigh. 'Look, all the pros are on this stuff. You take your Pronobal and Sustanon – or whatever it is – same as you're doing now and add a shot of Deca once a week.'

Nick looked away from the shiny point. 'I just don't like even looking at fucking needles.'

'Hey, I'll do it for you. No problem, mate.'

'And it'll really lift me?'

'Could take a few weeks to kick in, but once it does you can lift a fucking car.'

'Right, you do it and I'm up for it.' He unlocked the door and sat down on the seat. He held his arm out. He felt the prick and the longer, squeamish-making pain as the liquid was injected, then another sensation as the hypo was withdrawn.

'You're done,' said the man.

Nick could smell his own sweat. He looked at the guy and saw that his face was also glistening. 'Do these roids make you feel like you've got flu?'

The dealer shrugged. 'Different strokes for different folks.'

'But this Deca'll make a difference?'

'Sure will. Once it builds up you'll have the strength of two men.'

Nick nodded weakly, liking the sound of that. At the moment he had the strength of half a man.

'Next week, same place, same time?' he asked, trying to sound casual. He hoped the guy didn't think he was a pansy, being so scared of a jab.

'Up to you. I'm in here at eleven most mornings. Some guys take Deca once a week, some take it every five days.'

In five days he'd have his next giro. 'Meet you here in five,' Nick said. The guy told him that his name was John. Nick bet that wasn't on his birth certificate. John also told him the cost and he mentally started to work out what he could cut back on or steal to pay his way.

He'd be superman soon. He walked all the way back to Yurek's with his offering of wine for the old fucker. In a few weeks he'd be strong enough to lift a car – or knock Con and Betsy into the middle of next week.

CHAPTER
TWENTY-EIGHT

'I'll get it,' Ralph said as the doorbell pealed through the house.

'Cheers,' Ben muttered and returned to sipping his triple vodka. He'd started diluting it with a little organic lemonade in the hope that it was less likely to give him a sore head.

He coughed as a little of the liquid went down the wrong way. God, he was a mess. He had to start exercising soon or lay off this stuff. He looked down at his stomach, protruding slightly over his jeans. Today they'd felt so tight at the waist that he'd left the button undone. What did it matter? Dawn had chucked him and he couldn't imagine ever wanting to date anyone again.

He looked up as Ralph popped a worried-looking head around the door. 'Police for you, Ben.'

'For me?' He got to his feet, wondering if they were here about his mother. Since being raped, he'd worried about her working in a shop on her own. It only took one desperate robber to push her out of the way as he went for the till...

As he walked towards the lounge door two constables sauntered in. One was a middle-aged male, the other a very thin and extremely young female.

The older one introduced them both. 'We're making enquiries about a recent incident, sir, and wondered if you could help?'

For a moment the drink fogged his brain and he decided that Ralph was setting him up, that the policewoman would soon whip out her tits and start singing. He glanced out of the window, saw the panda car and suddenly knew it was for real.

'What incident?'

The man ignored his question and said, 'We can talk here or down the station.'

'I'll piss off upstairs,' Ralph said nervously and promptly did just that.

'Ask me anything,' Ben said with a lightness he didn't feel. He sat down in his chair and the constables sat on the settee opposite him. Ben wondered if they were here about the rape.

Shame washed over him again and he glanced down, noticed that his jeans' button was undone. Rather than start fumbling with his flies, he took the cushion from behind him and transferred it to his lap.

'If you could tell us where you were on Boxing Day?

'I'd have been at work.'

'It was a holiday.'

'Not if you're working to a deadline and you work in industry.'

Both police people grimaced and looked unconvinced. Ben searched for a further explanation. 'Oh, and we were offered double time.' Not that the money had been his main motivation for going in – since Dawn had chucked him he'd spent most of his life at work.

The policeman leaned forward slightly. 'And can anyone verify that?'

'Half the firm. All the single engineers came in,' Ben said and gave them several names.

'Phone numbers?'

'I've got them in my diary. I'll get it.' He walked slowly up the stairs to his room, feeling like he was taking part in a play.

The constables – or whatever they were – were murmuring to themselves when he re-entered the lounge. 'It's got an addresses section,' he said, then wasn't sure why he'd said it. Shakily he gave them the details of everyone who'd been working overtime on December 26th.

'What about October 6th last year?'

'That's in a different diary,' Ben laughed but neither of them grinned. He looked at each serious face. 'Do you want me to go and get it, too?'

'It would help eliminate you from our enquiries, sir.'

Aware of four eyes trained on his front and then on his back, Ben walked from the room again, hurried up the stairs and rifled through his bedside cabinet. He kept his diaries as they had various art editors' phone numbers jotted down in them.

He had a feeling Ralph's eye was blocking the keyhole as he walked past his door. God knows what the neighbours would make of this police visit. Unless they were visiting every house in the street?

'So, has something bad happened around here?' he asked as he walked back into the lounge.

'We're investigating crimes in Salisbury, that is correct, sir.'

'I meant in this particular district?'

'No.'

'Right.' Ben flicked through his diary till he found the start of October, which had lots of entries pencilled in.

'Sorry, what date was it in October?'

'October 6th, sir.'

Ben looked at the entry, which said to meet Dawn outside The Odeon.

'Oh, I met my girlfriend – well, my ex – at the cinema.' He named the film. 'And afterwards we probably went on to a pub or to her house for a drink.'

'And what time would you have gone home, sir?'

'Let's see.' Ben turned the page to find the entry for the next day. Sometimes he wrote that he hadn't gotten home till 5am, that he'd slept in. He looked at the next few days and froze. They had the words *Off Sick* scrawled through them. The only time he'd been ill had been after that man… They must be investigating the fact that he'd been raped.

He must have flinched or paled for the policeman said, 'Anything wrong, sir?'

'No, nothing.'

'So you went home at…?'

Dawn had thrown him out that night but it was hard to remember the exact time. 'The early hours. Maybe one or two am.'

'Could it have been three or four?'

It probably was by the time that bastard had finished with him. Plus he'd lain there for ages because his legs wouldn't work – and the eventual journey home had been agonisingly slow.

'It could have been.'

'And do you remember bumping into anyone?'

No one that I'm prepared to tell you about. He shook his head.

'Are you sure, sir?'

Maybe someone had seen him with the rapist. 'Well, there was a man asked me for a cigarette, but as I don't smoke…'

'And what did this man look like, sir?'

I'll bet you already know. 'I couldn't tell you. I mean, it was dark. I hardly glanced at him,' Ben said.

'And this meeting took place…?'

'In the park beside the river.'

'And did you see anyone else in the park that night?'

Ben shook his head emphatically. 'No.'

'What about after you left the park?'

Ben thought back, started reliving the scene. He'd broken into an odd half-run when he reached the street and had almost cannoned into a large girl with a tear-stained face.

'Yes, there was a girl – a very large girl. She looked upset. I literally ran into her.'

'And where would this be, sir?'

'Just as I left the park.' He thought about it. 'Did something happen to her?'

There'd been a murder in Salisbury around that time but he thought it was at the industrial units much further along the Southampton Road.

'No, but she may have seen the murderer.'

'Oh, right.'

'She gave us a very good description of the man she bumped into.'

Ben nodded encouragingly then his brain kicked into gear. 'But that was me.'

'Which is why we're here.'

Ben wanted to reach for his vodka but realised it might look suspicious. With the can sitting next to it, his glass probably just looked like it contained organic lemonade.

He tried to piece together events. 'I bumped into her and apologised then went on my way. I didn't harm anyone.'

'Can you explain why you were coming home so late, sir?'

'I'd had a row with my girlfriend.'

'And her name is?'

'I'd rather leave her out of it. She's my ex-girlfriend,' Ben said.

'You split up that night?'

'Yes… well, no. She called round after a couple of days and we got back together.'

'And she'll be able to verify that you left her house after 3am.'

'It was definitely earlier than that,' Ben said.

'Well, our witness places you at the park gates after 4am, so if you left your girl's much earlier, where did you spend those unaccounted-for hours?'

'I walked in the park,' Ben said.

'Can anyone verify that?'

No one I know. He shook his head.

'You didn't walk out the Southampton Road?'

'Yes, my route took me along the Southampton Road, then I went into the park and walked around for a while. It was a very nice night.'

'And then, sir?'

Then I got bum-fucked.

'Then I walked all the way along the park till I emerged at the other side, which is where I bumped into the girl you've been talking about.'

'The large girl?'

'That's right.'

'So, what was the row with your girlfriend about?'

Ben thought back. It was something about Dawn's sponsored child, something trivial. He didn't want to talk about it. 'I can't remember now.'

'But it was enough to make you walk out?'

'She told me to get out.' He aimed for a laugh. 'You know how women's hormones are.'

The policeman apparently didn't and the policewoman looked too young to have started her periods yet.

'So you were angry when you left her house?' the constable said.

Ben looked at him helplessly. 'I really don't see where this is heading.'

'It's just that there was a murder on the Southampton Road that night. Our witness puts you in the vicinity. You don't have an alibi for the early hours.'

'Does anyone?' Ben asked bitterly. He forced his mind to think. 'Look, I was upset. Nature always calms me down. I sat by the ducks. I might have dozed off. There's no big mystery.'

'According to our witness you were dishevelled, panicky and out of breath.'

'I didn't expect to meet anyone that late. She gave me a fright.'

'She said that your shirt was untucked from your jeans.'

Both constables looked at his crotch and Ben suddenly realised that his jeans were still unbuttoned. They probably thought he'd been wanking over some corpse when they arrived.

'After the fight with Dawn I got dressed in the dark.' He couldn't tell them about taking it up the arse from another man – he just couldn't. They'd see him as such a wimp.

'If this Dawn can verify your story then you really have to give us her address. It may eliminate you from our enquiries, sir.'

He wanted to be eliminated so he didn't have an option. 'She's called Dawn Reid,' Ben said, then gave her home address.

'And she's your current girlfriend?'

'No, we split up again recently.'

'How recently?'

Ben checked his diary and named the day.

'You had another row?'

'No, she sent me a Dear John letter.'

'Can we see it?'

'No, I tore it up and put it in the bin.' He'd only read the first few lines, something about him having changed. It was the truth incarnate. He hadn't replied, not yet having the courage or even the energy to explain.

'Right, well, we'll talk to Ms Reid and possibly speak to you again. Thank you for your time, sir.'

'No problem,' Ben croaked then walked them, his jeans' button still undone, to the door.

CHAPTER
TWENTY-NINE

He'd recently had his latest Deca injection but it still wasn't kicking in. Nick stared at his lower arms as he gripped the handles of the cross-training machine. They looked white and puny. OK, so his biceps were bigger but they didn't feel as firm as he'd have liked. His legs were stronger, though, probably because he spent most of the day walking around Wiltshire, trying to keep away from Betsy and Con.

Con was a shifty bastard, so he was. He brought in cans of Carlsberg and bottles of sherry to keep Yurek sweet but wouldn't give Betsy any until she gave him a tongue bath. Nick had walked in on this twice and had almost puked. If Con was willing to let that haggard old cow suck him off then he was as mad as a fish.

Mad-as-a-fish people had to be kicked to the kerb, otherwise they brought you down with them. With Con lifting booze from the shops almost daily, how long would it be until the pigs were battering at the door? They'd see Nick and check him out, find he had previous involving pussy. And if someone had seen him in the area when either of these bitches were killed...

'How's it going?'

Nick flinched and almost fell off the cross-trainer then focused on the boy. Ah, it was that Rob, the rich kid.

'Hanging on in there,' he said and wondered if it was true. He tried to think of another sentence but came up with zero. He just wasn't firing on all cylinders these days.

'I've lost ten pounds,' Rob said.

Thinking he meant money, Nick was about to commiserate.

'I've had to buy shorts in a smaller size,' Rob continued, flicking at his waistband and looking smug.

It was fucking typical, so it was. People like himself had a couple of pairs of jeans – and a nicked suit – that they wore to damn near everything whereas the Robs of the world bought new gear on a whim.

'In my day we just tied a knot in the waistband,' he said then realised that he sounded like one of his mother's boyfriends. He'd hated that particular bastard but was sounding more and more like him as he aged.

'Uh huh,' said Rob, who clearly didn't know what it was like to have empty pockets. Now there was a thought. Maybe he could tap the not-quite-so-fat kid for a few quid?

'I could do with some shorts myself,' he said casually then stopped as one of the newer trainers came rushing over and gestured towards a parcel on the desk.

'Rob, a courier just brought in your polar watch.'

'Got me a Timex,' said Nick, not wanting to be outdone.

The trainer laughed. 'You wear this beauty with a heart monitor. You know, so that you can work within your zone?'

'Cool,' the uncool boy said and trotted off after a mumbled, 'See you later, Nick.'

Nick hit the stop button of the cross-trainer and wiped his brow. Then he wiped his face, neck and upper chest. God, he felt disgusting. But maybe a go with this polar watch thing would sort him out.

He lurched over to the trainer who immediately stepped back. Nick moved forward again and for a few seconds it felt like they were waltzing.

'See those watches, mate? Can I try one?' Nick said.

'They're for sale – but we can order you one like we did for Rob. They're a hundred and thirty pounds.'

'For a watch?' He jerked a thumb towards the piles of exercise magazines. 'I've seen sports watches on sale for thirty.'

The trainer smiled weakly. 'This is top of the range. The sensors that go round your chest pick up your heartbeat. It'll tell you the number of calories burned.'

He knew that already – far too many. He still looked like he'd recently escaped from a concentration camp.

'Is that so? I'll talk to my accountant,' he said in his pretend-posh voice and stalked away.

He could feel the man watching him so he tried to act sophisticated-like as he headed towards the treadmills. Fuck it, every single one of them was occupied. He looked at the bikes but each already held a smug pedalling bastard. Nick stared frantically in all directions but it was the same story on every piece of machinery.

One treadmill slowed and he moved towards it but the woman beckoned to a middle-aged female who was closer. The cunts had clearly set up a system where they let their pals go next. Now that he was standing still he could feel his sweat cooling. Within minutes he was frozen and started to sneeze.

One of the designer-fucking-everything youths walked past, pulled a Reebok step from a cupboard and quickly assembled it. Christ, why hadn't he thought of that? The exercises the guy was doing looked great for building up your thigh muscles. You could kick hard if you had a strong thigh or stamp down on a face with equal strength.

A poncy tune played for a moment and the guy fumbled in the pocket of his branded shorts.

'Hello?' he said in a ridiculously loud voice. 'Ah, greetings, Bruno.'

He'd give him fucking Bruno. A new burst of rage sweeping through him, Nick plucked the mobile from the ponce's hand and threw it across the gym.

'Oops, sorry,' he said, staring into the youth's widening eyes.

The colour drained from the designer guy's cheeks and he swallowed twice. Nick stared around. The people on the treadmills hadn't seen what he'd done as they were facing in the opposite direction – but everyone else in the room seemed to be staring at him.

Screw them, he was out of here. Nick strode across the gym and took the stairs three at a time, only stopping for a moment to get his jacket from his locker. He scored his knife along the other lockers in an extra-quick move.

He left the gym and hurried along the street – then remembered that Rob had money. He'd wait till the kid came out and permanently borrow enough so that he could have a chicken madras and all the trimmings, a proper treat.

For half an hour he walked up and down the frost-slicked road feeling like shit. At last Rob came puffing out of the gymnasium door, letting it swing closed behind him.

'Hiya, mate,' Nick said.

'Oh. Hi.' Rob stopped and stared up at Nick.

'I'm still remembering you'd like to be a biker. Next time I've got my machine, I'll bring it here.'

'Well, my mum probably wouldn't like...'

'We wouldn't be taking your mum.' There was a joke about a ride in there but he decided not to say it. Rob seemed a bit rattled so he'd have to get him on his side.

Silence. Rob shifted his sports bag from one hand to the other. It was a good one, Nick thought assessingly. Any pawn shop would give him four quid for it.

'Thing is, pal, my bike's being fixed in Andover.' He didn't have a scooby where Andover was but it was where Con had been living. 'And my transport's let me down so I need the coach fare to get there to pick it up.'

'You could go to the bank,' Rob said.

'Being new to the area,' Nick said in his very best voice, 'I haven't yet availed myself of banking facilities.'

'Surely your parents'll lend you the money?'

Christ, the kid really was clueless. 'They're dead,' Nick said. Well, they were to him.

'An auntie, then?'

Was Rob about to work through Nick's entire fucking family tree?

'No relatives,' Nick explained, 'I'm on me own.'

'It's not yet pocket-money day.'

Hell, the kid got money once a week yet he was still complaining. He, Nick, had never been given pocket money, which was another reason he'd been picked on at school. If a kid gave you some of his sweets one day he wanted some of yours the next. But as he never had any cash…

'So how much do you get on pocket-money day?'

Rob blushed. 'Not much.'

'If you could even see your way now to lending me a fiver?'

Rob hesitated. Nick stepped closer and Rob immediately stepped back. It was getting to be a habit, people backing away from him. If only it would apply to Torvill and Dean back at Yurek's flat.

'A fiver? Oh, OK,' Rob said, his lips drooping downwards. He pulled out a wallet that looked like it had cost five times that. He held the leather close to his chest as he pulled out a five-pound note.

'Thanks, pal.' Nick took the note. 'I'll give you a shot on the bike when I see you.'

'There's no need,' Rob said in a strained tone.

It was just as well – he didn't fancy nicking a Yamaha. 'Well, you want a training partner at the gym or something then I'm your man.'

It was time to eat, drink and be miserable. He already had a bottle he'd filled with water earlier at the gym – but now he needed to get his strength up and a fiver wouldn't get him the curry he craved. Nick went to the supermarket and bought a wholemeal roll, a tomato and a cut-price roast chicken breast. Walking to a bench beside the river at The Maltings, he sat down and turned the ingredients into a giant sandwich. The ducks, pigeons and an especially adventurous seagull all tried to join in his meal but he ignored them. Everything was going wrong so he had to fend for himself.

It just wasn't right. Here he was, scraping by from day to day and trying to keep himself on roids and food and Yurek on booze, all off a tiny giro. And here was this kid getting loadsa money for shorts and gym memberships from mummy and daddy every week. Rob had just spent a hundred and thirty quid on a polar watch – but had tried fucking hard not to give his mate, Nick, a fiver. Nick thought about the fat kid and his mood grew black.

CHAPTER THIRTY

Dawn hurried home from work, desperate to cook herself something to eat. Since finishing with Ben she'd felt almost permanently hungry. She wanted very fast food – but it would also have to be cheap food. She could open a tin of beans, fry an egg and serve them with a box of microwave chips…

She was mentally adding sweet pickles and tomato sauce as she walked up the stairs to her bachelor-girl pad. She looked up as she heard high heels tapping on the stairwell, then smiled as her young neighbour appeared.

'How's life?' Dawn asked warmly. When the first Salisbury murder victim had been found, Dawn had immediately thought of this particular club-loving girl next door. Since then she'd been especially nice to the young woman, glad that she was still alive.

'Fine.' She lowered her voice. 'But there's a couple of police outside your flat.'

'There are?' Hell, they must have traced her earlier call. 'Well, I hope you'll bring me a file in a cake,' she added shakily and made her way up the remaining stairs to greet the men in black.

They were standing on the balcony outside her lounge window and peering in. One of them was a woman in black.

'I'm Dawn Reid. Can I help you?'

'Ah, Mrs Reid – your neighbour was just saying that you were due home. If we could have a few words about a friend?'

They'd do her for obstructing justice if she said no. Dawn invited them in and looked longingly in the direction of the freezer. She settled for an apple from her usually-ignored fruit bowl.

'Can you tell us about your relationship with Ben James?' the policeman said.

The policewoman looked covetously at the apple but when Dawn offered her one she declined.

'Well, we went out together for a few weeks.' Dawn thought back then gave them the approximate dates.

'And was his behaviour ever unexpected?'

'You know it was. You must have traced my call.'

The policeman frowned. 'We're here because Mr James told us that you were his ex-girlfriend. Which call did you think we'd traced?'

'I phoned Crimehalters anonymously and gave his name. That's presumably why you were talking to him in the first place,' Dawn said.

The police had presumably figured this out already but the man didn't give anything away. 'So when did you start to suspect Mr James?' He whipped out a small notebook and began to write things down.

'He... well, he started acting strangely after that girl was stabbed on the Southampton Road. You know, drinking more, taking time off work, cancelling nights out.'

'Did he talk about the murder?'

Dawn thought back. 'No.' They seemed to be waiting for more. 'He acted distant. My friend commented that he looked really like the photofit but I just laughed it off.'

'Had he been violent towards you?'

'No, he was very thoughtful at first – that's the odd thing. But after the murder he began to change.'

'He says you had a row that night.'

Dawn felt her ears redden with embarrassment at the memory. 'Yes, it was my fault. I wasn't feeling very well and overreacted to something he said. I told him to leave.'

'And he left at…?'

'I'm not sure. Maybe midnight or one in the morning?'

'It couldn't have been four?'

They hadn't been in bed long when the row had started. 'No, it definitely wasn't that late.'

The policeman was scribbling so fast now that Dawn wondered if he'd been on a speedwriting course. Her mouth felt tense and she tried to relax it by nibbling at her Cox's Pippin. Both police people stared.

'And did you see him the next day?' the policeman asked.

'No, not for ages after that. He went down with a cluster migraine. You know, the type that goes on for several days?'

The policeman looked blank but the policewoman nodded. 'We can check if he had a doctor's note,' the constable said. He turned to Dawn. 'So you next saw him…?'

Dawn fetched her diary and named the date. 'I went round. He'd been drinking.'

'And did he seem pleased to see you?'

She'd worn new underwear but he hadn't been the least bit interested. 'No, but he was ill.'

The policeman nudged the policewoman and muttered something. She said, 'What?' then, 'Oh, right.' She turned to Dawn. 'Mrs Reid, when it came to your sex life, was there anything unusual about Mr James' requests?'

The policeman was pretending to study his notes. *Yeah, like his big ears weren't twitching.* Dawn mentally relived her sessions with Ben. 'No, he was very sweet, very caring. It was only after the row that he went off sex.'

'You didn't have sex after that?'

Dawn leafed through her diary. 'Well, we almost did after a meal that I cooked here. But he said he had a cut on his penis. He just...' It felt ridiculous saying this to strangers. 'He just brought me off with his tongue.'

The policeman's saliva must have gone down the wrong way because he choked. The policewoman looked enviously at Dawn. 'Did you see this cut?'

'No, but he was between my legs. I wasn't looking.' She suddenly remembered something. 'Oh, but he had a long red scratch on his back after the first murder. I remember because I got into the shower with him.'

It was the policeman's turn to look envious. He flicked through his notes then seemed to recover his thoughts. 'Did he tell you how he came by this scar?'

Dawn marvelled at how stiltedly police people put things. 'Yes, he said a friend at work had hit him with a metal ruler whilst fooling about.'

The policeman turned the page. 'What about Boxing Day – were you still seeing him then?'

Dawn knew that was when the cemetery body was found.

'No, we split up as soon as we came back from Brussels.' She told them her holiday dates.

The policeman cleared his throat. 'Mr James' work – is it a place that you can leave for an hour or so without anybody noticing?'

'I was never there. I've really no idea,' Dawn said.

Both PCs looked slightly disappointed. 'Well, I think that's about it,' said the man and they both stood up to go.

'Do you think it's him?' Dawn asked.

'We're keeping an open mind.'

'Could I be in danger? I mean, if he's stabbed one woman and suffocated another and realises I've shopped him to the police?'

They might give her a whole new identity or, at the very least, a personal bodyguard.

'It's best to play safe so don't be alone with him,' the male PC said.

The bodyguard wasn't an option, then. 'And if he comes round?'

'Don't let him in and ask him to leave. If he doesn't we can get a restraining order.'

'What if I see him at art shows? We're both artists,' Dawn said.

'I thought you worked in the post office?' The policeman started to fish out his notebook again.

'I do, for the cash. But I also produce the graphics for various adult comics. Ben draws for another comic. We might end up at the same event.'

'Again, just act normally but don't let yourself be left alone with him,' the PC said. He gave her his card and the policewoman gave her a sympathetic smile. 'If you remember anything else, please call us,' was his parting shot.

It wasn't looking good. Dawn double-locked the door behind them, then sank onto the settee and stared at her fast-browning apple. Had she been licked and fucked by a double killer for the past few months? At this very moment he could be walking around Salisbury planning his next murder – and he knew where she worked and lived.

CHAPTER
THIRTY-ONE

'Told you it was him,' Angela said lightly into the mouthpiece. She tried to keep her voice natural but could feel her heart beating really hard. God, had Dawn really been to bed with a double murderer? There had been nothing about Ben that suggested such rage. Hell, she'd fancied him herself that time they'd all met up in a cafe, and had hoped she'd meet up with him again when Dawn wasn't around.

'I don't think the police are sure about the cemetery death. He might have been at work then,' Dawn added, sounding shaky.

'What, on Boxing Day?'

'Yeah, software engineers work really odd hours.'

Angela turned sideways in her chair so that she was facing the clock. She didn't want to speak on the phone for too long as she was expecting an important visitor. 'So how do you feel?'

'I feel sick, Ang. In fact, I was sick about half an hour after the police left that night. I keep thinking of how good it felt when he touched me – then I think of these same hands holding a knife.'

'So are you getting police protection?' Angela asked. She felt a hollowness somewhere behind her breastbone and realised that it was envy. Dawn had had an orgasmic few months with Ben and now had the new excitement of police visits and possibly a court case. She, Angela, took Jack to nursery three mornings a week and was ignored most nights by the bookish Zoe and Rob.

'No – I just have to make sure that I'm not alone with him,' Dawn said, sounding small and scared.

She spoke for another ten minutes whilst Angela commiserated and wondered how to tell Dawn her own news.

At last Dawn seemed to run out of words and Angela took a deep breath. 'Dawn, you know how I've been wanting to work but couldn't because of Jack? Well, I bumped into Richard in town while you were in Brussels and he offered me some freelancing on *Crisis.* '

'Why didn't you mention it before now? That was ages ago,' Dawn said.

Angela hesitated. 'Yes, I know – but we agreed on a trial at first. I didn't want to tell you till it was definite. But now he's okayed my work so I'll be producing some of his graphics from now on.'

'Does that mean I'm sacked?' Dawn asked in an even smaller voice.

Angela felt a surge of power followed by a smaller surge of guilt. ''Course not. I'd never queer your pitch, girl. It's just that Rachel will be leaving him soon.'

She heard Dawn's sharp intake of breath. 'They've split up?'

'No, nothing like that.' She couldn't resist killing that particular fantasy. 'He seems really happy with her. It's just that she'll be moving on workwise to a more permanent job.'

'Oh, right. So how are you getting on?'

'I just finished my third Mandroids strip.' Angela looked at her watch. Richard was due round to collect the work in half an hour. She decided not to tell Dawn in case she too wanted to come round. God knows, it wasn't often that Angela had a man about the house nowadays – and three was definitely a crowd.

'Some of the newer writers can be a bit unsophisticated – so if you think of an improvement to the dialogue don't be scared to jot it down,' Dawn said.

Angela immediately felt guilty – her friend was always so bloody nice to her. But it was easy to be nice when you had a job, no ties and a freelance interest that you really enjoyed.

'I'll put my thinking cap on,' she promised.

'It's a mid-twenties male readership so just target your thoughts at them.'

'That's no hardship.' Angela laughed suggestively then asked Dawn where she was going tonight, assuming she'd be dating the policeman who'd interviewed her or something like that.

'I'm not really sure. I mean, I should really renew my library books but I don't feel like wandering around Salisbury in case I meet Ben.'

'Right, well make it happy whatever you get up to,' Angela murmured, preparing to hang up.

'I could take a taxi to your place,' Dawn said.

'No, I... I've got things to do,' Angela mumbled. 'But I'll come round to you tomorrow night if Zoe can babysit.'

'Oh, OK. I'll stay in and paint a female version of The Scream,' Dawn said.

Angela said her goodbyes and hung up the phone. It made a nice change to have Dawn doing the screaming. Knowing that her life was at last improving, she stared critically into the pyramid-shaped mirror on the lounge wall. With her long auburn hair and mascaraed eyes she looked more exotic than her friend and she was at least ten pounds slimmer. Had Richard noticed that yet?

When the doorbell rang she finger-combed her fringe and hurried to let him in. 'Hi, everything's ready.' It was too – she'd changed the duvet cover, just in case.

'Any problems?' Richard asked as he walked in.

Just the usual one of having no money, no fun and no sex life.

'No, I'm really getting into the characters now. Everything's great.'

She watched nervously as Richard studied her work. 'Once again it's exactly what I'm looking for. Thanks, Ang.'

Ang now, was it? She wondered if she should call him Rich.

'Can I get you something?'

'Mm? A water would be nice.'

Angela ran him a glass from the cold tap, wishing she had a slice of lemon to garnish it. 'So, you suddenly allergic to tea?'

He grinned. 'No, Rachel's been reading up on health. Seemingly tannin robs you of energy so I'm cutting back.'

'Ah. And how is Rachel?'

Down with thrush, I hope, she thought sourly.

'Oh, a bit low because she didn't get this job she went after,' Richard said, sitting down at the lounge table and sipping his drink.

'The art therapy one?'

'No, that was last month. This was for the design arm of a clothing firm.'

'Right. Does she know that there's a place in Poole looking for an artist in residence? Dawn applied months ago,' Angela said.

She watched Richard rear back as if a wasp had flown at him.

'Dawn's moving to Poole?'

'Well, if she gets this job she'll have to.'

'She didn't tell me,' Richard muttered, pushing his glass away.

Angela took a deep breath and tried to sound casual. 'Oh? Have you seen her recently?'

'Not for months. I called in one day at the post office but she'd nipped out to do some shopping in her break. And the last time she brought round her *Crisis* strip I was with my accountant so Rachel answered the door.'

'Well, she's doing great,' Angela said. She looked at Richard and wished that he was drinking wine rather than ignoring his water. She wished that he was curled next to her on the settee rather than sitting at the table in a plain wooden chair.

'Does she know you're working for *Crisis* now?'

'Yes, I told her when she phoned tonight.' Angela sat opposite him and straightened her shoulders in a bid to make her small breasts look larger.

'What did she say?'

'That it was fine – that I could think up some dialogue if I wanted to.'

'Right. She does that all the time. She's a natural,' Richard said.

Christ, weren't men supposed to call their ex-wives names? Angela looked at Richard and thought that Dawn had been mad to let him go. He'd always been tall, dark and handsome. And now that he'd lost the baseball cap and a few pounds from his midriff he looked great.

'So, what else did she say?' Richard continued with what was clearly hard-won casualness.

Angela hesitated, then decided all was fair in love and war and single parenting. If she told him that Ben was a murder suspect then he might go round and comfort his ex-wife. 'Not much. She was cooking for someone so had to go and prepare.'

'I can guess who,' Richard said heavily and pushed his chair back, clearly preparing to leave.

Men didn't escape from her web that easily. 'Talking of food, I was about to make myself a tuna sandwich. Should I make two?'

'Great – just don't tell Rachel,' Richard said with a grin.

'She doesn't like you to eat out?'

'She doesn't like me eating fish or meat. She's a strict vegetarian.'

'Oh, she should team up with Zoe's boyfriend, Rob. His parents are organic freaks,' Angela said. She realised that Richard and Rachel probably wouldn't last. Men liked their burgers. 'Want to live dangerously and have it with a cup of tea?'

'Make it a pot,' Richard replied. Angela was surprised when he followed her into the kitchen and started to set out plates and cups on a tea tray. If he was this domesticated she'd have to marry him.

It had started as a jokey thought but as they chatted it became an increasingly pleasant one. Oh, she didn't want the certificate or the ring – but the sex and the house would be nice. Most nights she longed for adult company. She and Rich could talk about most aspects of art.

He'd long since split up with Dawn – and it sounded as if he'd soon tire of Rachel. Why couldn't she, Angela, be the one who lived and worked in Richard's house? It was big enough for Jack and Zoe to have their own rooms – and knowing Zoe she'd be moving to live on a kibbutz or something similar soon.

Angela flaked the tuna and hoped that Richard wouldn't find out that Dawn no longer had a young lover. She wanted this particular catch all to herself.

CHAPTER
THIRTY-TWO

'You've gotta give it time,' John said.

'It's been weeks. Christ, I'm burning up again.'

They were sitting in the gents changing rooms of the gym and Nick was sizzling like something on a barbecue.

'You remembering to take them all?'

''Course.' It wasn't as if he had much else to do.

He looked sideways at John. 'Thing is, I've still got these two wasters dossing down at my place. They don't want to leave. I need a bit more muscle and I thought the Deca would help.'

'How fit are they?' John asked.

Nick shrugged into his training T-shirt before he spoke. 'Well, one of them's no problem – she's an alkie. But she's shacked up with this guy in his twenties and he's done time, possibly for GBH.'

'Doubt if he could handle two of us,' John said.

For the first time in months Nick felt surprised. He'd been looking to make himself stronger so that he could conk out Con. It hadn't occurred to him to involve this dealer. He was just so used to being by himself.

'Thing is, John, we'd have to scare them good or they'd just come back. The guy has a mate in the army. I'm not looking to get my head kicked in.'

'You want them out of the way for good?'

'Yeah.' It was what he fantasised about each morning when Con and Betsy walked in on him. It was what he thought about each time he heard Betsy using her rotting mouth to suck Con off.

'I'd do it for a grand,' John said.

Nick felt his stomach flip. It had been just talk until now. 'Thing is, pal, I'm on a giro.'

John stared at him for so long that Nick felt ready to take up smoking. One of his eyes started watering especially hard.

'There's a couple of us going shopping after the shops shut on Monday night,' John finally added in his usual downbeat way. 'A third pair of hands would speed things up.'

'I'd get a grand for it?' It was months since he'd had that much cash.

'No cash, but you'd get my help to the tune of a thousand. Put it this way – you'd never see those two dossers again.'

Ask no questions, hear no lies. Nick thought about it. He'd never actually planned to kill anyone before, except his dad if he ever met him. But it John was willing to do the deed then he, Nick, wouldn't exactly throw himself on Con's funeral pyre. The Andover Man was always hanging around, always looking him up and down, always entering his room in the mornings. Christ knows what he had in mind...

'It's a done deal,' Nick said. They shook on it and Nick flexed his fingers all the way home until the pain finally ebbed.

The next few days crawled by and he came close to kicking Betsy to the kerb when he found her being sick in his sports shoes. But he reminded himself that soon she'd be gone for good.

At last it was 1am on ram-raiding night and he put on the dark clothes and gloves that John had given him and waited around the corner from Yurek's till John picked him up in a four-wheel drive. There was another large man in the back who John said to call Gerald. He had a roll of binliners beside him on the seat.

John drove slowly so it was quite a few minutes before Nick realised that they were heading out of Salisbury. 'Where we going, mate?' he asked, trying to sound casual. There was a bad atmosphere in the Land Rover. What if John was really a friend of Con's and this whole thing was a set-up to get him, Nick, on his own in a lonely place?

John named a nearby town. At least Nick hoped it was nearby. 'And I just go for the designer labels?'

'It's all designer labels – but concentrate on the suits and leather jackets,' John said patiently.

'So,' Nick looked back at Gerald then at John, 'you guys done this before?'

'The less you know the less you can tell,' said John.

He was right, of course, but Nick just wanted them to like and rate him. Or rather he wanted them totally on his side. He kept talking, knowing that his voice sounded too high, too fast, too fucking everything. He knew he sounded girlish, really weak.

At last they reached the store. The bodybuilder turned the vehicle around and reversed till he was facing the shop's front window. 'Get your heads down,' he said and put his foot on the accelerator. Nick felt the vehicle catapult forward, heard the crash then the tinkling that went on and on. John reversed out of the window but kept the ignition running as he turned to Nick.

'Go, go, go!' he shouted. Gerald was already jumping to the kerb. Nick opened his own door and his ears were immediately filled with the sound of an alarm ringing. He raced through a carpet of glass and into the main shop, started throwing suits into binliners. At eight hundred quid a suit you didn't need many to make it worth your while.

'Go, go, go,' John shouted again from the driver's seat and he and Gerald raced back to the vehicle. John drove along for a few minutes until they came to a double garage next to a detached house. The garage was open. John parked the vehicle there then they walked down the drive.

'Aren't you forgetting something?' Nick said, realising they'd left all the bags of clothes in the back seat. He found that he was grinning manically. It had all gone like a wet dream.

'No, someone will deal with them,' John said. 'The getaway car's over here.' They followed him to the adjacent street where he walked towards a faded brown Mini. Moments later they were driving back to Salisbury.

They dropped Gerald off first. Nick was impressed at the area the guy lived in. He felt ashamed when John reached the half-boarded-up flats where Yurek lived.

'Thanks, mate.' Nick made to get out of the car.

'Hang on, I'm coming with you,' John said.

'How come?'

'Well, you've earned your cut. Thought you wanted some business sorted out?'

'What, now?' Nick asked haltingly.

John looked at his watch. 'Yeah. They're likely to be asleep. So's everyone else. And I don't know about you, but I'm still wired.'

'Same here,' Nick said. 'The way your truck went in… it was just so fucking magic.'

'So magic that you'll have forgotten all about it by tomorrow,' John said, staring hard.

'Forgotten what?' Nick joked quietly as they stood on the street outside Yurek's flat. 'There's an old man in the room on the right – just ignore him. The other two will be dossing down in the room on the left in a big sleeping bag. You want to roll the guy first or he'll put up a fight.'

John nodded and they walked silently to the darkened flat. Nick turned the key. He led the way, pointing out the correct door to his bodybuilding friend.

John slid the door open and tiptoed in, Nick a couple of feet behind him. The moonlight showed two figures snoring under blue quilting. John crossed the remaining floor and knelt. The snoring changed to a frenzied gurgle then there was a popping sound followed by a very loud crack.

'Uh?' a female voice said. It was Betsy's last understandable comment as John apparently transferred his huge hands from Con's broken neck to her throat. Again Nick listened to the ghastly animalistic sounds as crushed tubes tried to suck in a little oxygen. Again he heard the cracking noises then John said, 'Help me get them out of here.'

'Where to?'

'Just to the Mini.'

'Then what?'

'Then you don't need to know any more.'

He was right, of course. He was the type of person who was always right. Nick gazed at the roids dealer and felt overwhelmingly grateful. 'I owe you one, mate,' he said.

'We'll take the guy first. No, leave him in the bag. Just get the girl out.' He switched on the light and added, 'Jesus, that's never a girl.'

'She's been on the streets,' Nick explained. He looked at Betsy's protruding eyes and tongue then quickly looked away.

'I'll pull her out. You get a blanket or something to cover her while we're gone in case your other mate looks in here.'

'Yurek? He's not big on going walkabout,' Nick muttered but nevertheless found Betsy's coat and covered her with it once John had laid her on the floor. He watched in disgust as urine ran across the bare floorboards, swiftly followed by a more bowel-based swill.

Panting, they carried the sleeping-bagged Con to the Mini, unzipped him from it and stuffed him in the boot. Then they took the sleeping bag back and put the soiled Betsy inside it. She was much lighter than Con but also much more pungent. Nick could also smell his own heavy sweat and that of the wet-faced John. He felt sick.

At last they got the bagged Betsy into the back of the car.

'Go back there and clean up,' John said. 'Like it never happened.'

'And I'll see you...?'

'At the gym same as usual. But don't ever mention this.'

'Gotcha.' Nick wished there was some way he could show John that he was just like him, a survivor. He settled for a, 'See you soon then, mate.'

He could still smell Betsy as he walked back to Yurek's flat. Gone but not forgotten. He walked into the room where she and Con had lain and stared shakily at the wet-tened floor. Yurek's wasn't a shake 'n' vac kind of a house so there was no bleach or disinfectant. Tap water would have to do.

Soaking his oldest pair of underpants in cold water, he scrubbed at the liquid for a while. Then he opened the window a couple of inches. OK, so it wasn't Ideal Homes but it would do.

He tiptoed into the room he shared with Yurek. As usual, the old bastard was lying in his chair, mumbling rubble. Nick sat down, still trembling, and watched him for a while.

Slowly the moonlight turned to sun. A bird made a half-hearted call. No other bird answered. They'd probably been made into pies by the neighbours, Nick thought wearily. He went into his bag for something to eat and found a blackening banana. He ate it but still felt weak. Reaching into the zipped pocket of his bag he found his roids. He was due to take a couple in three hours. Nick decided to take them now – and swallowed down six.

CHAPTER
THIRTY-THREE

She'd never liked swallowing – and she was damned if she'd do so tonight. Rachel had been moving her lips down Richard's cock but now she stopped as he bucked upwards, clearly close to completion. Pulling her mouth free, she straddled him and put his shaft tip against her sex.

'Jesus,' Richard whispered.

Rachel felt a momentary annoyance at his sudden blasphemy. She'd been brought up to never take the Lord's name in vain. Still, there would be plenty of time to eradicate things like that when they were married. She'd want their child to be christened for a start.

'How's that?' she murmured, sliding down so that she took him all the way inside. Richard had teased her for being silent during sex so now she tried to think up the occasional comment. Really, she'd have been happier doing it lying down in the dark.

'Perfect,' Richard whispered.

'Good.' She really preferred him to go on top but he'd been so close to coming that she was scared he might ejaculate into the air if she took too long to change positions. Tonight was going to be the night.

She jiggled about, feeling self-conscious. Richard drove his hips up. She pressed down again, noting her breasts looked very small.

'You look like a model,' Richard said with obvious pleasure. Gazing at his half-closed eyes and wide-stretched mouth she could tell he was almost gone. Reaching a hand back, she brushed at his balls and he cried out and raised his chest half off the bed like some corpse come to life in a bad horror film.

He looked old tonight, Rachel thought with a shudder. When he moved his head a certain way his flesh creased near the neck and his skin looked loose and mottled. Maybe if he lost a few more pounds on their vegetarian diet it would help.

'What about you?' Richard murmured a few minutes later, putting two fingers on her clitoris.

'Me? I'm fine,' Rachel whispered, pushing his hand gently away. She put off the bedside lamp before snuggling up to him, just like a loving child cuddling up to her dad.

And she was indeed fine – for the contraceptive pill was now out of her system. A moment ago she'd been filled with Richard's sperm during her most fertile time of the month. Even as she lay here her body could be starting the cycle to produce a baby. Then Richard would marry her and Dawn would never get him back.

CHAPTER
THIRTY-FOUR

Dawn stared at the phone, willing it to ring. She'd been phoning Angela a lot since Ben became a murder suspect, but Angela often had her answering machine on. Was she ever going to return her calls? The other woman clearly had a new man to entertain her. She'd actually been dusting when Dawn last called. She'd mumbled something about not having much time to socialise now that she was a working girl.

Dawn stared morosely at the too-familiar walls. She could phone Richard, of course, and ask him to come round and collect her latest cartoon strips. She'd finished them early, had the time now that she was no longer spending her nights with bionic-tongued Ben.

Ben the murder suspect. Would she ever tell Richard about that? It would make her seem so pitiful. Richard still had Roach but she had no one at all.

She'd play it by ear – or by eye, if he invited her round. She'd need ten minutes to freshen up and five minutes to travel there by taxi. They could have a really nice evening. Angela had said that he didn't see Roach every night.

Dawn phoned the number that had until recently been her number. Her spirits faltered slightly as the answering machine clicked on. 'Hi, it's me,' she said. 'I've some more artwork for you so just give me a call if you want me to bring it round.' She hesitated, hoping that he'd pick up the receiver, then added, 'Tonight would be good as I've got nothing on.'

She put down the receiver, wondering if her last words had been a Freudian slip. Then she wondered if Richard would even think about her being naked. After all, he'd had months of the nubile embryo in his bed. There again, Rachel was fairly dim – and Richard had always craved intelligent conversation. Rachel was fixated on carrots whereas Richard enjoyed red meat.

Ben was now a mad murder suspect so could anyone blame her for wishing she was back with her very sane ex-husband, a man whom she'd loved all her life? A man who'd adored her? Dawn lay on the settee and thought about ways of getting Richard back.

CHAPTER
THIRTY-FIVE

'You want me to come with you now?' Ben stared at the two detectives monopolising his doorstep. 'If you could, sir. Just to answer a few questions.' 'What about?' He already feared he knew the answer.

'With regard to your whereabouts on 6th October last year,' the taller detective said.

He was a big man and Ben suddenly felt very small. 'Am I under arrest?' In films people always asked to phone their solicitor but he didn't have one to phone.

'No, sir.'

Ben shifted from one slippered foot to the other. 'How long will this take?'

The tall detective opened his mouth but the smaller one gave him a stern look. 'It needn't take long,' the six-foot three man said. They'd given him their names when they rang the doorbell a moment ago but Ben had been too shocked to take the information in.

'Fair enough.' There was nothing fair about this. He reached for his calfskin jacket, which was hanging up behind the door, and spent an awkward moment forcing one arm into the wrong sleeve. His every movement was being watched by both detectives. Ben wished that one of his flatmates was in, that he could tell someone he was going to the station. He wondered briefly if Dawn knew about this.

The police headquarters looked even bigger than they had on the few previous occasions that he'd walked past. The car park was almost full but the smaller detective seemed to have his own space. Ben sat in the back beside the tall 'tec, feeling like the Incredible Shrinking Man.

'This way, sir.'

He followed them up a few steps and through a reception. The WPC on reception hardly glanced at him.

'This way,' the DC said again and they turned and went down a very few stairs and approached a much larger desk. Two policewomen were in the room behind it. Both were studying files.

The smaller detective said something to the nearest policewoman and she brought over a book. Ben could see that it had various spaces. She introduced herself as the Custody Officer. 'Your name please, sir?' she added in a soft, polite voice.

'Ben James.'

'Your date of birth?'

He answered the few questions that she asked, reassuring her that he wasn't a drug addict or a diabetic.

'You have the right to speak to an independent solicitor free of charge and the right to consult the codes of practice covering police powers and procedures,' she said.

At the formality of it all, Ben felt his heartbeat speed. 'Am I under arrest?' He was sure he'd asked this before.

'No, you're simply here at our invitation,' the small detective said.

Ben hesitated. Finding a solicitor would take time and cost money. Plus he'd done nothing wrong and he wanted to keep this as low-key as possible.

'I don't think I need a solicitor,' he said.

'You're free to change your mind at any stage, sir,' the Custody Officer explained.

Ben looked at the detectives who'd brought him here. 'I've never even been inside a police station before,' he added helplessly.

'No problem. The interview room is this way, sir. Would you like a tea or a coffee?' one of the DCs asked.

'A coffee, please.' He'd had a couple of whiskies before they turned up at his door and desperately wanted a third one. 'Black, no sugar,' he added. He looked back at the policewoman and smiled. She looked quickly away.

The three of them walked a few more steps to a large black iron gate that was made up of a series of bars. It was exactly like the bars you saw on old-fashioned police cells in TV westerns. Ben shivered as the smaller man unlocked the gate. They walked through it and he locked it behind them. A short walk took them to an exact replica of the gate and the detective unlocked it too.

'If you get this when you're innocent then God knows what you get when you're guilty,' Ben joked.

'It's just standard security procedure, sir.'

'Can you call me Ben?' he asked, not sure if this would contradict some formality law.

'Ben it is. You can call me Tony and my colleague Ross if you like,' the friendliest detective said.

Tall Tony. That was easy to remember. Ben tried to think up a moniker for Ross that would help him to recall his name. It suddenly seemed very important that both DCs like him. The sooner he could convince them that he was a good guy, the sooner this would all be over with.

Tony opened a door and ushered Ben into the interview room. It held a wooden table and four wooden chairs. He sat down in one of them and both detectives sat opposite him. The room was small and Ben immediately felt the walls closing in. He looked covetously at the door and saw an illuminated red bulb above it, wondered what it meant.

Tony slotted three tapes into the huge black tape recorder at the far end of the desk. He switched the machine on and introduced himself and his colleague. He gave Ben's name and the time. Ben could see the time for himself on the large round clock on the wall.

'You do not have to say anything...' Tony said. He continued using the words that Ben heard on television crime programmes every week.

'Am I under arrest?' he asked yet again.

'No, sir. It's just a caution.'

Ben reminded himself that he had nothing to be cautious about. 'I told two constables all I know when they came round before.'

'They followed up your story, Ben. There's just a couple of things don't check out.' Tony spoke whilst the smaller Ross opened a notebook and looked at Ben expectantly.

'Like what?' Ben tried to push the desk forward slightly to give himself some breathing space but the desk's legs were bolted to the floor. Christ, they must get some violent prisoners in here. He pushed his chair back two inches instead.

'If you can just take us through the night of 6th October last year?'

He did, being necessarily vague when it came to the time spent in the park.

'So you think you left Ms Reid's at around midnight or 12.30?'

'Something like that.'

'And it took you – what? – fifteen minutes at most to walk to Churchill Gardens?'

Ben nodded.

'For the benefit of the tape, Ben James is nodding,' Tony said. 'So you enter the park some time between 12.15 and 12.45. What did you do then?'

'Walked by the water for a while.'

'Were you on your own?'

'Of course I was on my own.'

'You didn't bump into anyone?' Tony asked, staring steadily at Ben.

'Just that girl I told your colleagues about. She was overweight. I think she'd been crying. I almost crashed into her and we both got a fright.' He felt happier now that he was talking about the girl. It took his thoughts away from… from the full horror of what had happened to him that night.

'She says you encountered her at about four.'

'It wasn't that late,' Ben said weakly.

'She has witnesses who can verify the times she gives on her statement. She had a falling out with a lady friend ten minutes before she saw you and was back in her mother's house by 4.10am.'

'How can you be sure it was me she saw?' Ben asked.

'She gave a description to the police the next day and we immediately issued a photofit. It's the spitting image of you,' Tony said.

Ross was now writing so quickly that Ben was sure he'd get cramp.

'OK, so she saw me leaving the park. So what?' he asked tiredly.

'So you enter the park before 1am yet you don't leave before 4am. Are you telling us that you walked by the river for over three hours? It's not exactly the Nile,' the detective said.

'I sat down and fell asleep.'

'Was that before or after the man approached you?'

'What man?' Ben asked sharply, sitting further back in his chair.

This time Tony consulted a book. 'You told our colleagues that a man approached you in the park and asked you for a cigarette.'

'Oh, him. It was after that when I fell asleep.'

'So, you're telling us that you crash out on a bench in the pitch-black when there are strangers walking about. Weren't you scared that they'd steal your wallet?' Tony said.

'No.' He thought about telling them that he'd left his wallet at home but decided to follow the old engineering maxim of keeping it simple. 'I didn't have much money on me,' he explained.

'So you were happy in the park?'

'Happy enough.'

'Happy despite the fact that you'd had a fight with your girlfriend?'

'Well, not happy exactly, but glad to be out in the fresh air, just walking,' Ben said.

'You must have felt frustrated, her kicking you out of bed.'

'I was more hurt.' That made him sound like a wimp. 'I was surprised that she'd gotten so angry.'

'And maybe you felt angry too, wanted to retaliate?'

'I didn't hit her if that's what you mean.' He suddenly wondered what Dawn had said. Didn't some women get mad after a relationship had broken up and pretend the man had abused them? 'Is that what this is about?' he said.

Tony looked at him steadily. 'We have a young girl dead on the Southampton Road. You're on that road the same night, having been kicked out of bed by your girlfriend just before sex. You're frustrated and angry and pissed off with women...'

'I was upset, yes, but I didn't hurt anyone,' Ben said.

'You're telling us that you were happy?'

'Well, I was stable.'

'Yet the girl you bumped into says that your shirt was out of your jeans, that you looked really wild,' Tony explained.

'I dressed at Dawn's in the dark.'

'That doesn't explain your wild look.'

'I got a fright when I crashed into her.'

'Are you sure she's the only girl you ran into? Couldn't you have walked out the Southampton Road in the other direction, maybe to go to the 24-hour supermarket? And you see this girl walking with her high heels, all dressed up and sure of herself. And you've just had a fight with your girl that's made you so mad...'

'I wasn't in that part of the Southampton Road.'

'What part?'

'The part where they found the body.'

'So you know what part of the road she was found on, do you, Ben?'

'It was on the news.' Ben felt his heart speed some more. 'She was found at the industrial end of the road – like you said, near the supermarket. I entered the road beside Salisbury College and immediately crossed into the park.'

'Did you have a weapon on you, Ben? You know, for protection?'

'No, I've never carried any type of weapon.' They were big on verification so he'd give them some. 'I'm sure that Dawn – Ms Reid – will clarify that.'

'I suppose that if you did carry a knife it could be used against you in a struggle,' Tony said. Ben shrugged. 'For the benefit of the tape recorder, Mr James is shrugging,' Tony explained.

Ben looked at the tape machine. Then he looked at the grey and blue walls, at the grey carpet. He wondered what would happen if he got up to leave. He hated it here, hated the closed-in feeling, hated the lack of things to look at or read.

'So, you've never carried a knife and never had a knife used on you,' Tony clarified.

'That's right.' He wondered where this was heading.

'So how did you come by the long scar on your back?' the detective said.

Ben froze then realised he'd already answered this. 'As I told Dawn, someone at work inadvertently hit me with a metal ruler.'

'And that person was?'

'I don't remember. There were a few people larking about,' Ben said.

Tony consulted his book. 'Only no one at your work remembers the incident,' he stated then stared at Ben some more.

This was getting worse. 'You've checked up on me at work?'

'Of course.' Tony nodded vigorously.

Ben thought about saying, 'For the purpose of the tape, the detective is nodding.' Deciding against it, he said, 'They'll tell you I've never been in trouble in my life.'

Tony leaned back in his chair. 'That's true of most people who kill. They only do so once, often under extreme provocation. Maybe this girl laughed at you or tried to con you out of money and you snapped?'

'I never met the girl.'

'So what did you do that night? You're in the area acting suspiciously and you've several hours unaccounted for.'

'I told you – I slept.'

'In the early hours of an October morning with strangers prowling about? I don't think so.'

'And I walked a lot.'

'For hours in the pitch-blackness, knowing you had work the next day? It doesn't make sense. And you didn't go into work the next day, did you, Ben? You didn't go into work for several days according to your Human Resources Department. Just what happened to turn you from the happy stable man you tell us you were, into this sick person with a long scar on his back?'

They were going to come back to the same points forever and ever, a Salisbury version of Groundhog Day. And he would never have a satisfactory answer. Ben realised he was going to have to tell them the truth.

He looked at them both, wondering if they'd heard a story like his before. 'That night, I went to the park like I said. I just wanted to walk by the water.' He took a deep breath. 'After a few moments I was approached by a man who asked for a light then demanded money. He... I think he was a drug addict. At least, I could smell chemicals on his breath.'

There was no air in this fucking room. Ben looked up at the ventilation shaft and wondered if it had stopped working. The tape was still spinning but Ross had stopped writing things down.

'He asked you for money,' Tony prompted.

'Yes, but after I gave him it he demanded my jacket. He was bigger than me so I gave it to him. Then he pushed me over one of the benches and...' He stopped, grazing his knuckles against his mouth to hide his trembling lower lip.

'Could you describe this man for us?'

Ben nodded. 'He was tall – about six feet. He was very thin yet strong at the same time. He had dark hair and a day's stubble. And he was wearing a shirt – no jacket – and jeans.'

Anything else?'

'He had a sharp knife. He held it to my throat and later cut me across my back. That's how I got the scar that Dawn told you about. Oh, and he had black boots on. He... there was something odd about his skin. He looked slightly yellow. And did I mention the chemicals? He had an odd scent.'

'He was foreign?'

'No, definitely British.' Ben felt on safer territory now. He could describe what the man looked and sounded like – but it was harder to talk about what he'd actually done.

'Accent?'

'Probably the south of England. He put on odd voices at certain times, like he was trying to act more upmarket than he actually was.'

'And did he say anything that sticks in your memory?'

Ben looked at them numbly. 'He just kept threatening me. He warned that if I didn't do what he said then he would cut my throat.'

'And what did he want you to do?'

There it was, the million-dollar question. 'He wanted me to take my jeans off, then my underpants and then he… he raped me,' Ben said.

He glanced at them in turn, expecting to see their discomfort.

'And do you have proof of this?' Tony asked.

This wasn't what he'd expected. Ben realised he was staring blankly at the man. 'What kind of proof?'

'What I mean is, did you go to hospital immediately after this event?'

Ben shook his head then remembered the importance of talking into the tape recorder. 'No, I just wanted to get home, have a shower.'

'You weren't physically hurt?'

He'd been damn near split in half. Ben fought to keep his voice from wavering. 'I was, bled heavily for days.'

Tony raised his eyebrows. Ben noticed that they were unusually dark and thick. 'Can anyone vouch for this?'

'Well, I didn't take part in any naturist parades, if that's what you mean.' He realised that Ross had started writing again, that the man wasn't big on irony. 'Look, I just wanted to be by myself so I mainly stayed in my room.'

'Your flatmates can back you up?'

Ben winced at the detective's choice of words. Why did so many phrases seem to hint at physical coercion? He shook his head.

'Mr James is shaking his head. You mean that none of your flatmates saw that you were in pain?' Tony pressed.

Christ, this wasn't going well. He'd assumed that once he told the police about the rape he'd no longer be a suspect. 'No, they went to work the next day, didn't realise I'd stayed home.'

'But you were off work for several days.' Tony clearly thought he was listening to a fairy story.

'I know – but I don't work the same hours as them so they didn't know I'd changed my routine.' He tried to find the words that would make them understand. 'I felt…

well, it hurt to walk and I kept wondering why he'd picked on me. I didn't exactly want to broadcast what had happened to other men.'

'You didn't even tell your girlfriend?'

'No, we hadn't been together long. I didn't want her to pity me. I just felt so fucking odd about the whole thing.'

'But she knew that something was wrong?'

Ben nodded wearily. 'She saw the cut on my back. She probably noticed that I was drinking more. She knew that I was ill, but I told her it was a migraine.' He paused, remembering the chain of events. 'Oh, and I avoided sex in case the bastard had made me HIV-positive, didn't want to pass anything on to her.' He realised this gave him proof that he'd had a bad experience. 'I went for an AIDS test, can give you the clinic's address.'

Tony cleared his throat and leaned back slightly. 'Have you had your results?'

'Uh huh. I tested negative.'

'That's good to hear.' Tony leaned forward again.

Ross suddenly found his voice. 'Did you keep the clothes that you were wearing that night?'

'No, I threw everything out.' Both detectives were frowning at him. 'I just didn't want anything to remind me of the attack.' They were still looking at him sceptically as if it was a crime to throw out a pair of Levis. 'Plus my shirt had a long tear across the back.'

'Exactly. It would have been evidence,' Ross said. 'And if you'd had swab tests taken at the time…'

'I just couldn't face it.'

Ross grimaced. 'It's just that, with this being a murder enquiry, we can't take your word for everything.'

At the moment they weren't taking his word for anything. At this rate they'd lock him up – and let him out in fifteen years as the latest miscarriage of justice. 'But you can check I had the AIDS test,' Ben said desperately.

Ross scribbled down a few more words. 'We can, but you might have gone for it after having sex with a prostitute. Or you might have invented this whole story and had the test to help back it up, give you an alibi. You can see our point, Ben. We need concrete evidence.'

Tony looked sadly at him. 'Ben, it would help clear your name if you'd consent to an immediate physical examination.'

'But it was weeks ago. There won't be any...' He couldn't bring himself to say the word *semen*.

'There may still be scars that a doctor can document,' Tony said.

'Will you...' He felt ridiculous saying it. 'Will you be there?'

'No, there'll just be yourself and a doctor. He'll report back to us. This happens more often than you might think so they're used to the procedure, Ben.'

Beige walls, a grey couch, a metal trolley with a cloth half over it. Half an hour later he talked to a tall, slim white-coated doctor in the nearby medical suite.

'If you can undress below the waist and put on this gown.'

I can, but I don't want to, he thought. Then he remembered the option might be prison. He had to prove that he'd been raped that night, that he hadn't been the one to kill the girl.

He took off his jeans and underpants, shrugged into the white cotton gown. It was open all the way down the back, left him feeling like a transvestite-style rent boy. He looked at the couch, couldn't bring himself to clamber onto it.

'If you could lie on the examination couch on your stomach,' the doctor said, walking briskly back into the room.

Ben took a few faltering steps towards the couch. 'As I said, it was weeks ago.'

'I'm sure the detectives will take that into consideration. I'm not involved in the legal process, you understand? I just have to report what I find.'

There was going to be no exit. Ben got awkwardly into position on the couch. He was hugely aware of his naked buttocks and the brutalised opening that had brought him so much pain.

Slowly the surgeon pulled on a thin white rubber glove and smoothed a surgical jelly over it. 'I'm just going to examine you now.'

Ben closed his eyes as he felt the gloved fingers probing between his cheeks. This was all too familiar. He couldn't have gone through this within hours of being raped.

'Tell me if it hurts.'

Of course it fucking hurts. He mumbled his assent.

'I'm just going to check deeper inside with a proctoscope.' Ben heard an implement scraping against the metal table then his body was invaded with cold.

'What does it do?' He figured he knew but he wanted to talk, to distract himself from the shame and discomfort. He wanted to be seen as a person, not as a violated arse.

'It'll show up any internal trauma.'

'I bled for days after the attack,' Ben said.

'I can see that. There's been considerable external and internal tearing.'

'And you'll tell the police that?'

'Of course I will. '

'I couldn't have gone through this at the time.'

'We could have done more for you then if you had.' He was glad that the doctor sounded matter-of-fact rather than judgemental. 'Given you antibiotics and stool softeners as well as taking forensic evidence.'

Fifteen minutes later he was back with Tony and Ross in the interview room. 'The examination backs your story up,' Tony said, looking at him with obvious sympathy. 'We'll get a written report for your file but the verbal one confirms what you told us.' Ross's face remained impassive but he had put his notebook away. 'Do you feel up to continuing with this or would you prefer to come back tomorrow?' Tony continued.

He desperately wanted to clear his name forever. 'Let's get it over with,' Ben said.

'OK, we'll have a coffee then I'll ask you a few more questions about what happened,' Tony explained. He looked up at Ross. 'And if you could get Ben a leaflet about Victim Support?'

After another cup of instant, they started again. This time it was easier as he knew they understood something of what he'd been through. They'd seen this happen to various unfortunate men. He went over every detail of Nick's description then answered the supplementary questions they said would help.

'When he held the knife did he use his right hand or his left?'

'His right.'

'You mentioned he put on an odd voice at times – did he also use any words that sounded strange?'

'I don't think…' The words the man had used had been humiliating but unexceptional. 'If I remember anything specific I'll get back to you.' He hoped fervently that he'd never have to discuss the subject again.

'If you think of something, ask for me at any time.' Tony slid over his card.

Ross leaned forward. 'What direction did he head off in after he'd finished the assault?'

'He went towards the car park side of the Gardens.' He suddenly realised that if the man had kept walking in that direction he'd ultimately have reached the industrial units on the Southampton Road. 'Do you think that he could have stabbed that girl? I mean, I just assumed he hated men.'

'Some of these guys hate everyone,' Ross said.

Tony posed a few more questions then asked, 'Do you want to give a victim statement now or later? We can do so here or in another room upstairs.'

'I'll do it now if we can go upstairs,' Ben said.

'It's the soundproofing in here. Some people find it a bit claustrophobic,' Ross explained.

Half an hour later Ben stood up to go. 'Do you think you'll get him?' he asked.

Tony shut his file with a snap then nodded. 'You've given us an excellent description – and it tallies with other descriptions we've been given of a man acting suspiciously.' He stood up, looking tall and strong and ready to tackle anyone. 'These guys have a habit of drawing attention to themselves so we've got a good chance of catching him if he's stayed in Salisbury.'

CHAPTER
THIRTY-SIX

'Where they go?' Yurek asked. It was the fifth time he'd asked it today.

'To fucking Mars. Who cares where they went?' Nick felt the familiar closed-in sense of rage gripping his chest. 'They were no-good dossers.'

'They were good to me,' Yurek mumbled, lying further back in his chair. 'They bring me cans.'

He'd like the old Pole to can it now. When Yurek didn't have a drink he just went on and on until you got him some to keep him quiet. But he, Nick, had no money. He cursed himself for not having asked John for some cash.

'Need cans,' Yurek said again.

'So buy some. Thought you collected your pension today?'

Yurek nodded warily then pointed to his thin trousered legs. 'My feet are not working. I have to wait.'

'Hell, I have to wait, too. It's Saturday till my giro comes in.'

'You get me drink now, I pay you tomorrow,' Yurek said, leaning forward and releasing an armpit's worth of sweat.

Nick moved further back against the wall. The old guy's breath was as bad as Betsy's. 'I've not got any money till Saturday. I just told you that.'

Yurek's shaking seemed to intensify. 'I no feel good.'

'Tough luck. I no feel good either,' Nick replied.

'You get me some milk and rolls and four Carlsbergs?'

'If you give me the cash.'

Yurek sat there for some time and Nick wondered what the old soak was thinking. At last Yurek reached into the back pocket of his trousers and brought out a very creased and dirty benefits book. 'I give you my pension to get cans for me,' he said.

'Right, you have to sign it on the back saying you want me to collect it,' Nick told him. He'd done this for neighbours before when it was a stolen book.

Yurek signed his cross. Nick sighed then filled in his own name and asked for additional ID. After much scrabbling below his chair – movements that produced much belching and wheezing – Yurek produced a membership card for a pensioners' lunch club. It had his name and photograph on it.

'Good, man. Be back in an hour.' Nick did the two-minute mile to the post office and got Yurek's weekly pension. Then he went on to the gym and got another Deca injection from John.

'It's on the house,' John said when Nick reached for his wallet.

He took two twenty-pound notes from Yurek's pension. 'In that case, can I buy a couple of hundred roids?'

He did, then went on to do an hour-long workout. His arms felt good for a change and he managed a lot of reps. Afterwards he walked around town then treated himself to a chicken dhansak with pilau rice in an Indian restaurant. This was the life – good food, a couple of beers and a warm place to read the sports magazine that he'd lifted from the gym.

He stayed in the restaurant till three o'clock, when they started to vacuum around his feet. He paid, feeling too full to do a runner. Then he sat in the library for a while and read a book about the biggest cons of the twentieth century. He went back to the gym for an early evening workout. Rob was just leaving by the main door as the staff buzzed Nick in.

'How's things?' Nick asked.

'All right.' Rob looked like the before picture on a valium advert.

'Good. See you soon, eh?' Nick said.

Without waiting for an answer he sauntered into the building and went to the gents where he swallowed down another two roids, went upstairs and lifted weights like he was fucking Popeye. He felt ace.

He continued to feel ace until he got back to Yurek's that night. The old man was waiting behind the living room door when he walked in. Clearly, his legs had recovered.

'You take my money,' he shouted in a surprisingly loud voice. 'I wait all day but you no come.'

'Heavy traffic out there, pal,' Nick said perkily. 'I got delayed.'

He figured he could say what he liked. Now that Con was cancelled, Yurek had no one to protect him.

'You bring my Carlsbergs?' Yurek said.

Shit, he'd forgotten to bring his unlikely landlord anything – no milk, no rolls and definitely no booze.

'I'll go out again in a minute and get everything, right?'

'No right. You give me my pension. I go,' Yurek said.

Nick stalled. He'd planned to give Yurek his money when he was drunk and incapable. A sober Yurek would immediately see how much he'd spent on a meal and on roids.

'S'all right, I'll go for you pal.' He backed away.

To his surprise, Yurek sort of cannoned forward into him, his chest pushing into Nick's whilst his feet stayed immobile on the floor.

'Get off, you cunt!' Nick shoved the unwashed man away and Yurek ricocheted back and hit the side of his chair. He slid down it.

'Pension. You no keep my pension,' he screamed.

A baby started to cry then a window opened and someone shouted for them to shut the fuck up. Nick felt his heart beating faster. 'Shut it, Yurek.'

'I go tell Con,' Yurek yelled.

He couldn't tell Con – but he could tell others about Con and about Betsy, about the fact that they'd suddenly disappeared.

'Just calm down, will you? You'll get your cash.'

'I go to polis,' the old man said. 'I tell them that you cheat.'

Nick shook his head then winced as a needle-sharp pain flashed through it. 'No one grasses around here.'

'I tell,' said Yurek again, trying to stand up. Nick looked down at the old man's matted hair, sweat-crusted clothes and badly-shod feet. 'I go now,' Yurek warned, and Nick could see the pale pink sockets where several of his teeth had been.

'Fucking loser.' He aimed a kick at the man's mouth, feeling a moment of wonder as his toecap connected. The elderly lips seemed to open to receive the training shoe.

'Uh,' Yurek made an odd half-grunting and half-gasping sound. Nick kicked him again, harder, this time aiming for the throat. He so wanted safety. Yurek was going to the police and he, Nick, would get done for stealing his pension. Christ knows how he'd pay the fine.

Worse, Yurek might tell the cops that Con and Betsy had scarpered and the police would analyse the stains. They'd find he had previous for sorting a woman out, start looking at him more closely. How long after that would it be before they collared him for the Southampton Road murder and for that cemetery death? No, people around here didn't usually grass so Yurek deserved to have his very big mouth kicked in.

244 Kiss It Away

Nick kicked and kicked and kicked. At last he became aware of a dull pain in his right ankle and another pain in his hands, which were both tensed. He moved back, panting, and flexed his sore feet and fingers. Then he glanced down to see that the old man no longer had a face.

Hell, he hadn't meant to do that. He'd just wanted to stop the old soak complaining. Now his thin chest wasn't moving. Nick toed the man's limp arms. No response. He nudged a toe at his nearest thigh but again the pensioner didn't move.

'Wake up, you old bastard,' Nick said.

He didn't like being here alone with a possible corpse. He felt... uncertain. His bowels stirred and he hurried to the bathroom, used his bag to hold the door shut, just in case. For half an hour he sat there on the loo, wishing that his bladder would produce something but it seemed that nowadays most of the liquid in his body came out in the form of water from one of his eyes or from heavy sweat.

Now what? Nick cleaned himself up then tiptoed back to the living room. He peered around the door. Yurek was still in the exact same place.

'Are you fucking with me?' he asked but he already knew the answer. The alkie was stone-cold dead.

Not wanting to look at the bloodied features, Nick went into the other room and sat on the floor staring ahead of him – staring at the very place where Con and Betsy had been strangled to death.

CHAPTER
THIRTY-SEVEN

Now that he'd told the police everything it might be easier to tell Dawn. Ben walked past her flat for the third time that night. There was a light on in the lounge window. She was definitely in – but was she alone?

He'd started to dial her number twice but had put down the receiver halfway through. He might say 'Dawn, it's me,' and she'd hang up on him. But surely if she saw his face she'd know that something awful had happened, that he was now ready to explain?

If he waited long enough he might not have to explain. Tony had phoned to tell him that the BBC were going to cover the crimes on a monthly programme. They'd reconstruct the man's attack on him – and the man's second murderous attack that same night on the girl on the Southampton Road. Dawn would recognise the date and figure out the rest – she wasn't stupid. The question was, did he have the courage to tell her now to her face?

She'd been good to him, deserved to know she'd done nothing wrong. She must need answers. She'd be wondering how he'd transmogrified from a nice guy into the boyfriend from hell.

He had to tell her he'd been raped. He practised various speeches in his head but they all sounded like the dialogue from some bad Gothic movie or *Play For Today*.

A tall youth walked past and for a moment he reminded Ben of the chemical-breathed and hate-fuelled rapist. He hurried home, remembering that the police had said the killer might still be living here in Salisbury.

CHAPTER
THIRTY-EIGHT

John would surely help him dispose of Yurek's corpse. Nick sat in the gym and watched the changing room doors, ready to greet the strong, sure dealer. Various poncy boys came and changed into their best baggies or Persil whites.

Where the fuck was John? For the first time he realised that he didn't have the guy's address. Hell, he didn't even have a surname. He simply knew that John was here each morning – except today.

Someone had left a comb lying on the opposite bench. He'd have that. Nick picked it up, went over to the mirror and combed his thick dark hair. For a moment he thought that he had fleas, for the air around him filled with fluttering blackness. Then he realised that it was his hair breaking away from his fringe. Christ on a bike. He'd always had thick hair. He'd have to ask John what was going on.

He waited, more and more questions swimming around his head. At last he went upstairs to reception.

'You seen John?' he asked the stick insect on the desk.

'John who?'

'Big guy. Dark hair. Wears black-and-white baggies.'

'Sorry,' the little bitch said, not sounding sorry at all.

Nick went to the gym's coffee bar and sat there trying to eat and drink and be anything except terrified. What was he supposed to do with the body under the blanket back home? By teatime the staff were giving him increasingly strange looks so he left and walked to the area where they'd dropped Gerald off. Again, he waited for hour after hour, hoping to see his fellow ram-raider. Again, no one appeared.

Now what? As darkness descended on Salisbury, Nick walked home wishing he had someone he could talk to. Not drunken Yurek or mad Con or blowjob Betsy, but someone reasonable, someone who was going somewhere. He wanted to get fit, to get some cash, to live in a decent piece of property – and he needed a girl who wanted the same things.

He reached Yurek's building and walked slowly to the old Pole's door. Thank Christ that no one had broken in and found the dead man. He walked reluctantly into the bedroom and checked that the body was still lying there. It was – and it didn't even smell too bad, probably because Yurek hardly ate anything.

What the fuck should he do now? He could put the body upright in the walk-in cupboard and nail the cupboard shut. He'd read of a guy who had done that once and the body had mummified. The main thing was, no one knew it was there. But eventually some social worker from Yurek's pensioner's lunch club might notice he was missing and check...

He could try carrying the body out of here by himself but where would he put it? It was obvious that Yurek's face and neck had been in close contact with a boot so again the police would come round. Nick sat there, thinking so hard that his head began pulsing. Suddenly he came up with a plan.

Of course, it was totally simple. He just had to leave the body here where it would rot. Everyone would think

Yurek had died of natural causes brought about by too little food and too much drink.

Water would help speed the process up. Nick used a wad of chewing gum as a bath plug then filled the tub with freezing water. Gagging, he took off Yurek's clothes. He put them in the water first, as if the old man had been washing his cardi and had fallen in and drowned.

He lifted the dirty naked body and let it drop into the tub. It made a bigger splash than he expected. Then he shut the door and permanently left Yurek's flat. Tonight he'd stay in one of Salisbury's hostels. Tomorrow he'd... well he'd think about that tomorrow. The main thing was to get out of here, to establish an alibi.

He'd have liked to leave the city now, to return to Brighton or even give Bournemouth a second chance, get a job in a club there. But he wanted to see John once more before he left. John had good gear for sale and had the muscle to make things happen. John was the kind of guy he wanted to be able to phone any time a problem arrived. Yep, he'd stay here for a few more days and get his stack well up and get his strength back. He'd get himself some money and some ass and he'd be just fine.

CHAPTER THIRTY-NINE

'I felt so fucking weak,' Ben said, forcing himself to look directly at Chris, the male-rape-support counsellor. He realised that he'd been swearing a lot throughout the past hour in a desperate bid to sound tough.

'These attacks – it's not about you, it's about them.' Chris spread out his arms in an expansive shrug. 'They feel threatened all the time, convince themselves that everyone else is threatening.'

Ben nodded. 'The police told me that.' He looked down at his medium-sized fists and managed a wry laugh. 'Me, threatening? I'm not exactly a killing machine.'

Chris smiled back, then shook his head. 'Men like that can find a kid who questions their authority threatening. You were just in the wrong place at the wrong time.'

'In a park in the early hours. He said I was asking for it,' Ben added bitterly.

Chris grimaced. 'It can happen any time. I was raped at work on a summer's afternoon.'

'By a stranger?' Ben asked. He looked at Chris more closely. The man was in his late fifties and looked well able to handle himself.

'No, he was my boss. He'd been making passes at me for months though he knew I had a wife and baby. I suppose I didn't deal with it well, just kept laughing it off.' He paused, clearly searching for the right words. 'One afternoon both my co-workers were at an out-of-town conference. He came back from lunch and I could see he'd been drinking. He made another pass and I rejected him and he hit me in the face.'

'You feel so sick,' Ben said, remembering.

'Afterwards I went home in shock,' the counsellor said. 'My wife phoned the police. In those days they didn't know how to interview men who'd been raped. Even the doctors at the hospital were embarrassed. They made me feel like I was the one at fault, like I was a total weakling. I didn't leave the house again for almost a year.'

'I had to force myself to go back to work,' Ben admitted. He realised for the first time that he'd been braver than he'd originally thought. 'So how did you start to get over it?' he added. 'I still wake up most nights.'

'I read about a support group and my wife drove me there,' Chris said. 'Talking to others who'd been through it changed my thinking. Until then, I'd been going over and over it, blaming myself.'

'I might join the group later. It's just for now...' Ben mirrored Chris's earlier shrugging gesture.

The older man nodded. 'There's no pressure to tell other people. I'm happy to see people individually like this.'

'I almost cancelled this appointment a few times,' Ben admitted.

Chris nodded. 'You've probably got a lot of questions. I know I did.'

'Mainly I kept wondering if it was something about how I looked, how I walked?'

Chris shook his head. 'Oh, sometimes an attacker will use that as an excuse. You know, say that the victim was cute and blond and acted girlish. But it's not about the victim. It's about how the rapist feels about himself.'

'But he really seemed to hate me.'

'At that particular moment he bloody well hated everyone. It's a mindset. Something's set him off and you were in the wrong place.'

'I think he'd been sniffing glue.'

'He might well have been – but these guys will also attack when they're sober,' Chris said.

'I wondered... I'm not exactly a muscleman.'

'It's not about your build,' Chris explained. 'I had a guy in here once, built like a Sumo wrestler. Six guys jumped him in a railway station and one of them raped him. Again, it was a hate crime – take the big guy down and feel temporarily stronger yourself.'

'With your wife, afterwards,' Ben said awkwardly. 'Could you...? I mean, I couldn't let my girlfriend near me.'

'It just takes time. Put it this way, I went on to father another three kids,' Chris said with a grin.

'I was worried about HIV but I tested negative.'

'A couple of the guys in the support group weren't so lucky,' Chris said.

Lucky seemed an odd word to use, Ben thought. There again, perhaps he was. He hadn't contracted a disease. He hadn't become completely agoraphobic like Chris had. He'd lost Dawn, of course, but at least he'd now found the bottle to write to her explaining everything. He was handling this.

'I probably will join the group,' he said.

'They're a great bunch of guys,' Chris promised. 'I joined fifteen years ago – and ended up running it.'

Ben smiled back, realising he was going to be OK. Then he voiced the thought that kept reverberating.

'I just hate the thought of him doing it again.'

Chris reached into a large file and took out a leaflet. 'One of the group runs a self-defence course here every Wednesday.'

Ben shook his head. 'No, not to me – to some other poor bastard.'

'You've done all you can now, told the police all you know.'

'But is he likely to…?' Given what Chris had said, Ben feared he already knew the answer.

The counsellor nodded. 'If he's still full of fear and hatred then he'll almost certainly rape again.'

CHAPTER FORTY

'So, how'd you manage to escape from them this time?' Dawn asked jokily, pouring Angela a glass of supermarket wine.

'Oh, Zoe's looking after Jack. Rob's at the gym but he's joining her later. I left them money for pizza – but she'll probably make them something with brown rice.'

'Will I get a pizza for us?' Now that Dawn was solo again she was no longer fighting the increasing roundness of her stomach.

'Not for me – I'm on a healthy eating kick,' Angela said.

'I spy a man,' Dawn murmured then was surprised when Angela stiffened. 'What's up, Ang? Is he married with triplets?'

'No, it's just… complicated,' Angela said.

'Can't be as complicated as dating a double murderer,' Dawn muttered with genuine irony.

'I know – to think I accused you of taking away young Ben's innocence,' Angela replied.

'He's history. Tell me about this new man,' Dawn said, realising she was becoming as strident as Angie. They said people became like their dogs – but maybe they also became like their friends?

'Not much to tell, we're just at the flirtatious stage,' Angela countered.

Dawn voiced her surprise. 'That's not like you – thought you'd have him stripped within seconds.'

'I'm playing it slow. He's worth waiting for,' Angie said mysteriously.

'So, did you meet him at Jack's nursery?'

'No, he's not one of the doting dads.'

'Anyone I know?'

'No comment to the point of infinity,' Angela murmured, looking sly.

'So where is he tonight?'

For the first time the other woman looked depressed. 'Otherwise engaged.'

'You sure he's not married?'

'Positive. but a lot of people would like him to be,' Angela said.

'If he called round at your place, would Zoe tell him that you were here?' Dawn looked hopefully at the door and at the telephone.

'Nah, she always hates the men I fancy. She'd make him stay and eat brown rice with her as a punishment,' Angela replied.

CHAPTER
FORTY-ONE

Maybe he should take Cheryl out again. Cheryl had really liked him. Cheryl had let him shaft her up the chocolate freeway, plus she had a nice little cottage with room to spare.

He'd sweet-talk her at the cafe now. It would be perfect. Nick sat on the sagging bed in the hostel and thought it all out. Around him, men groaned and snored and mumbled, filling the room with the stench of regurgitated beer and whisky. He'd only been here a night but he already wanted out. Nick showered, staring through a gap in the curtain to make sure that no one arrived to nick his bag or have a go at him. He put on his suit, noting dully that it hung on him more loosely than before.

He should really take it easy, burn less calories, but he felt wired. He walked at a fast pace, stopping briefly in the public toilets to wipe the sweat from his brow, his back and his underarms. Reaching Cheryl's workplace, he peered through the steamy window until he saw her emerge from the staff quarters. She had her back to him, wiping down a customer's table, when he sauntered in.

'Hi, pal,' he said, touching her somewhat chunky arm. She turned around, blushed and backed away.

'I'm just off the rigs this morning,' he said. 'Wanted to see you asap.'

He watched her Adam's apple move up and down. It seemed enlarged for a girl.

'No, you didn't – I've seen you in town three or four times.'

Fuck it. He'd have to win her over some more. 'Yeah, I was back for a bit to sort some business. You know, flying visits.'

'Well, fly off back there now, then,' Cheryl said. He realised that she was shaking hard.

'Pal, what's wrong? We're good together, aren't we? I'd hoped...' He spread his arms out then brought them swiftly in again when he breathed his own heavy scent.

'Leave now or I'll call Mrs Meacham,' Cheryl warned.

Nick glanced around. Both middle-aged female customers were already staring at him, though they looked away when he eyeballed them back.

'No need for that, pal. I just wanted to see you again.' He stood there trying to think up some magic parting shot, some special cruelty. But his mind was blank.

He left and walked fast along the street they realised he didn't have a scooby where he was going. He couldn't work out at the gym 'cause he was wearing his suit and he felt too jumpy to sit down and eat. Maybe he'd walk to Gerald's area again, try to find the man.

He tried. He failed. He walked all the way back to the gym and sat in the cafe there. John didn't appear – and nor did anyone else he could talk to. Sitting there on his own in his suit he felt different to everyone else, a total prick.

He tensed some more as he felt an unfamiliar pain spiralling through his bowels. What the fuck? He only just made it to the gents before the floodgates opened. When it was all over he felt even weaker, as though the very marrow had been flushed from his arms and legs. This wasn't right. He had to feel strong in case someone at the hostel had a go at him. He had to be able to talk a good game or to escape.

He went into red alert as the cubicle next to him opened and closed and he heard two low male voices, a zip going down. Were they about to bum-love each other? 'It's better than muscle popping,' one of the guys said.

Nick relaxed against the toilet seat. Muscle popping was when you injected roids directly into the muscle. It was what most bodybuilders did as it gave you a direct hit. What could be better than that?

He cleaned himself up and was washing his hands when the first guy came out.

'Can I have what you've just had? I've got the readies.'

'Fucking hurts,' said the guy. He battered on the door. 'Kenny – you got another customer.'

'A new friend, you mean.' A guy with a broken nose who Nick vaguely recognised came swaggering out of the john. He looked at Nick. 'What you on at the moment?'

Nick described his stack and the dealer nodded. 'I've got this stuff from France.'

'And you inject it…?'

'In the spine.'

Nick leaned back against the washbasins, feeling even weaker than before. 'No kidding? I've been getting these Deca injections from John in here.' He pointed to one of his biceps then added, 'You seen John around?'

'He's had a bit of bother. I reckon he'll be back by next week,' Kenny said.

That was fair enough – he could stay in Salisbury for a few more days, though he'd do what he could to find someplace better than that hobo's hostel. No way was he letting this guy spike him up the backbone, though.

'Mate – just put my spike in my arm.'

'It's your call,' the guy said and they went back into the cubicle and Nick paid up.

He looked away as the needle entered his muscle, but felt the thin hotness entering his system. It made him feel so queasy that he had to close his eyes.

'How long till it kicks in?'

'Within the hour,' the dealer said. 'Vets give it to horses so it's really strong stuff.'

There was a joke in there somewhere but Nick couldn't bloody well think of it.

'See you on Wednesday morning?' he asked, glad that he'd found someone to replace jilting John.

The guy grunted something that Nick chose to translate into yes. He went back upstairs to the cafe and sat there waiting for his legs to flood with energy. When they did he'd go back to that poxy hostel and change into his exercise gear.

Aware of a new itchiness in his calves, he bent to scratch them. But the itch moved up, causing him to tear at his thighs, his guts, his chest. Aware of an increasingly bad taste in his mouth, he used his fingernails to clean between his teeth but when he pulled his hand away it was smeared with blood. His mum had had all her teeth taken out when she was thirty. Nick hoped he wasn't heading the same way.

He hated fucking dentists and he hated sitting here sweating in his suit. And he hated the stuck-up bint on reception. And he couldn't stand all those flashy bastards cycling and running on the loud machines.

His pulse speeded even more as the familiar figure of Rob appeared in his slimmed-down shorts and rich-kid's training watch. He glanced at Nick then looked away and hurried to a stepping machine. How dare he diss him like that? He'd soon get his.

Nick picked up a muscle mag and pretended to read it, all the time watching the teenager out of the corner of his eye. Rob was a hell of a lot fitter than he'd been a few weeks ago – but still no match for a full-grown man.

He watched the boy's plump buttocks jiggling as he walked on the treadmill machine. He had an arse like a girl. He could just imagine yanking down the perfectly ironed shorts and displaying the cheeks that Rob tried so hard to keep hidden. He'd part the boy's buttocks and teach him all about respect.

Were there bushes near Rob's house? Rich people usually had huge gardens and lived near pretty parkland. All he needed was some hidden spot in which to sort the little bastard out.

It took a long time, but at last the youth finished his workout and left the gym. Nick stayed where he was, giving the kid time to shower and clothe himself. Only when five minutes had elapsed did he creep halfway down the stairs and sit there, looking through the banister at the changing room door.

A grey haired man left, followed swiftly by a twenty-year-old. Nick wondered if they'd been jerking off together. Then the door opened again and rich little Rob appeared.

He strode out of the front door. Nick counted to twenty then followed him. He ducked behind a parked car, pretending to tie his shoelace. Peering around the bonnet he could see the boy walking away from the town centre, towards a less populated part of Salisbury.

Magic. He followed at a safe distance, hiding in doorways whenever the boy turned to cross a road. Maybe he could actually follow the kid into the house, get more than his wallet? Providing Mummy and Daddy were still at work…

He frowned as the boy stopped at a street-facing door. This didn't look right. This was a bog-standard ground-floor flat. Rob knocked and the door was opened by a smiling dark-haired girl.

Aha, this must be Rob's girlfriend – a girlfriend who Rob admitted had a very begging-for-it mummy. Nick could be in there yet.

He waited for ten minutes, scratching his legs and arms and wondering if he'd caught fleas, then rang the bell. The girl answered real quick, so she couldn't have been in bed with the boyfriend. 'Hi, Rob's expecting me.' He stepped into the hall.

'Oh? He's in there.' The girlfriend pointed to a half-open door.

Nick strode in. Rob was sitting on the sofa reading a women's magazine. He looked up and started to smile – but his smile froze.

'How you doing?' Nick said.

'Fine, thanks,' the youth mumbled, not sounding it. The girl had walked back into the living room and was standing in the doorway, staring from one to the other.

'Aren't you going to introduce us?' Nick said.

'I... Zoe, this is Nick. I know him from the gym. Nick, this is my girlfriend, Zoe.'

Nick felt himself start to grin as he heard the strain in the teenager's voice. 'So, Rob, where's this classy older woman you told me about?'

Rob blushed. 'Forget about that.'

Nick turned to Zoe. 'He said that your mum was a real looker. Where you hiding her, then?'

'She's out,' the girl said in a somewhat haughty tone.

'But she'll be back at any minute,' Rob added quickly.

'You sure?' His bullshitometer told him that the boy was lying through his beautifully looked-after teeth. 'Well, we'll just have us a little party till she gets back.' He felt a rivulet of sweat run down his back and took off his jacket, throwing it on the settee. 'Let's just get comfortable.' He forced his fogged brain to concentrate. What did he want to achieve? Oh yes, to get the spoilt brat on his own for a few minutes. 'So, Zoe, you going to make us all tea?'

He watched as Zoe looked at Rob. The boy hesitated then nodded slightly.

'What do you take in yours?' the girl asked.

'Nothing. Black.' He was feeling real spaced, maybe needed some calories. 'With biscuits, preferably chocolate,' he said.

'We only have wholemeal digestives.' Zoe left the living room. Nick turned back to Rob and punched him in the jaw. Rob went down fast. Nick bent and grabbed the kid's wrists, put them in front of him. He bound his jacket sleeves around the kid's limbs and tied them tight.

Now he needed rope – or at least string. He walked quietly into the kitchen and grabbed Zoe by the throat. 'Tell me where to find rope or I'll break your neck.' For a moment he thought that she was defying him so he got ready to strangle her. Then he realised that she was trying to speak but couldn't because of the pressure on her throat.

He relaxed his arm slightly. 'Th… there's spare washing line in the third drawer,' Zoe gasped.

Nick brought her over to the built-in cupboard with him. 'Open it.'

They bent together so that she could do so and she brought out a coil of white nylon rope.

'Put your hands in front of you.'

She did. He grabbed them and wound the rope round and round. She was shaking so hard that at first it was difficult to keep her wrists together. But as he added more and more coils, the movement ceased. The rest of her body continued to shake and he had to prod her several times before she walked in front of him to the room where Rob lay.

Or had lain. As soon as he walked in, he could see that the boy was sitting up. 'Sit down,' Nick snapped at the girl, indicating the settee. He got his knife out and cut away the unused coil of rope still hanging from her bound wrists then he knelt in front of Rob and replaced the jacket binding with lots of the white cord.

'My wallet's in my sports bag,' Rob slurred, looking pale-facedly up at Nick. There was a purple mark beneath one corner of his mouth.

'What makes you think I want your cash? D'you think I'm cheap?' Normally he had to work himself up into a rage but today it came natural.

'No.' Rob seemed to consider saying more then clearly thought better of it.

'There's lots of food in the fridge,' Zoe added tremulously.

'Did I ask you for your opinion?'

She licked her lips then shook her head.

'Then don't speak till you're spoken to, all right?'

He thought about threatening to fill her mouth with his cock then decided against it. It was the boy who had dissed him, the boy who deserved to take the rap. But he'd better tie the girl's ankles together so that she couldn't kick him whilst he taught her man a lesson he'd never forget.

He finished tying her up then helped her move to the chair opposite the settee. He wanted the settee for Rob, ordered the youth to lie along it on his stomach.

'Please don't hurt my girlfriend,' Rob said shakily.

'You trying to give me orders? You know what happens to kids who give me orders?' Nick asked.

He pulled down the boy's grey flannel trousers, bringing his underpants at the same time. The boy tried to push himself up but Nick threw his own weight over the youth, knowing that this would knock the breath from his body.

'Leave him alone!' Zoe screamed.

Shit! He'd forgotten about her. What the hell had he done with his knife after cutting the rope? Yep, he'd put it in his sock for safety. Nick got the blade out and held it to Rob's throat. 'You scream again, girlie, and I'll slice this blade right through his neck.'

Zoe whimpered then the flat went quiet. Spitting on his hand, Nick prepared to invade the rich kid's arse.

CHAPTER
FORTY-TWO

'One of the highest teenage pregnancy rates in Europe,' Dawn exclaimed then attempted to whistle. She switched the documentary off.

'I blame today's music,' Angela said, reaching for the second bottle of wine. 'It's so boring that they can't dance so they have to go out and get laid.'

'Or these virgin sex-education teachers,' Dawn added. 'Talking about love and marriage for an hour then mumbling for a half-minute about tadpoles and eggs.' She glanced over at her friend. 'I suppose Zoe's had all that at school?'

Angela shrugged. 'I had to sign something once to say she could watch an instructional video. But she doesn't give me details. She's always such a prude about such things.'

'Hell, did you tell *your* mother?' Dawn asked cynically.

'Mine? She was virtually a bride of Christ. It's a wonder she ever had me,' Angela said.

'Yeah? Mine was a bit out of her depth but she bought me a little book on the subject.'

'Zoe probably learns all she needs to from the library. She virtually lives there,' her friend replied.

'But she's not there tonight,' Dawn prompted. She hated the thought of Zoe getting pregnant. The girl had little enough fun already without becoming a teenage mum.

'No, she's with Rob.' Angela at last seemed to follow Dawn's train of thought. 'You're worried that... no, Dawn. Zoe wouldn't.'

'I remember this really prim girl who went to Sunday school with me,' Dawn told her. 'No one could believe it when she got pregnant at fifteen because she had never even had a boyfriend, came straight home from school each night.'

'An unidentified fucking object?' Angela joked.

'Oh, an identified one. Turned out that she'd fancied her Sunday school teacher and they'd done it in his car.'

'So you think I should be manning the fort?' Angela asked with what was clearly a drunken grin.

'No, just give them a ring, make sure Zoe's not being pressurised into anything.'

'All right, Mum,' Angela said sardonically and picked up the phone. A few minutes later she put it down. 'No answer. They must be immersed in a video.'

'Or creating your first grandchild,' Dawn said.

CHAPTER
FORTY-THREE

Who the hell was that? Nick lay across Rob and stared at the ringing phone. After a few minutes it cut out and all he could hear was both teenagers whimpering.

'You really should have been nicer to me,' Nick said and parted the boy's buttocks again.

'Oh, please,' said the boy, as so many other boys had said.

'Spare me the sob story,' Nick warned. He saw, with a dull sense of shock, that his words were accompanied by bloody spittle. He must get himself some vitamins. He felt fucking strange.

Maybe shooting his load up this little runt would help him relax. He drove in, enjoying the boy's screams. He was vaguely aware that the girl was also crying. It had been a while for him so he came quick. Afterwards he rested, lying heavy-limbed over the teenager and telling him what a little prick he was. The words came easy – he'd heard them all before.

'You know you were asking for it,' he said. 'Why can't you ever do what you're told?'

The boy made odd little sounds but didn't answer.

'Am I not good enough to speak to now?' He tried to raise his hand to slam it into the boy's head but only succeeded in lifting his forearm a few inches before the effort became too great. 'You've fucking wore me out,' he muttered. 'You little bastard. But you'll learn.'

He'd learn... hell, he couldn't remember what he'd learn, what he had to teach him. But he had his knife right here in case the boy played up. He'd gone silent now – which was more than could be said for his snuffling girlfriend. He'd just lie here for a few more minutes then sort her out.

CHAPTER
FORTY-FOUR

'I've got to go,' Richard said, looking at the clock. He watched Rachel's smile turn into a pout. 'Why can't I come too?'

'There's no point – I'm only going to Angela's to pick up her artwork.'

'Well, I'll wait here for you then.'

'No, I have to get some work done,' Richard said.

That was a lie. It was also a sort of lie that he was going to see Angela. Oh, he was going to her place to collect her assignment, but only Angela's kids were going to be there. He'd phoned the flat at teatime and Zoe had said that Angela was round at Dawn's for a meal but that her art was ready for him to pick up.

'I don't feel right,' Rachel said, sitting down firmly on his settee.

'All the more reason for you to be tucked up safely at home with a hot chocolate,' he replied, pulling her to her feet again.

He realised that he was treating her like a child – but then she was acting like one. He increasingly knew that he wanted to finish with her, but couldn't bring himself to kick a dog when it was down.

'See you here for work tomorrow,' he added as he reached the hall and shrugged into his old suede jacket, 'It'll do us both good to spend a few hours apart.'

'But I don't know what to do at home.'

Richard felt his very brain sighing with frustration. 'Then find something – that's what adults do. They make a life.'

He saw that her lower lip was trembling but pretended not to notice as he stepped behind her and steered her through the front door.

'Are you driving?' Rachel asked.

'No, I fancied a walk.'

Her voice was tight. 'Right, I'll just look out for a taxi.'

'Rach – it's only a fifteen-minute journey to your place.'

'But I'm not feeling right.'

'In that case I'll drive you home.' He knew damn well that she wanted him to tuck her into his king-size bed, to bring her supper and adult comics. No way was he going to play her game.

He drove her home then drove back to his own house, parked the car in the driveway and set off on foot for Angela's flat, taking long lungfuls of the mild night air. It was just as well, he thought, that he was in no particular rush.

He reached the flat and briefly rang the bell – Zoe had told him to just give a quick ring as Jack would be sleeping. He waited for two full minutes, realised she couldn't have heard him, and pressed the buzzer for a longer time. He listened hard then knelt and peered through the letterbox. There was light shining from under the lounge door.

He rang again and again, suspecting that something was wrong but not being able to prove it. At last he did what he wanted to do and phoned Dawn.

She sounded slightly drunk when she said her number.

'Hi, it's me,' he said, forcing a casual note into his voice, 'Zoe said that I could go round to Angie's and get her art. I'm there now, but there's no answer. D'you think everything's OK?'

Dawn's reply sounded slightly perturbed. 'It's funny you should say that. Angie phoned home a while ago and no one answered.' He heard her speak to Angela then she came on the line again. 'Rich, stay there. We'll both come round.'

CHAPTER
FORTY-FIVE

'Please let him go. Oh, please. You're suffocating him.' Nick opened his eyes. At first he thought he was at home in Brighton, that the voice had been part of a dream, but then he realised he could still hear it. 'Please, he can't breathe,' the voice said.

He looked in its direction and saw a girl sitting in a chair. Her wrists and ankles were tied, her face was pink and tear-stained.

'What you on about?' he muttered, then wondered why he had such a terrible taste in his mouth.

'Rob – he can't breathe.'

As she said the words he became aware of the snuffling sound beneath him. He realised he was still lying on top of the boy.

'Fucking wimp.' He pushed himself away from the kid, saw the dried blood smeared on both their thighs. Christ, he needed a bath big time. His legs itched like crazy. It was driving him nuts.

Maybe he'd feel better if he had something to eat. He walked stiltedly to the kitchen and found the pack of digestives that Zoe had put out earlier. He ate six, stuffing the crumbling sweetness into his mouth and washing it down with water as he rubbed his itching calves against the nearest table leg. He could just sit down and close his eyes for a few minutes... He shook himself alert as he remembered the danger in the next room

Nick hurried back to the lounge and stared at the little runt on the settee. He was lying on his side now, facing the girl and talking to her quietly.

'You'll be laughing on the other side of your face in a minute if you keep this up,' Nick said. He leaned against the doorjamb and wondered what had made him say that. It was something that Vince had often said to him. He hadn't understood it then, though he'd thought about it for ages in the days when he was still trying to figure out what mum and Vince wanted, trying to get it right.

He walked a few steps until he reached the boy's head, hunkered down and stared into his face. The kid looked hurt but not defeated. He wanted... wanted... He felt a low pull of disappointment but didn't know why.

'You doing what you're told?' he asked in his most threatening voice. The kid nodded. ''Cause you know that if you annoy me I'll cut your girl's throat.'

Rob winced and swallowed hard. Nick looked at Zoe but she was staring down at her lap. He wondered if she was still a virgin. When he was younger he'd really wanted a virgin, someone who couldn't compare him with anyone else. Now, he just wanted peace and quiet. But he couldn't let down his guard in case the boy rushed him and... and did what some men did.

'You shouldn't have dissed me,' he said, knowing that he had to keep the young man scared. 'I'm older than you. You should respect your elders.'

'I didn't mean to diss you,' Rob whispered. 'I'm really sorry, Nick.'

'I thought we were mates,' Nick said.

'We are.'

'I thought you were going to fix me up with her mother.' He jerked his head back at the girl.

'She'll be home soon if you want to meet her,' Rob said.

'Nah, she won't. If she's out on some date she'll not be back until well after midnight.'

He looked at the clock. It was only 8pm. He'd stay here until about ten then take some food and leg it to the station. By morning he'd be somewhere far away where he could start again.

Zoe lifted her bound ankles slightly. He wondered if she wanted to kick him.

'You all right, doll?'

She nodded, still staring at the floor.

'Is mummy due back?'

She nodded again.

'When would that be?'

The teenager shrugged.

'An I not good enough to speak to now?'

He watched her mouth open and shut. A fresh tear ran down her face and dropped onto her jumper. It was a boring navy jumper that didn't show the outline of her tits.

'I think you should be really nice to me.' He pulled himself across the carpet till he was sitting at her feet. She made a strange little cry when he produced his knife.

He should really kneel up or preferably stand so that he towered over her. He should look more threatening. He sent the signals to his legs but they refused to move. He stared down, noticing that she wore socks but not slippers. 'I could cut off your toes,' he said, grabbing hold of one of her feet.

He listened for her scream – but it didn't come. Rob said something and he muttered for him to be quiet. He flicked the blade out of the knife, wondering at which stage she'd lose her cool. He heard a bang, a woman's voice shouting Zoe. Then someone was on top of him, pushing him down onto the carpet, forcing him to drop the knife.

His legs still weren't working so he tried to get his arms out from under him, to hit back. His face was buried in the rug but he could sense that someone was next to Zoe. He could hear them both crying hard.

The male voice on top of him ordered, 'Dawn – phone the police.'

Someone said, 'He's all right. Oh, thank Christ. He slept through the whole thing.'

The pressure on his back intensified. *Oh God no, not that.* He suddenly knew what the man was going to do.

He hadn't known during his second week in prison. Oh, he'd heard all the jokes about not bending down in the showers – but he thought that applied to being fucked by other prisoners. He'd felt thin and weak – but safe – when showering in front of a guard. But the guard had had other guard mates and they all knew what Nick was in for. Suddenly there were three of them grabbing him, lifting him, holding him over one of the wash-hand basins. They'd posted a lookout so that no one else came in.

The first man had been strong, tearing into him with his cock and squeezing at his nipples at the same time. It was like being a kid again only worse. At least when mum's boyfriend shot his load he knew it was over. But this time his bleeding rectum had been shafted by the second guard and then the third. They'd torn him open so badly that he couldn't walk or shit, had been leaking bowel fluids for days.

He had to take charge, couldn't let this happen again. He struggled against the man's weight and a new, dry heat flushed his body. He tried to open his eyes but his lids wouldn't obey. He could taste new blood in his mouth and realised it must also be clogging up his nose as he couldn't quite breathe.

Grey, then greyer still. He tried to move beyond the weight, beyond the darkness. He could vaguely hear both females crying – but not for him, never for him – as his inner picture went increasingly black.

There was no need for any of this. He was a good kid, really. If the man would just hold him gently then everything would be all right...

CHAPTER
FORTY-SIX

'They'll be here at any minute,' Dawn said into the room. She didn't know who she was trying to reassure – herself or Angela and her family. Zoe was still weeping quietly, Angela holding her around the waist. Rob had locked himself in the bathroom and Rich was lying on top of the attacker, holding him in place.

'I'll just check on Jack again,' she added and hurried to the child's bedroom. He was still asleep, his little face relaxed and pinkly healthy. Thank God the man hadn't come in here. After what he'd done to Rob…

She tiptoed to the window and peered out onto the street. Two police cars were drawing up. Dawn rushed to open the door to a gaggle of constables. 'My husband's holding the attacker.' She ran before them into the lounge.

The first thing she saw was that Richard had moved away from the rapist, who was now lying on his back. For the first time she saw his face. He looked young but strangely wasted. Rich was holding the man's wrist. 'He's just stopped breathing,' he said.

'There's an ambulance already on its way,' one of the policemen said. Dawn realised it was meant for Rob. The other policeman started resuscitation techniques, his air making the youth's chest rise and fall in a parody of normality. But the man's still limbs and greyish pallor didn't change.

'I think he'd taken drugs,' Zoe said shakily. 'He was acting very strange. He smelt of chemicals.'

The policeman kept compressing the man's chest and then giving him air, though it was clear that he wasn't going to revive.

Rob came limping back into the lounge just as the ambulance arrived.

'No way am I travelling with him,' he said shaking his head violently. So the ambulance took Nick away and another was requested for Rob and for Zoe, who appeared to be going into shock.

At 3am that morning, Rich and Dawn finally left the police station. Rob and Zoe were being kept in hospital overnight for observation, and Angela had been given a bed in Zoe's room. Rob's anxious parents were sleeping in Rob's room. Counselling was already being arranged.

Nick had been pronounced dead at the scene. One policeman had told Rich that the medics had found two kinds of steroids in his jacket pocket and needle marks on his arms.

Dawn shivered as she walked through the car park beside her white-faced ex-husband. Her own face felt tight with tiredness but she knew she couldn't sleep.

'Where to?' Rich asked as they reached his car.

'Can you think of an all-night coffee bar?' she replied hopefully.

'I can.' He named the bungalow's address. 'The service is good and for you it's free.'

'Won't the Roach be there?'

'No, she's ill. I sent her home when we finished work for the day.'

'Hope it's nothing trivial,' Dawn said.

They grinned at each other across the roof of the car, then both got in.

'I know I have to finish with her,' Rich said. 'It's just that she's so depressed, I can't bring myself to do it.'

'What's she got to be depressed about, looking like that?' Dawn said.

Rich turned the ignition key. 'Well, she's not the best artist in the world so she's really struggling to find a job.'

'Thought she worked for you?'

Rich raised his eyebrows. 'She does – but I've told you before that it's temporary. If I'd wanted her to stay with *Crisis* I'd hardly have taken Angela on.'

'Thank God you did,' Dawn said, wrapping her arms around herself. 'If you hadn't gone round tonight...'

'Bloody drug addicts,' Rich said.

Dawn nodded. 'It sounds stupid, but at the end I almost felt sorry for him. He looked so thin.'

'Save your pity.' She saw that Rich was driving faster than he normally did. 'Poor Rob needed stitches. And Christ knows what it's done to his confidence.'

'I know. I... Angela leaves them alone so much that I worried about something happening to Zoe or Jack. It never occurred to me that something might happen to Rob.'

She relaxed slightly as Rich drew up outside the bungalow. It felt right being here. Her flat felt like something temporary.

'Shall I do my famous croissants?' Rich said.

'Providing you serve them with indigestion tablets.'

Richard was always too rushed to reheat his croissants in the oven so he microwaved them.

They took the microwaved dough into the lounge. Dawn sat next to him on the settee and took a very deep breath.

'So Rachel isn't the love of your life, then?'

'No, it's never going to work.' Rich looked thoughtful. 'She'll make someone a nice wife but she's not for me.'

'That day I saw you kissing her, I just went into shock.'

'I know. It's just... the way you'd been glaring at me and sending me up about everything. I'd even started wondering if you wanted a divorce.' He sighed. 'And I suppose I was scared of growing old, and she made me feel young and... Textbook mid-life crisis stuff, right?'

'I should have been more understanding,' Dawn said, wanting to put her arms around him but not yet daring to. 'It was only when I met Ben that I realised I had my own fears about age.'

'He's still around?'

'We're not together, if that's what you mean.' She searched for a brief version of the truth. 'He was a suspect for that Southampton Road murder as he couldn't – well, wouldn't – account for a couple of hours. But it turned out he'd been raped that night and felt too upset to tell anyone for ages. He sent me a letter explaining it all the other day.'

'Another nutter? And Salisbury used to be such a safe little town.' She realised he was staring at her more intently. 'But you don't want him back?'

Dawn shook her head so earnestly that something clicked in her neck. 'No, it was more of a fling that anything else. I mean, it was exciting at the time but I couldn't imagine growing old with him.' It was now or never. She took a deep breath. 'Rich, I treated you badly and I really regret it.' Now for the punchline. 'I really want you back.'

She held her breath, waiting for him to say that he had a different life now, that he preferred being single.

'Good. In that case you can do the dishes,' Rich said in an uneven voice.

She looked at him more closely and realised that his eyes were watering.

'Can I have a hug?' she asked.

They held each other for an hour, dozing fitfully, then Rich said, 'We old people need our sleep. Would you mind if we went to bed?'

Dawn stood up then pulled him up with her. 'I could sleep for a week.' She remembered the Roach. 'But won't Rachel be here for work in the morning?'

Rich nodded glumly. 'I'll phone her answering machine now and tell her not to come in tomorrow, that I've had a late night.' He came back a few minutes later. 'Mission accomplished. Let's hit the sack.'

'So what happens now?' Dawn asked sleepily as she curled into his side in her beloved familiar bed.

'How d'you mean?' Rich mumbled sleepily.

Dawn felt equally tired but she wanted to know what the next few days held in store for her.

'Well, what happens with Roach?'

'I'll finish with her as nicely as I can the next time that I see her.'

'Yeah? Will she still be working on *Crisis*?'

She heard Rich laugh softly into the dark. 'Oh, that would make for a brilliant working environment.' He ruffled her hair. 'No, of course not, though she's so broke that I'll make up some story about severance pay, give her a couple of hundred quid.'

'She'll blame me,' Dawn said tiredly.

'Well, she shouldn't. I'd have finished with her before if she wasn't in such dire straits.'

'You're a regular charity,' Dawn said cheekily then yelped as he aimed a slap at her backside.

'Will you move back in now?' Rich asked. She could sense that he'd stilled, knew that the answer was important.

'I'd love to.'

'Tomorrow?'

'Tomorrow afternoon after we finally wake up. You can come back to the flat with me and help me pack.'

She settled down to sleep in his arms, knowing that they'd been incredibly lucky. They'd both been childish and uncommunicative for a stupidly long time. As a result, they'd drifted apart and almost lost each other – but now everything could go back to the way it was before.

CHAPTER
FORTY-SEVEN

She didn't often feel this spaced. Rachel groped for the bedside light, switched it on and squinted at her alarm clock. It was 6am. Wondering if thirst had woken her, she sipped from her bedside tumbler. A wave of nausea followed in the water's wake.

Oh oh. She only just made it to the bathroom before she started retching. Her stomach heaved but there was virtually no food for it to bring up.

At last the heaving subsided and she managed to eat a slice of toast. Her usual cup of tea didn't appeal so she settled for more water. As she shivered in her small lounge, she noticed that the answering-machine light was flashing to indicate one call.

She pressed the button. 'Rachel – it's Rich here. Two friends of mine were attacked last night. I've been at the police station and the hospital for hours. It's after five now and I'm only just going to bed.' There was a pause then he added, 'I need to sleep so I don't want you to come round tomorrow at all. I mean it. I need to rest.' There was another pause then he said,

'Sorry, Rach. I'll phone you tomorrow night about everything.'

Damn, now she'd be stuck here all day feeling sick and it was only… only early morning. *Of course, she had morning sickness.* Rachel was suddenly certain that was why she felt so strange. Oh, she'd noticed that her period was late but it had gone away before when she didn't eat enough or when she was worried about finding work.

Wasn't there a chemist opened at eight to dispense prescriptions? Rachel dug out the free paper and checked the public service ads. Yes, there was – and it was within walking distance. She had a slow, warm bath, ate some more toast then put on her mock-leather coat.

'How much?' she echoed when the chemist told her the cost of their over-the-counter pregnancy tests.

The man repeated the charges. 'But you can get it done for free by your doctor.'

'No, I want to know now.' Friends had been tested on the NHS before and she knew the results took days.

She went to the cashline machine and came back with a twenty-pound note, got the test kit. Then she walked home, feeling fragile and hopeful and totally different.

She did the test and left it in the bathroom, walked back into the lounge. It would take fifteen minutes. She wondered what to do during these minutes, couldn't think of a single thing. Life was a bore when you had no friends living locally and very little money. Only her time with Richard changed all that.

She sat staring at the clock, willing the hands to move round. The result could change her destiny. She'd definitely manage to keep Rich if she had his baby, would almost certainly become his wife.

The liquid would turn blue if she was pregnant. She walked back into the bathroom and made herself look, trying to shore herself up for the pale worst – but focused on a liquid that was the bluest colour imaginable. *She'd done it.* She was going to become a mother, give Richard his first child.

When could she tell him? She listened to his message again. He was saying that he had to sleep. Fine, she could sleep alongside him. She'd let herself in with her key, tell him her amazing news then they'd both rest. Impending fatherhood would take his mind off the fact that he'd spent half the night at the police station, that two of his friends had been attacked.

It was almost nine. He'd have had four hours' sleep so would be feeling less stressed, be pleased to see her. She was singing inside as she neared the bungalow, preparing to give Richard his biggest ever surprise.

Shrouded

Douglas likes women – quiet women; the kind he deals with at the mortuary where he works. Douglas meets Marjorie, unemployed, gaining weight and losing confidence. She talks and laughs a lot to cover up her shyness, but what Douglas really needs is a lover who'll stay still – deadly still.

Shrouded is a powerful and accomplished début, tautly-plotted, dangerously erotic and vibrating with tension and suspense.

Safe as Houses

NEW EDITION WITH AUTHOR'S INTRODUCTION

Women are vanishing from the streets of Edinburgh and only one man knows the answers. David is a sadist with a double life. He divides his time between the marital home – shared with devoted wife, Jeannette and young son – and his Secret House.

The Secret House is where fantasies become horrible real and where screams go unheard. Slowly Jeannette begins to realise that all is not well...

Noise Abatement

A typical street in Edinburgh... Stephen and Caroline Day are an active young couple until the neighbouts from hell move into the flat above. Suddenly every day becomes a living nightmare and they're shocked from sleep every night.

After weeks of police inactivity, Stephen snaps and takes increasingly inventive and extreme revenge on his tormentors. But there are horrifying unforeseen consequences...

Recently published by THE DO-NOT PRESS

Grief by John B Spencer
'*Grief* is a speed-freak's cocktail, one part Leonard and one part
Ellroy, that goes right to the head.' George P Pelecanos
When disparate individuals collide, it's Grief. John B Spencer's
final and greatest novel.
'Spencer writes the tightest dialogue this side of Elmore Leonard, so
bring on the blood, sweat and beers!' Ian Rankin

No One Gets Hurt by Russell James
'The best of Britain's darker crime writers' – *The Times*
After a friend's murder Kirsty Rice finds herself drawn into the
murky world of call-girls, porn and Internet sex.

A Man's Enemies by Bill James
'Bill James can write, and then some' *The Guardian*
The direct sequel to 'Split'. Simon Abelard, the section's 'token black'
– has to dissuade Horton from publishing his memoirs.

A Dysfunctional Success by Eric Goulden
'A national treasure' – Jonathan Ross
Wreckless Eric first found fame in the 1970s when he signed to the
emergent Stiff Records. More than a biography. It's possibly the most
entertaining read you'll come across this year.

End of the Line by K T McCaffrey
'KT McCaffrey is an Irish writer to watch' RTE
Emma is celebrating her Journalist of the Year Award when she hears
of the death of priest Father Jack O'Gorman in what appears to have
been a tragic road accident.

Vixen by Ken Bruen
'Ireland's version of Scotland's Ian Rankin' – *Publisher's Weekly*
BRANT IS BACK! If the Squad survives this incendiary installment,
they'll do so with barely a cop left standing.

Green for Danger edited by Martin Edwards
THE OFFICIAL CWA ANTHOLOGY 2004
A brand new and delicious selection of the best modern crime
writing themed on 'crime in the countryside'.

Ike Turner – King of Rhythm by John Collis
At last, respected rock and blues writer John Collis has written the
first major study of one of music's most complex characters.

The Indispensable by Julian Rathbone
'Julian Rathbone's characters live; he writes with elegance, with wit
and with conviction' *Books & Bookmen*
At last! The collected work of one of Britain's most successful and
accomplished literarists, chosen by the author himself.'

The Do-Not Press
Fiercely Independent Publishing

Keep in touch with what's happening at the cutting edge of independent British publishing.

Simply send your name and address to:
~~The Do-Not Press (KIA)~~

Withdrawn

NB '03

A...   se of
d...   ere is
n...